Visitation Rites

VISITATION RITES

Diplodocus Press 2014

published by Diplodocus Press
Bangkok • Los Angeles
Main Office • 48 Sukhumvit Soi 33
Bangkok 10110, Thailand

about this publisher
www.diplodocuspress.com

ISBN: 978-1-940999-00-5 (trade paper)
978-1-940999-01-2 (hardcover)

0 9 8 7 6 5 4 3 2 1

P.D. CACEK

Visitation Rites

DIPLODOCUS PRESS
BANGKOK · LOS ANGELES

To:

The Bark House Society

Visitation Rites

He's here.

APRIL

She was doing better.

This time she almost managed to swallow an entire sip of lukewarm coffee when her desk phone rang again. It'd been that way since she walked in that morning.

Giving the much-needed caffeine a hopeless look, Tess took a deep breath and set the mug back on its company-logo coaster. Although it was an annual event, like Christmas and Groundhog Day, from the way the phones had been ringing off their collective hooks it seemed that April 15th, aka "Tax Day," had taken most of Montgomery County by surprise.

This was good for an accounting company, like the one she worked for.

Bad if you liked hot coffee and preferred dealing with clients as numbered files on a computer screen, instead of having to actually talk to them.

Especially since, as Vince was quick to remind her, she had a voice a weak as a mouse fart.

Clearing her throat, even though she knew it wouldn't help, Tess activated her headset.

"Good morning, Mayrdal and Associ—" Her voice broke. "—Associates. Excuse me. This is Tess Warren, how may I hel —"

"Don't you *ever* check your e-mail?"

It took her a moment to recognize her brother's voice and then panic set in. He never called during tax season. Tess felt her stomach flutter as she leaned forward, gripping the edge of the desk.

"What's wrong? Are you okay? Did something happen to Chuck? What—"

"Fine," he interrupted, laughing. *Laughing?* "Everything and everyone's fine. Better than fine. Check your e-mail and call me back. Or I'll call you back. No, it took four tries; ten minutes of listening to Pachelbel's greatest hit and three transfers to get you...I'm not going through that again. Just check it now while I'm on the phone."

"But—"

"I know, you're busy, its tax time...just—check—it."

Robby had switched from speed-talking to 'big brother'. Tess let go of the desk and gave the narrow corridor beyond her cubicle "door" a quick look. The cubicles had been laid out as mirror opposites, so instead of being able to see directly into the cubicle opposite, all you saw was an uninterrupted view of beige pressboard. It was supposed to give the illusion of privacy.

And it worked, for the most part, although she'd never taken advantage of it before. Vince never called her while she was at her desk. If he wanted to speak to her, he waited until lunch or while she was on a break and called her cell phone. He knew her schedule down to the second.

Tess turned back toward the monitor and rested the heels of her palms against the keyboard without actually touching any of the keys. No one would notice, and probably not care if she checked her e-mail—she was sure everyone did—but it *felt* wrong. It felt like she was cheating.

Curling her fingers away from the keys, she checked the time on the bottom of the computer screen and watched a minute slip away. Gone forever.

"Robby—" She dropped her voice to a whisper. "I have lunch in a couple of hours, can't this—?"

"No, it can't wait. Please, I'm begggggggggggging you."

He wasn't going to be reasonable.

Tess looked at the small drawing tacked to the wallboard behind the monitor. Chuck, Robby's partner, had drawn it for her when she first got the job, going on six years now. The cartoon was a variation of the old "Hang in There" image and showed the end of a frayed rope and a wide-eyed, very surprised looking kitten from the nose up peeking up over the bottom edge of the paper. The caption, in red balloon letters, read:

DO I *STILL* HAVE TO HANG ON?

Vince hadn't thought it was very funny and she had to admit it was sort of silly, but everyone in the office who'd seen it liked it, so maybe she was wrong. She usually was about most things.

Tess pressed the e-mail icon key.

When the Yahoo screen came up, she mouse-clicked to MAIL and gasped. "The attached file's huge... What did you send me?"

"Just *open* it, already!"

Tess gave the corridor another quick check, then opened the file and instantly realized why it was so large. There were four pictures, each showing some aspect of a large Federal-style stone house. The first showed the house decorated for autumn—orange pumpkins, dried cornstalks and coppery mums in oak barrels displayed at intervals along the wide raised fieldstone porch that ran the full length of the front of the house. The second picture was of the back of the house in winter, as if time has somehow sped up between the two shots. Steam ghosts rose from the in-ground pool to dance across the snow-covered patio.

The other two shots were of (1) the massive (empty) front room with its twin fireplaces, stone floor and spiral staircase that led up to a black-railed balcony, and (2) the kitchen and sunken, window-lined dining area (with another fireplace).

A standard seducement/description followed the pictures:

Montgomery County History—Exceptional picturesque stone farmhouse on fifteen gorgeous acres in Montgomery County overlooking Wissahickon creek, mill race runs through property. Perfectly located 40 minutes from Philadelphia, 90 minutes from NYC, original stone farmhouse dates back to 1818; completely renovated with additions. The home sits 250' off the road and includes a hand-split cedar shake roof and rafters (all new in 1990), open beam ceilings in main room, wired for Ethernet LAN, includes Panasonic Phone System, dual feed DishNet Satellite; spiral staircase; three large stone fireplaces, two with original beam mantle; gas fireplace in dining room; new high efficiency windows throughout. Original millhouse fully restored with electric and water service, road grated. Priced to sell at only...

Tess barely even flinched when she read the price. In the nine years Robby and Chuck had been together, she'd managed to glean a little knowledge of the real-estate business but it still amazed her what some people would spend on a house.

"Beautiful. Chuck will make a pretty good commission when he sells it."

"What do you mean sell? We're *buying* it."

Tess looked at the pictures...and price again.

"Robby, I—I thought you guys love your place."

"*Loved* it and we did. But, honey, did you read the description? I mean the pictures don't do it nearly enough justice. Oh my God, it's breathtaking and if you're worrying about the price—"

"I didn't mention the price."

"No, but I can hear you think it."

He knew her so well...in some ways.

"Look, baby, I know your little eyes are probably bugging out right now, but Chuck and I are a two-income family, remember, and with all false modesty aside, they're pretty decent two-incomes. Besides, what's the use of living with one of the best real estate agents in the county if you can't take advantage of a find like this, huh?" He took a long, ragged breath. "Tess, I actually cried when I saw it. You know how I've always wanted to live in the country."

He did?

Tess closed the e-mail screen just in case someone walked by and tried to remember if Robby had ever told her that before. She forgot things sometimes—*more* than sometimes—but even if he had mentioned it it still came as a bit of a shock. They were city kids, born and raised in Philadelphia, first living in a row-home off Cottman Avenue, then, after their parents' death, into their aunt and uncle's crowded but wonderfully comfortable two-story Victorian just off Germantown Pike in Chestnut Hill.

The "country" for them had always meant the thrilling Dutch Wonderland rides in Lancaster County and shoofly pie.

When she married Vince and moved into his condo, King of Prussia was still considered by many, her brother included, to be "the boondocks." Robby had tried his best to talk her out of it.

And she still wasn't sure if he meant the marriage or moving to King of Prussia.

Tess blinked and realized his voice was still echoing through her headset. "What?"

"What do you mean what?"

"I— Robby, when did you decide you wanted to live in the country?"

"Since I saw the place, okay. But you won't believe how fantastic it is. Our nearest neighbor...is a herd of deer. We're smack dab in the middle of Fort Washington State Park. Wait 'till you see it."

"Can't wait." Tess caught movement out of the corner of her eye—*co-worker? Supervisor? Fed-Ex?*—and cupped one hand

around the mouthpiece. "Look, Robby, I've got to get back to
—"

"Work, okay, and I'm sorry I called, I know it's a bad
time, but it all happened so quickly I just had to tell you. The
house only came on the market this morning and—"

"This morning?" Tess checked the computer's on-screen
clock again. Almost ten minutes had passed. "Aren't you
rushing this?"

"Had to, baby. Chuck sent me a FAX as soon as he saw it
and... He and I have been talking about getting a bigger place
for about a year."

It never dawned on Tess that her brother might have
secrets of his own.

"Okay, go back to work and I'll call you tonight—"

"Tonight might not be—"

"—know if our bid's accepted. It has to... God wouldn't
be that cruel. But keep your fingers crossed anyway.
Loveyabye."

"Robby, don't call after nine—" But he was already gone.

Tess turned off the headset and stared, unseeing, at the
row of figures on her screen. It was just like her big brother to
drop a bomb and then wander off without bothering to see
where the shrapnel hit. Or what the body count was. If he
called tonight and bragged to Vince about the house and the
price...

She closed her eyes and took a moment to pull her
thoughts together. Robby wouldn't do that. He knew Vince...
he wouldn't brag even though it was too much house and too
much money, even with two "pretty good" incomes and his
success as a software designer.

He wouldn't brag because he knew Vince.

When the phone rang again Tess noticed another three
minutes had vanished and the mug of coffee she didn't
remember picking up was cold against her knuckles. She set it
down and cleared her throat.

"Mayrdal and Associates. This is Tess Warren, how may I help you?"

The man on the other end of the phone wasn't her brother and, by the time she answered three of his four questions another ten minutes had passed.

If she was lucky the rest of the day would disappear as quickly.

**

He's here.

Tess finger-combed a tangle out of her shoulder-length hair and ran to meet Vince at the door, drinks in hand—scotch and water for him, small white wine for her—and smile on face.

She waited until he'd put his briefcase down on the entrance table and shrugged out of his coat before handing him his drink. Then she waited until he'd taken a drink and nodded—she'd get it right this time—before taking a sip. He seemed relaxed as he loosened his tie; tired but not upset, not angry, and he even returned her smile.

She didn't wait long enough.

"You'll never guess what Robby and Chuck did."

"Sign up for Planned Parenthood?"

She should have laughed, she realized that the second Vince took another sip and lowered the glass. It wouldn't have been perceptible to anyone except her, but even she saw it too late: the hardness that crept into his eyes while his face stayed calm and relaxed. That was her first mistake of the evening.

The second was laughing. Too late *(again)*.

"Did I say something funny?"

"Yes...no, I mean..." She stopped but didn't back away. That would have been a *fatal* mistake. "I—"

"Do you know how stupid you are?"

Tess nodded. "Y-yes."

"Did I say you could talk?" he asked, very softly and very gently because that was the kind of man he was.

Tess shook her head.

"No, I didn't. I hear enough mindless talk at work; I don't have to *hear* it in my own house." Vince finished his drink and handed her the empty glass. "Another, and put some scotch in it this time, will you? I come home after a hard day and all I ask is a little consideration. You think you'd understand that by now, wouldn't you? Are you going to stand there like a rock or are you going to make my drink?"

Tess hurried back to the dining room, but didn't run—making sure her wine didn't spill. That would have been a disaster. Vince followed at his own steady pace and she had the drink—done properly this time, she hoped—ready when he reached the liquor cabinet. He took the glass from her, but didn't raise it to his lips.

"Am I supposed to drink alone?"

"No, s—" Tess pressed her lips together, but it was already too late. There was nothing she could do now but apologize. "I'm sorry, Vince, I know you probably had a rough day and —"

"Probably?" It was the way he said, with a small chuckle in his voice that made the skin tighten across Tess' back. "Aw, but I am being a bear, aren't I?"

He leaned over and kissed her cheek. "I'm sorry, honey. Go on, pick up your drink." He clinked his glass against hers. "Cheers. Now, what were you going to tell me about your brother?"

Tess looked up, smiling. "He and Chuck—"

Vince glared at her. "You're not drinking."

"Sorry." She took too big a gulp and almost choked. Vince moved back, disgust on his face. "I...I'm sorry."

"Whatever." He took a sip to show her how it was supposed to be done. "Are you going to tell me or not?"

Tess wiped the wine dribble from her chin and mouth with the back of her hand.

"They're buying a house." She waited, *this time* she waited to see if he was going to say anything, and only continued when she was sure. "Robby called me this morning to tell me to tell me and…"

Vince nodded. She continued.

"He was going to call tonight to tell me if their bid was accepted, but he called this afternoon instead, the minute he found out. It's—"

Vince still seemed interested.

"It's out in the middle of Montgomery County and it's *very* expensive, but he said they can afford it and, it really is beautiful, Vince. It's an old stone farmhouse built in 1818 on fifteen acres with woods and fields in the middle of a state park, right across from the Wissahickon. And it has a pool and —"

"You saw it?"

Tess felt the temperature in the room drop.

"You left work to go see the *very* expensive house your brother and his *friend* are buying?"

"No! I didn't leave work, he… Robby sent me an e-mail with pictures and—"

"And you looked at them?" He took another drink and shook his head. "I thought we talked about all this when I let you take that job. When you're at work, you're supposed to *work*. Christ, what would have happened if your supervisor heard you, huh? What if he walked by and saw you looking at that *very* expensive house, hmm?"

Tess backed up a step before she realized she'd moved. "It was only a minute…"

"*Only* a minute? No, I don't think so." Vince finished his drink and set the glass carefully on top of the liquor cabinet. Tess jumped as if he'd slammed it down.

"What's the matter? Why are you so nervous all of a sudden?"

"I'm not, Vince, I—"

"I don't understand you, you know that? You don't seem very excited about this *wonderful* news. I mean, it isn't every day your only brother buys a *very* expensive house *with* a swimming pool on *fifteen* acres out in the middle of the woods...right? Why aren't you excited? I mean, your brother can afford it, hell; they could probably afford a house on *twenty* acres of land, right? It's not like he or his partner has to worry about money. Oh, hell, no...they're making money hand over fist. They can buy what they want, when they want. And I'm *really* sorry I can't do the same, but this is *me*...this is *all* I can do. And you don't even give a damn. You could have lost your job today and then where would we be? Huh? You think your fucking millionaire brother would take us into that nice, big, *very* expensive—"

Vince reached for her just as the phone in the kitchen rang, and it was the suddenness of the unexpected sound that made her jump, not him, but Tess knew he wouldn't believe that. He never did.

He looked down at carpet.

"Clean that up." He said each word as if it were a complete and final thought, not moving until she was on her knees, dabbing at the few drops of wine she'd spilled with a handful of cocktail napkins.

The phone rang three more times before he picked it up.

"Hi! Sorry...was helping Tess with dinner." He smiled and winked at her. "And I hear congratulations are in order." Pause. Still smiling." What? Yeah, Tess told me all about it. Wow, man...seriously, that it fantastic news. I always wanted a Gentleman Farmer for a brother-in-law." Laughter. "Right. What? Let me just check." He looked at her and his face went blank. "No...she's up to her elbows in dinner. Can she call you back tonight?" Shorter pause. "Sure, I'll tell her. Okay... Oh, our congrats to Chuck, too, can't leave him out of this, right?"

More laughter, none of it forced. He was very good on the phone. "Okay, I'll give her the message. Have a drink for us. Right. Bye."

His face was still blank when he hung up the phone.

"That was your brother calling to brag." Shaking his head, Vince finally smiled as he began unbuckling his belt. "Some world we live in, huh? It doesn't matter what I do or how hard I try, there's always somebody waiting to show me up. I don't think that's right." He pulled the belt loose. "Do you?"

Still on her hands and knees on the dining room rug, Tess shook her head. "N-no, but Robby didn't mean—"

"Did I ask for an explanation?" He doubled the belt over, holding both ends in one hand. "Come here, Tess."

Tess put the wineglass and wad of napkins on the dining room table before she started to get up.

"No, don't," Vince said. "You're fine just the way you are..."

AUGUST

Tess tucked herself deeper into the narrow space between the spiral staircase and candle-filled fireplace and watched her brother greet the newest arrivals.

"You made it! See, I told you it wouldn't be that hard to find. Chuck! Tracy and Geno are here. Ooo, wine! You shouldn't have, but I'm glad you did. Thank you. Okay, buffet in the dining room, bar in the kitchen...grab a plate and a drink and relax. The next house tour won't begin for another ten minutes. Fifteen if I open this."

Pushing the couple ahead of him, Robby steered them toward the back of the house via her spot by the stairs.

"Tess, you remember Tracy and Geno, don't you?"

Of course she did—they were regulars, as were she and Vince, at Christmas parties, New Year's parties, birthday parties, and "dinner-with-a-movie" nights. That brought the number of people she actually *knew* to six. The other fifty or so guests at the "Gala Housewarming"—artists and actors and writers; software designers *and* jewelry designers, real-estate agents and theatrical agents who made up the ever-widening circle of Robby and Chuck's friends—were strangers to her.

And she to them.

"How you doin', kid?"

Tess looked up and watched Chuck high-kick down the stairs. Only one of the six people following—a house tour coming to an end—copied the move.

"Very Russ Tamblyn in 'The Haunting,'" she said as he stepped aside to let the tour wander back to the food and drink.

"Oh, that's right...I wanted to tell everyone. People!" Climbing up three stairs and shouting to be heard over the ambient background of voices, clinking silverware *(no paper plates or plastic forks for this crowd)* and soft-jazz coming from hidden speakers, Chuck clapped his hands for attention. "Attention everyone! Robby, turn off the sound system for a minute! YO!"

The music stopped and although dead-silence wasn't achieved, the background noise lessened a bit. Chuck backed up two more steps.

"Can everyone see me?" A murmur rolled through the room. Tess watched Vince, standing next to the fireplace at the opposite end of the room, turn from the two women he'd been talking to and lift his glass to his lips. "Great. Okay...*ghost* story time."

Robby's moan, echoing through the house, added a nice effect but the *"oh no, not that"* broke the mood. Everyone, including Tess, laughed. When he came out of the kitchen he had a wine bottle in each hand. "At least wait until they're all drunk."

Chuck waved him away. "Did either of us tell you that our lovely, wonderful home is haunted?"

Silence was spontaneously achieved.

"Yep. The seller didn't mention this little fact, but we knew something was going on the first night we moved in. The ghost made its presence known to Robby first."

All eyes shifted to her brother, who shrugged. "What can I say? I'm cuter."

The few ripples of laughter vanished when Chuck cleared his throat. When he started again, his voice was soft and low, the way a good storyteller's should be.

"We'd unpacked all day and were dead tired..."

He looked up suddenly, hands raised. "No offense."

There were a few acknowledging chuckles.

"And we tossed a coin to see who got the shower first. I won and Robby went downstairs to lock up. I swear, I didn't hear anything over the running water—" He crossed his heart. "—but when Robby was coming down the stairs someone knocked on the front door."

Robby sighed and nodded. "That's what it sounded like."

"You want to tell them what happened next?" Chuck asked.

"No...but I will."   He shrugged. "I was coming downstairs and I heard what *sounded* like a knock. We really don't have neighbors out here so I thought it was either Tess," he smiled at her, "or one of our more nocturnal friends who Map Quested the address and decided to pay us a surprise visit, so I really didn't think anything about it. I won't mention any names, but some of you *have* shown up at the wee-small hours. So, anyway... I didn't think about it or even bother to turn on the downstairs lights. The porch light was on and I could see...

"Yeah. Okay, I *did* see what looked like a man's...shape through the glass."

Tess looked across the room to the front door's inlaid frosted glass panel and shivered. She'd always loved ghost stories.

"When I opened the door ...there was no one there. I went outside; just to make sure whoever it was hadn't realized the time and left because they thought we were already asleep but...nothing. No one, no car...just a whole lotta night. And out here night is a completely different kind of dark. Needless to say I beat my feet back to the house, to find the front door not only closed but locked...dead bolt included."

Robby looked at bottles in his hands and shook his head, as if he'd just decided against drinking directly from them.

"We'd locked all the other doors earlier, and the windows were closed tight. Doorbell was suddenly and mysteriously not working...either that or Chuckles was singing opera in the shower and didn't hear it. I spent thirty minutes pounding on the door before he used up all the hot water and turned off the shower. And do you want to know what he asked when he finally came downstairs and opened the door? 'You lock yourself out?' "

"You really do have a ghost," someone said and it wasn't until Tess noticed a few people were looking at her and smiling that she'd been the one who said it. Vince was looking at her, too, but he wasn't smiling. He didn't believe in ghosts or weakness or making a fool of oneself in public. He always left those things up to her and she never failed to live down to his expectations.

Tess dropped her gaze to the scuffed toes of her high heels. No other adult woman that she knew still managed to scuff the toes of her shoes. Vince was a saint for putting up with her.

"Yeah," Chuck said and reached through the wrought iron banisters to lift her chin," we really do have a ghost." He winked. "And he's a real card, let me tell you. Our new roommate really has a thing about locking doors. We both had to start carrying our house keys around all the time because we would get locked out even when we made sure the doors were unlocked. Then, there were the bumps and thumps and moving shadows in the night."

"Shadows?" someone *else* asked. "Oh, my God."

"It got really bad, so I did a little research with a local group."

Robby raised one of the bottles in a toast. "Chuck's joined the Hysterical Society."

"His*tori*cal," Chuck corrected, "and I got a little information on Frank. That's not his real name, but it's a good strong name and we call him that because he used to be the bodyguard for the man who owned this house...about three owners back." Chuck reached up and bent his nose to one side. "Sort of a Godfather type, you know what I mean. Had some really...interesting business associates, if you catch my drift?"

A round of quiet gasps filled the room.

"Well, Frank lived on site, in what is now the office off our bedroom...best place for a guard dog, and it was his job to lock up and make nightly rounds…first time around midnight and then again at three in the morning. We know this because that's when the noises would start. You could hear him wandering around…upstairs, downstairs; I mean you could *hear* his footsteps on the stairs and stone floor. Then he'd go outside and walk around the house. Robby saw him once."

Robby backed into the kitchen. "Don't remind me. It looked like a big shambling pile of leaves."

"After that, he'd come back inside and we'd hear the door in the butler's pantry close and footsteps coming upstairs… then he'd rattle the bedroom doorknob just to make sure it was locked.

"He's a stickler to routine, is our Frank, which is probably what got him killed. Apparently someone else knew his routine, too, and he was gunned down out by the pool one night. I have a copy of the newspaper article about the murder up in the office if anyone'd like to see it." There were no takers. "Soon afterward the *boss* moved out, sold the house, but our boy stayed on. First few weeks where the hardest."

"Does he still…do that?" Jeannie, another of the regulars, asked.

"Well, he still lets us know he's around, but Robby took care of the nighttime shambling."

"What did you do, Robby?" Jeannie asked before anyone else could.

Robby came back carrying a large glass of red wine.

"One night, while he was thumping and bumping happily along, I went out to the balcony up there," he pointed, all eyes lifted, "and told him to shut the fuck up. And he's been very cooperative since. Okay, next tour about to leave—anyone who hasn't seen every inch of this place please follow Chuckles."

The sound of laughter followed Chuck and a half-dozen people back upstairs. Tess was about to join them, even though she and Vince had been given a private tour before the other guests arrived, when Robby waved her toward the kitchen. She nodded to let him know she'd seen him, but first glanced across the room to see if Vince needed...or wanted her for anything. He wasn't even looking in her direction. Vince had his back to her, as he enchanted his group of admirers. It had grown from two women to five—and why not? People, men as well as women, naturally flocked to him. He was tall and handsome, a blue-eyed, golden-haired All-American Boy who somehow, for some reason she still didn't understand, had picked her from all the other—better, prettier, more talented— women he could have had.

One of his new fans said something and he threw back his head and laughed. The polo shirt was just tight enough to show off the contours of his shoulders and upper arms, the flat plane of his belly. Vince always dressed for success no matter where he was.

Tess smoothed down the front of her leaf-green sundress, the one she thought Vince liked *("Where'd you get that thing—Wal-Mart? Jesus, you're bound and determined to let your brother know I can't afford to buy you decent clothes, aren't you? No...don't change; we're going to be late as it is.")* as she wove her way through the crowd toward her brother.

Robby was bent over the sound system, fiddling with one of a dozen knobs. He looked so much like the pictures she'd seen of their father at the same age—large, slightly almond shape eyes and baby-fine chestnut hair; wide smile and laugh lines like exclamation points that ended in nearly bottomless dimples. Of the little she remembered of their father, she remembered his laugh and it sounded like Robby's. He'd gotten their mother's sage green Irish eyes, Tess had gotten her black hair but that was all.

Their mother had been delicate and petite, Tess was 5'10" and bony. Where their mother had soft curves, Tess was...angular. Where their mother had strengths, Tess had weakness. She was a black haired, muddied-eyed, genetic fluke.

And part of her was happy her mother never lived long enough to see it.

Tess waited silently until he was finished because she knew men don't like to be disturbed when they're doing something important.

"Having fun?" Robby asked while the sound track from *Kiss Me, Kate* filled in the few empty spots in the background noise.

"Yes, it's a wonderful party and a fantastic house."

He linked his arm through hers and walked her back toward the kitchen.

"Even with all the track lighting and modern art?"

Robby liked chrome and smoked glass and art pieces that required long observations from numerous angles, Vince preferred framed photographs that he'd taken himself and IKEA Scandinavian...Tess really didn't have an opinion and it wasn't her place to say, except—

She glanced back to the Great Room with its monochromatic color-scheme—black leather sofa and white chairs fronting the fireplace next to the spiral stairs; white loveseat and clear plastic chair separated by a low black-lacquered table grouped around the opposite fireplace...a black-and-white cowhide on the floor between.

"This is a historic house and—"

"And you would have decorated it to match. Early Colonial-chic?"

Tess shrugged one shoulder as if she hadn't given it a single thought and looked down. "Do you really have a ghost, Robby?"

He laughed and she could already feel the blush starting, glad that Vince wasn't there to see it. She was always saying such stupid things...

When Robby leaned forward, Tess tightened the muscles along her back and shoulders before she realized he was only going to kiss her forehead. He winked at her as he straightened.

"Come with me. I've got something to show you."

Arm in arm, Robby walked her through the equally modern dining room, past the scattered groups of smokers on the patio, and deeper into the August night. It had to be almost eleven, she guessed, but it hadn't gotten any cooler and, after, the air-conditioned comfort of the house—and the wine—she felt herself immediately begin to wilt. *Why did you have to drink…you know you can't drink.*

They skirted the pool lined with people, some sitting along the edge with their legs dangling in the water, the underwater lights turning their skin pale. It looked like a wonderful idea and Tess hoped that's what Robby had in mind —her feet were throbbing—but he just called a few names, made a few jokes and turned them away from the pool and toward the thick line of trees beyond the patio.

In less than a dozen steps the concrete path gave way to uneven ground that made walking in heels more of a challenge than Tess had hoped to face that evening. She could still hear the party through the trees, but the sound was muffled and even the light that made it through the branches seemed dull compared to the last of the season's fireflies playing hide-and-seek with the dark.

At some point Tess noticed that the party sounds had been replaced by the tumbling rush of water at her side and immediately backed away…only to plant the heel of her left shoe in what felt like mud and stumble.

Tess had never been afraid of the dark before, and especially not with her brother near, but there was something about this particular dark…something that made it seem as if it were closing in on her.

Robby looped an arm around her waist to steady her as she pulled her shoe free.

"Where are we?" she asked. "The river?"

"Your sense of direction has never ceased to amaze me. The river faces the *front* of the house, *this* is the millrace. I apologize for the path...what there is of it. Former owners— *plural*—didn't really keep it up, but don't worry, it'll be easier once we lay down bedding stones and put in the lights."

Tess looked down and didn't see anything. "Lights are a good idea. Can you run electricity all the way out here?"

She felt him turn to look at her and even though she couldn't really see the expression on his face, she felt it against her own.

"That would be a bit much, especially with the depth of the water table here. No we're going to put in solar-powered lights all the way from there—"

Tess couldn't actually see where her brother was pointing, but nodded.

"—to there. Chuck wants to straighten the path out, but I sort of like meandering through the trees, don't you?"

"Mmm-hmm." She was afraid to give any recognizable answer. "So this is the mill race. Nice. Thank you for showing me. Can we go back now?"

"Go back? No, this isn't what I wanted to show you."

"It's not?"

"No. It's just a bit farther up the path."

The path? "I'm not wearing hiking boots, you know."

Robby tossed an arm around her shoulder and began walking. Tess had no choice but to go with him. If she tried to go back she might end up in the millrace. "The tree line ends just up there...then you'll see it."

Tess felt a shiver brush against the back of her neck.

"The ghost?"

"If we're lucky, but Frank usually stays closer to the house. No, I'm going to show you something *really* special."

More special than a ghost? Tess wanted to ask, but didn't get the chance before Robby began hauling her through the darkness again, the need for lights and a level pathway made all the more obvious as they stumbled along. Tess worried more about breaking a heel than about breaking an ankle. Vince loved the way her legs looked in the shoes and if she ruined them he'd—

"Oh my God."

Tess clung to her brother when they stopped.

The path continued past the trees to a field of whispering meadow grass, dotted with fireflies...but that's not what took her breath away.

It sat like a hunched toad on top of a small hill about 100 yards beyond the meadow—lopsided, ravaged, forlorn and hopeless. The pale light of the waning moon had turned it the color of ash.

The ruined building was an almost perfect, but incomplete copy of the bigger house. It had two stories with the same sort of hipped roof braced by stone chimneys at both ends, and six-paned windows, three on the second floor, two on the first... blind glass eyes staring out into the night. A small rain-porch, its roof sagging and canted to one side, covered the dark hollow of a recessed doorway. Dark tendrils of summer-dry ivy rattled like wind chimes made of bone.

A voice shouted and Tess turned around. A hundred yards or so across the whispering meadow grass, the main house shown like a diamond. Shadow people moved in and out of the light and the sound of laughter and music drifted on the breeze to blend with the constant soft murmur of water. It was beautiful and alive and Tess turned her back on it.

The house before her was dark and forbidding, and looked like every child's image of a haunted house.

"I love it."

Robby hugged her. "I knew you would. Really something, isn't it?"

"It's beautiful."

"Well, I wouldn't go that far, but it can be again with enough time and money and a few more ulcers." He sighed. "Probably the wisest thing we could do would be to tear it down."

Tess turned and laid her hands against her brother's chest. Now that they were out of the trees she had no trouble seeing him. "Oh, Robby, you can't!"

"Did I say I was? I said the *wisest* thing we could do is tear it down…and when have you ever known me to do that? Naw, we're going to be very *un*wise about it. Come here."

Robby took her hand and led her to the edge of a group of weathered planks that crossed the millrace. To call it a bridge would be about as accurate as calling the ruins a house. It felt solid enough when Tess stepped on it, but the planks shifted under her weight and she backed off quickly, shouting "heels" as if it was a viable explanation.

Robby nodded.

"Okay, I guess you can see well enough from there. *This* is the millhouse and over there…" He pointed toward a clump of shadows to the left of the house and Tess squinted. "Well, there's really not much to see, to be honest, just a couple pieces of the foundation, that's where the mill was. The original mill was built in 1779, the millhouse in 1816, and *our* house was completed five years later when the miller decided he wanted to boost his social status. You can't really see it in the dark, but if you look over there…"

He pointed to another clump of shadows.

"That's where the original mill was, but a flood took it back in 1907 along with a couple acres of land and about two dozen people." His smiled reflected the moonlight back to her. "Chuck isn't the only one into hysterical history, baby."

Tess looked back at the millhouse.

"But it survived the flood."

"Sure did. See how the land rises up? You can't really tell from here because the grade's so gradual from the river on this side, but if you stood on the other side of the creek you'd be able to see how high the millhouse sits above the water. It rode out the flood high and dry." Robby walked up to the building and thumped the exterior. Only a bit of plaster fell. "Yeah, it's been here a long time."

Tess forgot about her heels and took another step. "Is it haunted, too?"

Robby's laugh was soft, but it filled the part of the night that had settled between them.

"Yeah, baby, it's haunted. And pretty dramatically if the accounts are right." He suddenly jerked to one side and Tess backed up. "Darn mosquitoes. What was I saying? Oh yeah... the ghost. Well, according to the records, the ghost is of a miller who committed suicide in...uh, 1885 or 86. I have the file in my office. He supposedly hanged himself after his wife and child died."

A mosquito buzzed close to Tess' ear and she ignored it. "Poor man. Can we go inside?"

Robby shook his head and walked back across the bridge. "Not right now."

"You're afraid?"

"Me? I bad-mouthed one ghost already, remember? But I am afraid—of falling through the porch or coming face to face with the biggest, meanest looking Wolf spider I've ever seen. First time I came out here the damned thing chased me around the kitchen." He exaggerated a shiver. "First thing on the list is to call in an exterminator with extreme prejudice." Robby turned around and talked directly to the millhouse. "Besides the porch and a couple places of damp, it's pretty sound. It just looks like a nightmare. Somebody did a lot of work on the place, but not recently. It's been wired for electricity *and* they had the cables buried because I guess they didn't like the look of wires, God bless 'em; and there seems to be a pretty good furnace and hot-water heater down in the basement, but... I want to get someone out and look at the whole enchilada before I turn anything on.

"On record, the last person who was supposed to have lived here was Frank."

"Frank?"

Robby turned and pushed his nose to one side then pantomimed being shot. "Frank, the bodyguard."

"You mean your *ghost*?"

"One and the same, only we know where he slept. Chuck thinks this must have been kept as either a safe house for visiting..." He twisted his nose again. "...friends or, I don't really know. But, like I said, all that happened a while back and since then it's been pretty much left to the elements. The roof and porch have to be replaced, no question, and then there's the bathroom.

Tess met the millhouse's blank stare. "There isn't one?"

"No, there is...sort of. I don't know why, considering all the work that was done, but the bathroom is basically a reconverted closet with barely enough room to... Well, you know." He shook his head. "What do you think of black and orange?"

"For Halloween?"

"For a bathroom."

Tess gagged and swatted another mosquito.

"Exactly. How about pink and green?"

She thought a moment and knew that had once been her favorite color combination, but couldn't remember when. Or why. Tess made a face. "Sounds better."

"I'll tell Chuck you think so...personally I want to stay as close to the period as Sherman Williams will allow." Despite the fact that the light was behind her and her face dark, Robby had apparently felt her stunned look. "What? You think I only like uber-modern? Baby, this is a piece of history and I'd like it to reflect that. Besides, I think it's pretty the way it is."

He gave her a hug. "Great minds and hearts do think alike, don't they?"

Tess hugged him back and winked up at the windows before letting go. "So what are you two going to do with it?"

"Well, there's where we have a problem. We don't know, I mean the house is huge and we're still trying to find ways of filling it, but…Chuck would love to turn this into an art studio and I think an off-site home office would be to die for. Or we could try to rebuild our diminished bank accounts and rent the place out. Or…"

He smiled at her. "We can sell it to you and Vince."

"What?"

"Well, I don't mean right now, obviously. It might take a year to get it in shape, but once it is…all this—" He swatted a mosquito. "—could be yours."

Tess didn't have a chance to think of an answer.

"And *why* would we want it?"

For as big a man as he was, Vince could be surprisingly quiet when he wanted to be. Stepping away from her brother, Tess hurried to her husband's side. She'd left the party without telling him where she was going and he was probably… worried.

"I—"

"*I* was looking for you." Vince reached for her, his hand going to the back of her neck and resting there. For the moment. "I didn't know where you were. Chuck pointed me in the right direction and let the cat out of the bag about this… house idea."

"I—" Tess began and then his fingers tightened on her neck. It was dark enough and her hair hid what he was doing so Robby couldn't see. She licked her lips and managed not to flinch. "I'm sorry. I should have told you."

"Yes, you should, you silly." He pulled her close and kissed the top of her head. "I was worried you might have drowned. You sure have a lot of water around here, Roberto."

That was Vince's nickname for her brother, like *stupid bitch* was hers.

A mosquito landed on Tess' cheek and she ignored it.

"My fault, Vince," Robby said, "I just wanted to show Tess the millhouse."

"And to make her that offer. Wow, I don't know what to say." There was no emotion in his voice. "Two houses and you're offering to let us buy...one. I'm beyond words, brother-in-law of mine. But I'm afraid we'll have to decline, we have a home. Right, baby?"

Tess nodded as much as his hand would allow. "Right. I love our place."

"Well, Chuck and I thought just that if you two might ever got tired of apartment living—"

"It's a condo, not an apartment." Vince corrected, chuckling softly when he said it and no one, besides Tess, would have even noticed that his voice had changed, gotten harder. "Of course, it's not a *house*, but it's ours and we like it. Home sweet home."

Vince's fingers pressed deeper into her flesh.

"Well, if you ever change your mind."

"We won't. But thanks."

Robby looked like he was about to say something else but slapped his cheek instead. "Okay, the mosquitoes are winning...everyone back to the party."

They stayed for another hour and Vince never left her side. Dutiful husband that he was, he blamed himself for their having to leave so early—*"Can't party like I used to, know what I mean?"* and called her office the following Monday to tell them she'd come down with a case of food-poisoning over the weekend. *"No, there's nothing really anyone can do. Doctor said it should all be out of her system in the next forty-eight hours. Yeah, we went to a party at her brother's house on Saturday and neither of us has been very well since..."*

   And in between those two points, she was the total focus of his attention.

   "What the hell did you tell your brother to make him offer us a house? You tell him I can't support you? And look what he offers… some shit hole that's about to fall down. He's got more money than God and he offers us THAT? Fuck him."

   Vince took off his wedding ring before he punched her in the stomach—

   "What did you tell him? Answer me, you stupid bitch…what did you tell him?"

   —and he used his bare hands instead of his belt.

   Because he loved her.

CHAPTER 1
FEBRUARY

He's here.

The knife blade scraped against the cutting board as she turned to look at the clock above the stove. He was early. *Oh God.*

Picking up the knife, Tess scooped the quartered red potatoes off the cutting board and into the boiling salted water and did some quick calculations before setting the digital timer. Vince liked his potatoes barely warmed through, almost crunchy, with lots of butter and sprinkled with dried parsley flakes and enough paprika to give them a rosy glow.

And that's the way he was going to get them—perfect. For him. Because tonight she wanted everything to be perfect for him. The potatoes, the roast, the wine…everything.

Except her.

He'd come home early and she wasn't there to meet him and now his dinner would be late. And he wasn't whistling. For the last few months, ever since he'd been made project manager for a major account, he'd come home whistling— even though he couldn't carry a tune—and more relaxed than Tess had ever seen him. He hadn't even felt the need to "correct" her beyond a few quick slaps. It'd been a turning point in their relationship.

That's why tonight *had* to be perfect.

"Tess."

"I'll be right there, Vince." She made a grab for a kitchen towel to wipe her hands and fell forward against the counter as the dizziness took her. *Not now, please God, not now.* Prayers didn't help this time. There was nothing she could do but hold on until it passed. If she fell and he came in and saw her on the floor…

It would ruin everything.

Tess took a deep breath and felt the vinyl flooring tilt under her feet. She closed her eyes—*mistake*—only to open them instantly as the taste of bile filled her mouth. It took three deep breaths and a mouthful of tepid water before the taste went away…and through it all, she listened to the thumps and bumps coming from the next room.

"Anybody home?"

"Yes! Vince, I—I have wine out here. Your favorite."

The random thumping stopped and condensed into step. One after the other, heading for the kitchen.

The dizziness took pity on her and left as quickly as it had come, giving her the chance to be found standing in front of the steam-clouded oven door when Vince walked in.

Whatever mood had been building from the front door to the kitchen, it changed when he sniffed the air.

"Roast beef?"

"Medium-rare, just the way you like it." She caught her reflection in the glass and it wasn't pretty. She'd tried—changing into the pale blue velvet lounging set Vince had gotten her for Christmas and dousing herself with perfume (his favorite)—but it hadn't helped. Her hair was a mess and her face looked haggard. Tess touched the oven and kept her fingers there until they burned. "I'm sorry. It's still got ten minutes to go and I just put in the potatoes and—"

He waved her into silence and leaned back against the pantry doors opposite the stove. He'd taken off his suit coat but left his tie on, although he'd pulled it loose and opened the first two buttons of his shirt. And he was holding a drink in his hand. *He'd had to get his own drink.* The highball glass in his hand was half-filled, no ice; and he drained it as she watched.

"It's okay, don't worry about it." Vince looked down at the empty glass. "I'm early."

Tess exhaled and brushed her fingertips against a pants leg. *Thank you, God.*

"Did you say you had wine?"

"Yes!" She didn't run, exactly, but handed him the bottle as quickly as she could. And even managed to keep smiling when he pulled it out of her hand and replaced it with the empty glass.

"Oh. Chaumbourcin." He didn't sound enthusiastic.

Tess felt a subtle tightening across her shoulders as she walked slowly to the sink.

"I stopped at Clover Hill Winery on the way home and picked it up." She rinsed the glass quickly and set it in the rack before turning around. "You like it, don't you? I mean, you said it was your favorite when we had it at the Thompson's party."

"Well, when you're one of the fair-haired boys in the company you have to say things like that. But that doesn't matter anymore, not after today it doesn't."

The tightness in her shoulders expanded down her back. "Vince, did something happen? What's wrong?"

He chuckled as if she'd said something funny then went in search of their corkscrew. Tess picked it up off the counter and handed it to him before he managed to do more damage to the silverware drawer.

Tess jerked back as he stabbed the cork. "You...don't like the wine?"

"What?" Vince pulled the cork free and a few garnet-red drops splattered the front of his shirt. It would stain and he was usually so careful about things like that. "The wine? No, hell, this is good wine...fine wine, in fact. Top of the line fine wine. And since this will probably be the last we'll have in some time, we might as well drink up."

With a salute, he upended the bottle and took three long swallows before Tess could get it away from him.

"Vince! What's the matter with you?"

She got too close and he pushed her away. It wasn't a hard push, but it was enough to snap her head back at an awkward angle and reawaken the dizziness when she hit the oven door. The roasting pan rattled and Vince took another drink.

"God, I don't why I put up with you. You never think of anyone but yourself. Don't you *even* want to know how my day was?"

Tess ignored the pain where she'd hit the oven handle and the fact that she'd already asked him...no, she'd asked him if there was something wrong, not about his day. How could she be so selfish? She licked her lips.

"I'm sorry, Vince. How was your day?"

He cradled the bottle against his chest and looked at her. "My day? You *really* want to know about my day?"

"Of course I do."

"Well, then, let me just say it was special. I mean, how many times in a man's life does he get professionally castrated in front of his entire project team because some pencil-pushing V.P. from research is trying to save his own ass, huh? How many times can a man be called incompetent without being able to say one fucking word in his defense because the God-damned *client* is standing there smiling? Do you want to know? Well, I'll tell you...*as many times as it takes*, that's how many."

He pushed himself away from the pantry and walked to the oven, ducking his head to see through the glass. Tess moved out of the way slowly, sliding her back against the edge of the counter.

"Pretty fancy for a loser."

"You're not a loser, Vince." She dropped her gaze to the floor when he looked at her. He hated to be stared at. "You're not."

"Oh?" He took another drink. "Well, that's not what the V.P. said while I fucking stood there and then had to apologize to the asshole and client and promise to do a better job. And he was right. I am a loser. Only a loser would stand there and take it and not tell him what he could do with his goddamned job. Sideways."

Without thinking, Tess went to him and touched his arm. "You didn't quit, did you?"

"Quit?" His eyes suddenly grew soft. "No, I didn't quit, I couldn't…a loser can't afford to quit because he has a wife and mortgage and two car payments and bills….   No, I didn't quit."

Vince jerked the bottle toward his mouth and Tess flinched, her hands coming up to protect her face even though he'd never hit her in the face before. He liked places that could easily be covered—the belly, back, upper legs, arms. It was still early spring, perfect weather for bulky sweaters and leggings.

Perfect.

"I'm sorry, I didn't mean to. I—I—"

He backed her across the kitchen to the chrome side-by-side refrigerator/freezer he told everyone she always wanted. The heart-shaped magnet he bought her for Valentine's Day fell, the coupons it held scattering across the floor.

"I, I, I…God, you sound like a fucking broken record. Asking if I quit, shit." He shook his head. "You must not think very much of me."

"I love you, Vince. I have to get the salad ready."   It surprised her when he nodded and moved out of the way.

Grabbing the pre-packaged bag of mixed salad greens and blue-cheese dressing—*his favorite*—she carried them to the sink and was about to reach for the scissors to open the bag when—

Tess managed to move the bag and bowl out of sink before she vomited bright yellow-green bile across the spotless white porcelain.

"Je-SUS…"

Tess heard him back away as another spasm rocketed through her. He hated being around sick people, especially her. Sickness meant weakness and loss of control and those were things he couldn't handle. When she was sick he slept on the couch and ate his meals out to avoid contamination. On the rare occasions he got sick, it was understood she'd stay home to take care of him. Like any good wife would.

"It's okay, I'm—"

She shouldn't have tried to talk. Doing so required taking a breath and when she did the smell from the sink overwhelmed her. The digital timer went off while her stomach squeezed the last drops of bile out of her mouth.

The potatoes...I have to get the potatoes. But all she could do was hold onto the counter and lock her knees to keep from falling.

When the final spasm ended in an empty hiccup, Tess grabbed the dishtowel off the counted and ran it under the faucet. While she wiped her face, she used the sprayer to wash the bright splatters of bile down the drain before rinsing her mouth.

Without turning around, she pointed to the stove.

"C-could you turn off the potatoes, please?"

And heard his weight shift behind her.

"What?"

"They're burning."

Tess was surprised how normal her voice sounded, even more surprised when she heard him move to the stove and turn off the timer. The sound of boiling water seemed to fill the room.

"Just—just take them off the burner, okay?"

There was the scrape of aluminum against coiled iron, then— "What the fuck's wrong with you?"

"I—" Tess gave her face a final pass with the towel and stood up. If she hadn't known how badly he'd take it, she might have laughed.

Holding the near-empty wine bottle in one hand and the steaming pot of potatoes in the other, Vince looked utterly helpless and confused...like a little boy who'd woken up on Christmas Eve to see his parents, not Santa, putting the gifts under the tree. It was endearing and sweet and—

"They're ruined."

For a moment she didn't understand what she'd ruined. This time. "The potatoes? No, I think they'll be—"

"They're ruined."

Tess let her fingers tighten on the dishtowel. It wouldn't be much protection.

"I'm sorry. I can—"

He held the pot out to her. "Is it too much to ask that the food I pay for isn't ruined?"

"I bought the—" Tess pressed her lips together, but it was too late. "I didn't mean that."

"Really? Hmm. You bought these, huh? Well, guess that means *I* don't make enough money, doesn't it? I guess without the fourteen-dollars an hour you bring in we'd starve. Wow...I didn't know that." The bottle moved toward his lips, but stopped halfway. "Oh, did *you* buy this, too? Is this part of the bounty *you* supplied?"

He held the bottle out at arm's length and turned it upside down, letting it bleed out across the floor. When it was empty he carried the bottle to the sink and laid it down carefully.

But he was still holding the steaming pot of potatoes when he turned around. Tess looked down at the wine then at the doorway into the dining room.

"I'll get a mop," she said but he stepped in front of her and water from the pot slashed across the back of his hand.

It was the pain, he wouldn't have done it otherwise—especially not so close to her face—but he did and the sound that came from out of her mouth when the potatoes and boiling water hit her didn't even sound human.

What happened next was all her fault.

If she'd just laid there and been quiet it would have been all right. He would have realized how badly she was hurt and helped her upstairs. Maybe she could have even salvaged the roast...if she'd only kept quiet.

"The baby—"

It wasn't how she'd planned to tell him.

She'd wanted it to be so special—*perfect*. They were supposed to have a lovely dinner *(ruined)* by candlelight and toast the news with wine; then they'd go upstairs and make soft, gentle love for dessert while they talked about the baby, *their* baby.

Tess had kept it a secret for the last four months.

They'd talked about starting a family for almost ten years, but it'd never been the right time. There were always other things to consider first—job security, making more money, getting a bigger place...a house with a big backyard because Vince didn't want his son to grow up a condo-rat. Not *his* son.

She knew he wanted children, they both did, but until the "morning sickness" began at the end of her third, period-less month, Tess hadn't really considered the possibility that she was pregnant. She hadn't had a regular menstrual cycle in almost ten years. When you get hit in the belly enough times it can throw little things, like menstruation, off schedule.

A home pregnancy test confirmed it and tonight she was going to tell him.

Surprise, daddy.

But it wasn't really a surprise. She had known, somehow, and now it was too late to do anything about it. She'd done some research on the Internet during her lunch hours. No clinic would touch her now, not after sixteen weeks. It was too late. *LIAR! The articles said they can terminate up to twenty weeks...*

It's all my fault.

Tess curled into a ball as the empty pot hit the floor next to her. "Vince..."

"What did you say?"

There was a hushed softness to his voice as he bent down. It was the same gentle tone he used when he apologized. Tess couldn't stop herself from shivering in pain, but she smiled as best she could and turned onto her back, smoothing down the wet velvet so he could see the tiny bulge growing beneath her belly button.

"I'm—"

He didn't let her finish.

And, this time, he didn't care where he hit her.

His first blow was an open-handed slap that caught her across the ear. The second, closed-fist, opened her bottom lip and cracked the back of her skull into the floor's simulated bird's-eye maple finish. The third almost knocked her out.

Tess was still conscious enough when he kicked her in the stomach to hear the kitchen smoke alarm signal that the roast, like the potatoes, was ruined.

CHAPTER 2

"Tess? Oh my God, what happened? What did you do?"

"Fell…she fell."

"You bastard. Did you call an ambulance?"

"R-R—"

"Tess…Hi baby, yeah, I'm here now. You're going to be okay. Jesus, Vince."

Darkness.

Light.

Pain.

"I know it hurts, but we're going to help you. Jack, pump in the fluids, she's going into shock. It's okay, Mrs. Warren, just try to relax… Jack—"

Darkness.

Light.

Pain.

"Can you tell us what happened, Mrs. Warren?"

"Look, I told you this would have to wait until we get her stable."

"I know and I'm sorry, but the sooner we get her statement the sooner we can—"

"She's crashing, doctor."

Darkness.

Light.

Pain.   Darkness.   Light.   Pain.
Darknesslightpaindarknesslightpaindarkness light pain   darkness

MARCH

Tess blinked at the sudden intrusion of sunlight that filled the window and scooted to the shaded corner of the bench. It was already the middle of the month, but the March lion prowling the skies, shredding clouds and playing hide-and-seek with the sun. The middle of the month, but Tess couldn't remember the beginning of it...or what she'd answered that made her brother so upset.

Or exactly where they were.

The last thing she *could* remember, this time, was sitting in Robby's kitchen while Chuck poured coffee and told her to 'eat up, gotta get your strength back'...but she couldn't remember why she was sitting there, having breakfast without Vince.

Time kept getting away from her. Days would pass without her knowledge and then, she'd suddenly...*wake up* and discovered she was standing in line at the market or sitting at her desk or in the middle of a conversation.

Like now.

And not know what she was going to say next.

"What do you *mean* you won't appear?"

Tess glanced around as if she was just nervous that someone would hear him and time took pity on her. She remembered where they were (in the hallway outside a courtroom) and why (the preliminary hearing)...and couldn't, for the life of her, recall what she'd said to upset her brother.

She waited until the last echo of his voice faded from the halls of justice.

"Robby, shh..."

"I won't shh. We postponed this whole thing until you were strong enough *to* appear."

He was still yelling and now the two uniformed officers of the court at the far end of the hall were looking at him. If he didn't stop, they might ask him to leave…and then she'd be alone with her attorney—a man she'd recognized immediately from his television commercials, but met with only once before that afternoon, when he came to the hospital to take her deposition. All their other conversations had been over the phone.

"Robby, *please* sit down."

He sat down hard enough to send a jolt through the bench. Tess pressed her hand against the front of her belly and took a deep breath. Neither Robby nor her lawyer noticed.

"Okay, I'm sitting. Now, will you please explain why you're not going to testify?"

"I can't."

"Yes, you can."

"No, I'm afraid she can't." Both of them looked up, but Tess was sure she was the only who was relieved to do so. "A wife can't be forced to testify against her husband, Mr. Denton."

"Well, that's just great!" Robby slapped his knees and Tess saw one of the uniformed bailiffs at the far end take a step toward them. "As long as we're here, why don't you file for divorce and we can come back in six months and try this again. And just when were you going to tell me?"

Tess looked down and found she'd been spinning her wedding ring around and around her finger. It was the second time in her life she couldn't meet his eyes. The first time was in the hospital's Emergency Room while they prepped her for an emergency D&C and he asked her if she was all right. Vince had called him when he noticed blood pooling on the floor between her legs.

And Robby called for an ambulance, and police, because by that time Vince had passed out on the living room couch.

She shrugged because it was safe. "I—didn't want to upset you."

"*You* didn't want to upset *me*? I… Give me a minute."

Robby stood up and left her sitting on the bench while he went down the hall to the drinking fountain. When he came back, he cupped her hands in his and told her, very sincerely.

"This is bullshit."

"Robby."

"I'm serious. That bast... That man should already be in jail for what he did to you, and you know it." This time he sat down so gently Tess didn't feel a thing. "I'm just having a little problem accepting this whole...trial thing, okay? But I will."

Tess hugged him, whispering "Thank you."

"I know exactly how you feel, Mr. Denton," her attorney said. "There is nothing I'd like better than to put your sister up on that stand and let her tell the court exactly what he did to her, but as we both know most of her injuries can't be seen."

It was strange for Tess to hear herself being talked about as if she wasn't there... ghost eavesdropping at her own funeral. She laughed at the thought and quickly covered the sound with a cough.

"The court has copies of your sister's hospital records and the police photos. The judge isn't stupid; he knows what happened to Teresa."

Tess looked up. No one but strangers ever called her Teresa.

"The thing is, Teresa, there's no history of abuse up until that night. Is there?"

She sat back and kept her eyes down. Vince was somewhere in the building, maybe just behind the door across the hall, maybe close enough to hear. "No."

"That's...unusual," he said. "Generally domestic abuse is a gradual escalation of violence and from the severity of your injuries and the number of old fractures found on your X-rays —"

"What?"

Tess grabbed Robby's arm before he could stand up. She was suddenly very sure and very scared that if she didn't hold on tight to her brother he would find Vince and kill him.

"When I was a kid, remember, I was always… It was my fault, Robby. It was always my fault."

It took a moment, but when he finally took her shoulders, his fingers had stopped trembling. "But *he* hit you before, didn't he?"

"No. I mean, not like this."

"Oh God. Tess, why didn't you tell me?"

When she didn't—*couldn't*—answer, her lawyer filled in the silence.

"Unfortunately, even if she were allowed to testify it would still be her word against his. She never brought charges against him, she still hasn't, Mr. Denton. All your brother-in-law has to say is that she fell those other times or claims not to have any knowledge of those injures."

"Okay." Robby took a deep breath. "But what about the baby? He killed the baby- that has to mean something."

"Involuntary manslaughter."

"But he killed it and almost killed her."

"He says it was an accident. He was drunk and when you fell—"

"*Fell?* God, what a bastard!"

"—he must have accidentally kicked when he was trying to help you up."

Tess folded her arms across her empty belly.

"Accidentally kicked her…" Robby's voice had dropped to a whisper and somehow that made it worse.

"Mr. Warren also claims that he didn't know about the baby until the hospital told him about the miscarriage. Teresa, did you mention anything about a baby prior to the attack?"

I shouldn't have told him. I should have done something, gotten rid of it when I found out. It was my fault—I'm sorry—I should have known better. Or waited…God, why didn't I wait just a little longer until he was… I'm so sorry you never got a chance to be born I should never have told him.

"Tess!"

His voice sounded so much like Vince's she almost screamed.

"Tess, did you tell Vince about the baby before he hit you?"

It's my fault. I killed it because I told him. "No."
**

She got the call from her lawyer two days later.

It had gone as he suspected it would—Vince was found guilty of a first-degree misdemeanor and given a one year suspended sentence plus a $1000 fine. But he, her lawyer, didn't want her to worry. When the decision had been handed down, he'd asked for, and been granted, a restraining order against Vince.

In her name.

And, according to her lawyer, Vince hadn't taken it well.

"I think the judge began questioning his decision after your husband threatened him. His attorney tried to blame it on the stress of the trial combined with the trauma of...your accident, but it was a rather weak defense, shall we say. Your husband was charged with contempt of court and will be spending the next forty-eight hours as a guest of the taxpayers. Will I be able to reach you at this number if I need to?"

It was a subtle question. He had her work and cell phone numbers, but he'd called on the landline, the *home* line, and that's what he was asking about.

"Of course you can." There was a pause just long enough to make the hairs on the back of her neck stand to attention. "Why?"

Tess shifted on the couch, pulling her legs up to her chin. Robby paused the DVD just as Joseph Cotton began to suspect there was something odd about the way Jennifer Jones kept getting older every time he saw her, and leaned toward her. He'd been staying with her, at the condo, since she got out of the hospital.

She remembered that.

"What?" he asked.

Tess shook her head. Her lawyer was talking again.

"Is the house in both your names?"

Tess didn't correct him the way Vince would have. It wasn't a *house*, it was never a house.

"Yes… No. I mean— I really don't know. I'm sorry." She moved again, twisting away from her brother so he wouldn't see the blood rush into her cheeks. *God, it was pitiful.* She should have known the answer to that question. A good wife would have known. "Vince always took care of things like that."

"I see."

"But he can't come here, can he? You said there's a restraining order…"

Robby reached over her and took the phone. "Hi, this is her brother. What's going on?"

Tess could hear her lawyer's voice through the narrow gap between the receiver and Robby's ear, but couldn't make out any of the words. But whatever they were, her brother kept agreeing. "Uh-huh." "I see." "Okay." "Right."

A few minutes into the one-sided conversation, Robby got up and carry the walkabout handset into the kitchen. Whatever he was going to say, he didn't want her to hear. Tess lowered her feet to the floor and sat up straight when he came back into the room. Hands in lap, knees together, she kept her voice very calm and was careful not to look him in the eyes.

Vince taught her well.

"I was talking to him, Robby."

She heard him put the handset back onto its base on the end table and felt the couch sag as he sat down next to her.

"I know; you're right. I shouldn't have taken the phone and I'm sorry. But once a big brother always a big brother. Forgive me?"

Tess exhaled sharply. It was almost impossible and totally impractical to stay mad at him. She looked up and smiled. "So what did he tell you?"

"I guess the same thing he told you, more or less...about Vince's little dramatic outburst and time out. Nothing else, no secrets, but I get the impression he thinks it might be wise if you move and I second that opinion. Chuck and I have already talked about it and we want you to move in with us."

Her body turned and made her look up. "When?"

"While you were in the hospital." He shook his head, sighing heavily. "I know, I tried to talk him out of it, but Chuck likes you...probably only because he never knew you during your bratty little sister stage. Believe me, there were times I wished I'd been an only child."

"Liar."

"No, really. He likes you."

She unclenched one hand and touched his arm. "Robby, you know I love you and Chuck, and I appreciate it, but you don't need me constantly underfoot."

"You're right, we don't. That's why we're going to stick you in the millhouse."

The millhouse was the one thing time hadn't made her forget.

"You finished it?"

Robby's smile crinkled the corners of his mouth. "We finished it. So what do you say we pack you up and move you in?"

Tess smiled. "Wasn't it supposed to be a studio? Or your on-site office?"

"Who has time for a studio? Chuck's selling so much real estate he's barely home and if I worked off-site I'd never do the laundry on a regular basis. Please, it needs you. The ghost is lonely."

Tess folded her arms over her belly. *But I already have a ghost right here.* "Thank you, Robby, but this is my home."

"This?"

He looked around the room, his nose wrinkling as if she were living in a garbage dump. That made her angry. Robby had no right to do that, this *was her* home and it was beautiful. It was.

"I can't believe you're even considering staying here. Look... Okay, forget the millhouse. I can see where you might not want to 'live with your big brother' again... even though a half-mile is really not *that* close...but you need to get out of here."

"Why?"

"*Why?*" He looked at her the same way Vince did: like she was crazy and he knew it. "Well, besides the fact that he beat you and killed your baby not twenty feet from where we're sitting—"

"Robby!"

"—This was his place before you got married, so legally, unless he had it changed to duel ownership, which I doubt, it will go to him after the divorce."

Tess was still reeling from what he'd said about the baby, so she didn't immediately hear what he'd said. Or maybe time had gotten away from her again.

"Divorce? What divorce?"

Robby stood up, backing away from the couch but Tess wasn't frightened until he saw that his hands were clenched and the knuckles white.

"Please...don't."

But he misunderstood why she'd said it and just shook his head. "You can't honestly tell me that you plan to *stay* with him? After what he did? Jesus Christ, Tess!"

Tess felt her body relax. He wasn't going to hit her. He wasn't like Vince. He was just angry about what she said. *What did I say? Divorce...something about divorce.*

"I— No, I didn't say..." *He wants me to divorce Vince.* "I just... I just need some time to think about it, okay."

"Tess."

"He didn't mean to, Robby, he had a bad day and I... It was my fault, I should have realized he needed some time to unwind, but I kept—" She pressed her arms tighter into her empty belly. "It was my fault, Robby. He'd never been that angry before."

"How many times before, Tess?"

She shook her head, biting back the answer before it could form. There were some secrets she had to keep from herself. "He's my husband, Robby. And I'll handle it, okay?"

"Okay." He stayed across the room from her but nodded. "But I'm going to get a locksmith over here."

"But he can't come back here...not now, not with the restraining order." She had to keep her voice steady when she'd said that. She knew just how useless a restraining order could be. *Law and Order* was Vince's favorite show.

"Right." But he held up his hands when she leaned forward. "Okay, then let's just call this a precaution. If Vince *was* to come over—for any reason—the fact that you had the locks changed would actually insure that he *couldn't* violate the restraining order, right? Think of it this way...you're preventing him from doing anything stupid."

Venom dripped from the words, but it made the decision easy. And it would solve the problem of having to tell Vince why she did it, if...or when...the time came. "Okay, and get two sets of keys so you can have a set."

"Already planned to, baby. Now..." Clapping his hands together, Robby turned and headed for the kitchen. "So what do you have around here to celebrate?"

Tess waited until he'd left the room to explore the contents of her kitchen before stretching out on the couch. Her eyes closed and she took a deep breath. *Divorce Vince? That was crazy. It was bad now, but he'd forgive her...he was her husband and she loved him. Divorce? That would be suicide.*

        **

He hated beige, but...

The cell was beige.

The walls were beige, the floor was beige, the ceiling was beige. Beige, too, were the woven steel rods of his door, with locking pass-through, and the smooth-edged bed frame that held the thin mattress. Even the recessed mounting that held the security light was beige.

The urinal/john/sink combo, however, was off-white and it matched the thin foam mattress and over-bleached cotton sheet and pillowcase.

He, in his Hunter's Orange prison jumpsuit, was the only colorful thing in the cell. And he was sure that was on purpose.

Beneath his butt was the only other color in the cell, the cot's olive-drab blanket. He wondered how much the government had paid a "decorator" to find the one color that would clash with beige. And bright orange. If he didn't know they were watching him via some well-hidden monitoring device, he would have stuffed the fucking blanket in the crapper and tore the chlorine-scented sheets and jumpsuit to shreds.

But he knew they were watching. He knew the score.

They wanted to see him act like a criminal so they could nod and slap each other on the backs and congratulate themselves for getting "another felon off the street." Yeah, he knew the score: Cops 1, Vince 0. But he wasn't going to play their game and especially not by their rules.

He took a deep breath and heard a cot spring twang.

If he were a criminal, he'd be on his feet, pacing back and forth like some caged and mindless animal. But he wasn't a criminal, so he wasn't going to act like one. He was only there because he'd been too forceful about demanding his rights. No one was going to tell him where he could and could not go. Shit, this was still a free country, wasn't it?

The cot spring twanged again and Vince immediately relaxed. No, he wasn't going to get angry, he was just going to

sit there like he'd been doing—all nice and quiet and still...
forearms resting on his thighs, hands clasped between his
knees, sorrow etched deep into his face.

He'd practiced the look in the bathroom mirror while he
shaved the morning of the court appearance, planning to use
it, after he was acquitted, while he told the court and waiting
reporters how sorry he was and how he could never
intentionally hurt his wife or unborn child.

Sniff.

He'd even managed making his eyes water so it looked
like he was tearing up, but never got the chance to perform.

*Goddamn bitch, if she'd been there...I would have given them
something a real reason to put me away.*

At the sound of footsteps in the corridor Vince let his
shoulders slump forward another inch.

"Brought your dinner."

"Thank you." As he looked up one tear slide from the
corner of his eye. "That's very kind of you."

The female guard's face softened as he stood up and
slowly dragged his feet toward the cell door. He knew what
she'd been expecting to see—the wife-beater, the child-killer, a
monster.

It was amazing what one little tear could do.

"Well, there's no reason for you to be with the general
population. We thought it'd be easier if you ate in here."

There'd been the slightest pause when she said it. Vince
rewarded her with a sad smile so she'd know he understood
and waited until she'd slid the covered cafeteria tray halfway
into the pass-through before raising his hands to take it. The
tray was a light salmon-pink color, just like the ones they had
in high school.

He kept his voice soft and eyes lowered to the tray. "I...
appreciate it."

"Yeah, well, you won't be here that long." She tapped the
flat of her hand against the opening. "Sorry."

"Thank you."

He lifted his gaze slowly to the woman's haggard, pinched face. Mid-forties with smoker's wrinkles and crow's feet; blond hair, black roots and angry eyes of no discernable color—she was prematurely aged and mean from being overlooked by every male she'd ever come in contact with. He'd seen her type before and not just on television. She was a hard-ass like the rest of the women in her "chosen profession," a man-hater who'd been granted power and would be happy to prove it whenever necessary.

As long as she had a gun and there were beige steel bars between her and the real world.

"I don't know what happened..." Vince let his voice break since he couldn't count on anymore tears. "I ... God, I love my wife and ... I must have gone crazy, I would never have hurt her...and the baby. Jesus, I didn't know about the baby...."

Since the temporary insanity defense worked well enough in court he saw no reason not to stay with a proven winner. He saw the tiniest hint of a sneer tightened one corner of her mouth when he looked up.

"So you don't think that some women just need to be hit once and a while?"

Vince backed up a step from the "good-cop/I understand/just spill your guts" routine. *Does she really think I'm that stupid?*

"No! God, never! No woman should ever be hit!" *Where it can leave a mark.* "And I'll regret what I did..." *Not finishing the job and getting rid of the body.* "...until my dying day."

A frown deepened the gullies between the female cop's unplucked eyebrows and he knew he'd won. She believed him and even if she didn't add it to any "official" report, his denial would get planted on the prison system's grapevine.

"We did wrong by him, he's really suffering...so what if he threaten to break the judge's neck, shee-it, poor guy gets told he has to stay away from the woman he loves...the mother of his poor, dead baby? Hell YAH, I'd say he had the right to be angry!"

More than a right.

"Thank you again for..." He lifted the tray and nodded, his sad smile dipping slightly as she walked away.

Then let it fall—*slowly, because they were watching*—as he walked back to the cot and sat down. With a sigh, he removed the cover and looked at his meal. Couple of chicken patties, mashed potatoes and gravy, gray beans and a berry-ish cobbler. Beige, white, gray and purple-ish.

Vince opened the cellophane packet containing his plastic cutlery—white—twin-packs of seasoning and paper napkin and ate every bite just like the good little boy...no, like the *innocent man* that he was.

CHAPTER 3
APRIL

"Hey!"

The can of tuna slipped out of Tess' hand and rolled across the aisle. He stopped it with his foot and smiled as he picked it up. In two steps he was at her side, holding the can out to her. An empty shopping-basket dangled from his other hand.

"Here." He lifted the can a little higher as if she hadn't seen it. "Well, go on...take it."

But when she tried, he pulled the can away and frowned, shaking his head. "No, you don't want this one, it's dented."

Vince put the can on the top shelf next to a row of corned-beef hash where it could be easily seen and plucked a new one from the stack. The frown didn't leave his face as he studied the label.

"This isn't our usual brand." He tossed it into her shopping cart and smiled. "Is it better?"

"It—it's on sale." Tess nodded to the sign in front of the display and stood there, waiting, unsure what to do next. She couldn't just *thank him* and walk away, even though she knew that's exactly what she should do. If she didn't and someone saw them, he could get into trouble. And it would be her fault. "I have to—"

"Go?" He reached out, tapping the flat of his hand against the side of her cart. He didn't grab it, he didn't have to. "Have someplace special in mind?"

"No. I...I just have to get some things..."

She took a step back and he followed as if he were anchored to the cart.

"For dinner? You having *tuna* for dinner...or is that just for the appetizer?" He leaned in before she could get away and began examining the few items scattered across the mess bottom of the cart. *Why did I get a cart? I didn't need a cart. A basket would have been easier to get away...* "Have a big evening planned, do you?"

"No! I...I just like tuna."

"Really? That's strange; I don't remember you liking tuna all that much. Interesting how much a person can change, isn't it?"

His smile grew edges.

"I have to go, Vince. Please."

He moved his hand from the shopping cart to her arm and squeezed just hard enough to make her gasp before he let go.

"So who's stopping you?" But she didn't move even after he stepped away and began contemplating the cans of *Dinty Moore Beef Stew.* "So what do you think is the better bargain... one big can or two of the smaller ones? I'm not used to having to buy or *cook* for myself, but I'm sure that doesn't bother you."

"Vince, you can't..." The words froze in her throat when he turned. "You're not supposed to be here."

"Where? In the market?" He looked confused. "Where else am I supposed to go food shopping?"

"You don't live near here."

"How do you know where I live? Have you been stalking me?"

She'd almost forgotten how quick and clever he could be. Everyone always joked he should have gone into politics, the way he could twist facts around; but they'd never had to live with the results of that skill. And he was doing it again. Of course she knew where he lived—a studio apartment in Norristown even though he could have easily afforded a high-rise in Conshohocken overlooking the Schuykill. The address, along with a list of items the court agreed he could take from the condo, was presented to her by his lawyer, via her lawyer.

That was three weeks ago.

And since then she'd seen him, *thought* she'd seen him twice.

Before now.

The first time was in the parking lot of the shopping center near the condo. She was coming out with a load of dry-cleaning and saw *someone* who looked like him near her car. But he turned and walked away when he noticed she'd seen him.

There was a scratch along the driver's side door, the kind a key would make, where the man had been standing.

A week later a dark blue Lexus sedan, just like his, followed her to work. The driver kept flashing his high beams each time she took a curve, momentarily blinding her, then honking when she slowed down. The car sped away when she pulled into the parking garage.

"Well, if you must know...I had dinner with some clients at *Shiraz* and this was the closest market. So..." He lifted his empty basket. "But what are *you* doing so far away from home? Got coupons?"

Tess lowered her gaze to the scruffed floor tiles. The night staff had just begun polishing the bakery when she walked in just before midnight. She'd driven to the twenty-four hour Acme in Paoli, because it was so far away from the condo she never thought he'd find her there...and because, up until that moment, she wasn't sure he had been following her.

"Please." She whispered above the piped in *Musak*. "Leave me alone."

The empty basket swung in an arc as he moved his hands in a *'who me?'* gesture. "I'm not doing anything."

"Yes you are. You're not supposed to talk to me." She tried to keep her voice low and steady, but it kept catching in her throat. "If someone saw you and called the police..."

"Who would call them?" Vince laughed. "And what would they say? That they saw me pick up a can of tuna?"

Tess glanced past his shoulder to the far end of the aisle. It was empty; there was no one to see what was going on or what he was doing. No one to help her. Movement caught her eyes and she glanced up into a security mirror as a man in an Eagles sweatshirt and jeans hurried past the end of the aisle behind her. The man disappeared, but left them behind in the glass so small and far away, but it was enough. If Vince did anything someone would notice.

He was smiling when she looked down.

"I know you've been following me, Vince."

He cupped his hand to his ear. "What? Speak up, honey, I can't hear you."

Tess cleared her throat even though she knew he'd heard her perfectly.

"I said I know you've been following me. I've seen you."

"You have?" He picked up a can of hash and dropped it into his basket. Vince hated hash. "Did you tell anyone?"

Tess shook her head.

"Just as well for you...and that's not a threat, sweetheart, so don't go making it into one. The honest truth is that I'm worried about you, I really am. You sound like you're getting a paranoid. Why would I be following you? This was a chance meeting. It happens all the time."

"Not if there's a restraining order."

He took a quick step forward and she closed her eyes, bracing against the blow to come. Nothing happened. But she knew it still could, that he might be waiting for her to open her eyes, to challenge him with a look...as she'd done it before. So often before. Tess silently counted to three and opened her eyes.

For a moment she thought she saw fear in his eyes, but that was stupid. Vince wasn't afraid of anything. It was something, though, a look she'd never seen before and it grew as he took a step toward her.

"What do you say to me?"

Her mouth opened—to plead, to explain—and she was almost more shocked than he was by the sound that followed. Vince backed up, eyes wide, and lips trembling, face pale as the scream swept out across the canned meats/soup aisle to fill the near empty supermarket.

The sleeve of his coat brushed against hers as he ran past. It wasn't more than a touch, but it would have added a new dimension to the scream if Tess hadn't noticed the woman at far end of the aisle. Bundled up against the cold in a fluorescent-yellow fleece jacket, one hand lifted toward Wolfgang Puck's smiling face, the other knuckle-white on the handle of her shopping cart, she was staring at Tess the way people did when suddenly coming face to face with a crazy person.

Her face.

The scream ended with almost surgical precision. There was no sobbing gasp at the end, no trembling intake to refill her empty lungs, nothing—except the look on the woman's face. It took a moment for the echoes to stop reverberating and then the store's ambient sounds returned: Musack's version of *Muskrat Love* accompanied by the hurried squeaks and thumps of rubber-soled shoes.

When the night manager and two of his aproned male employees did a stumble-slide into the aisle, the soup-loving woman in yellow was gone and Tess took a deep breath. Her throat felt like it been scoured with sandpaper; which made her whispered explanation—a lie about having seen a spider— sound pathetic but real. She couldn't take the chance of telling them the truth, because Vince might still be there, listening.

Maybe she was getting a little paranoid.

Tess couldn't tell if they believed her or not, but the Night Manager apologized and asked if she'd like him to call someone for her...all of which he did while personally checking her out.

Tess thanked him, but held up her cell phone by way of an answer and had punched in a number before her total for the single can of tuna appeared on the register's digital screen. She paid the fifty-three cents and asked if she could wait inside the well-lighted entrance until her ride showed up. The manager was still very polite and said that she could, but kept finding things to do near the front of the store so he could keep an eye on her.

Robby arrived forty minutes later, a long winter coat over his pajamas, and followed her back to the condo.

**

Vince sat in the dark nursing a neat scotch and his growing anger. He still couldn't believe what happened. *The bitch called the cops.* And he'd been so happy when he got home...

"Wrong." He took a sip, correcting himself.

This wasn't home; *she* was living in his home. *This*, be it ever so humble and furnished, was just window-dressing. If he'd moved in with friends—and he'd had a number of offers, most from buddies he'd known all his life, and a couple from female co-workers who'd made less than subtle hints about spare rooms and understanding shoulders to cry on—

As if I want to break in a new model. The idea, especially the *breaking in* part almost made him smile, but he swallowed it along with a mouthful of scotch.

If he moved in to a reasonably nice place with friends, or possible lovers, his situation wouldn't seem so obviously horrible.

And he wanted her to suffer for what she'd done to him.

Was still doing. *She. Fucking. Called. The. Cops!*

Vince took a deep breath and another drink to steady himself. It was the last thing he thought she'd be capable of doing, but it just proved how much she'd changed from the sweet, innocent, malleable woman he'd married. And that, more than the fact she'd actually...

"Hang on, hang on, hang on."

Vince shook his head. He was letting what happened get the better of him and that wasn't productive. If he was honest with himself, and he always tried to be, her calling the cops—*bitch*—probably worked to his benefit.

Yeah, her screaming like a banshee in heat had startled him, but he made it out of the market and into his car without being seen—he was sure of that. And the forty minute drive from Paloi to Norristown had transformed the momentary alarm he'd felt (he refused to call it panic) into exhilaration. He'd scared the crap out of her.

So he was feeling pretty good when the cops showed.

He'd toasted himself a stiff drink even though he generally didn't drink on a work night—but this was a special occasion—and was crawling into bed to enjoy Bruce Willis dying hard on cable when the two cops came a'rap-tap-tapping at his door.

The drink saved him. It made him cool and calm and collected and a much better actor. But the pj's and ruffled hair were the icing on the cake.

Even the shock when he opened the door worked for him. *"Oh my God, what happened? What's wrong?"* When they told him, he didn't have to pretend anymore. Vince went cold inside.

The Goddamned bitch.

"My wife said what? That I've been following her? No, sir, I haven't. Tonight? Uh, well…I had a business dinner in Wayne after work and… um…came back here. Sure, I can give you their names. No sir, I haven't seen my wife in…some time. We're having some trouble and I've been ordered to stay away from her. I don't know what to tell you, except that she's been under medical care recently…"

Nothing he said had been a lie.

Vince knew the cops had probably already memorized his file, so if he hadn't mentioned "the trouble" between them, they would have been suspicious. He wasn't stupid. He gave them solid facts and never explained *what* sort of medical care his wife was under. It was her word against his. He had witnesses to his whereabouts, she didn't. That was the beauty of late night shopping.

The policemen took his statement, mumbled the required warnings about "obeying the terms of the restraining order' and left with an apology for having woken him up.

The end.

For the moment.

Vince raised the glass to his lips. When he hit nothing but empty air he opened his eyes to make sure. Getting up to fix another wouldn't be a good idea, he was going to be fuzzy enough from the two he'd already had, so he sat there holding the empty glass and staring out at the flickering neon sign across the street. The bar was closed, but the light stayed on.

Enticing. Teasing. Offering a promise that couldn't be fulfilled. Lying.

Like her.

Bitch.

She'd made a promise to him and God to love, honor and obey... and he'd made sure that she'd kept that promise. True, sometimes her trembling deference got on his nerves, but that didn't mean he didn't love her. Of course he loved her, she was his wife and it wasn't like he *constantly* hit her, there were lots of times he let things pass without even making a comment.

Hell, he even forgave her—a little—for the whole court thing because he knew her brother had put her up to it. Robby never did like him, but this...this was all *her* doing.

She'd betrayed him; it was as simple as that. He couldn't let it pass. Not this.

Vince leaned back into the chair. It was clean, reasonably modern and moderately comfortable; but it wasn't *his* chair and this wasn't *his* home...and there was nothing he could vent his frustration on that wouldn't have to be explained and replaced. He couldn't call anyone—*not at 2:30 fucking A.M—*

and it wasn't the sort of neighborhood a man could go for a walk to help clear his—*anger*—mind. He was trapped.

And it was all her fault.

She thinks she's going to get away with it. Stupid bitch...stupid, stupid bitch.

Setting the empty glass on the bedside/end table as he stood up, Vince shuffled the few inches from chair to sofa/bed. In the morning—*early, before work*—he'd call his beloved brother-in-law and help build another snare. There was no doubt in his mind that Tess would have already told her brother, but he wanted to give Robby another possible scenario to worry about. *"God, Robby, I don't know what to do. Is she on drugs or something? I mean, she's gone paranoid...thinks I'm stalking her, for God's sakes. Oh, she told you that? Dear Jesus, my poor Tess. She needs help, Robby, what can we do?"*

It was perfect.

Vince pulled the new, but still unfamiliar bedding up over his shoulder and crushed the Wal-Mart pillow into an almost comfortable lump. He'd stop following her for a while. A couple of weeks, at least, to let any surveillance team she set on him get bored with watching a perfectly innocent man go through his daily—and lonely—routine. He'd check with his lawyer and then, when he was sure it was safe, he'd go have a little chat with her.

And straighten everything out, just like old times.

Vince smiled as he closed his eyes. "Goodnight, sweetheart."

Goddamn bitch.

CHAPTER 4
MAY

Tess moved the cursor's tiny arrow to SEND, finger poised above the left-click button, and felt time jerked away from her.

He's here.

She should be in the kitchen finishing—*no*—no, standing near the door...but not too near so he doesn't feel crowded and —*NO*—no she should be....

Tess stood up and felt the file slip from her hand, reshuffling the color-coded pages and text like misplaced autumn leaves across the top of her desk. They made soft rustling sounds and that's what brought time back, the sound...because it had been a sound, a thump or a scratch or something just enough out of the ordinary that had taken it away in the first place.

*Out of the ordinary...*what a ridiculous choice of words. Everything was *out of the ordinary* now. There hadn't been an *ordinary* thing in her life since...

Tess made herself stop by looking at the wall clock above her desk. She'd only lost a few minutes this time...another poor choice of words.

"What am I doing?"

What are *you doing?*

Good question. She was supposed to be working.

Tess began gathering up the file, putting the pages back in their right order, when she heard another little sound near the front door and grabbed time with both hands so it wouldn't get away.

He's *not* here. It was just a sound.

Are you sure?

No, she wasn't.

Leaving the file in more or less a completed stack, Tess walked to the loft's half-wall and took a deep breath, then slowly leaned forward over the clear pine railing until she could see down into the living room. It was empty and front door was locked, the dead bolt engaged.

Just the way she'd left it the night before, and double-checked it that morning.

He wasn't here and he wouldn't be. Whatever else Vince was—vicious *(not without cause)*, vindictive *(only when he's right)*, violent *(stop it)*—he wasn't stupid.

Time quivered just a little, but Tess hung on.

She hadn't seen Vince in weeks, not since the night he attacked her in the market... *No, now who's being vindictive? He didn't attack me, he didn't do anything. Not really.* He was probably angry, Robby said he'd called him the morning after and told him about being visited by the police *(I shouldn't have done that)*, but he wouldn't come to the condo. Besides, he wouldn't know she was there, he'd still think she was working at the office. Whatever she heard or thought she heard to make her think he was there was gone now...or probably never was. In the six weeks since she'd joined the ranks of telecommuters, she'd discovered just how many sounds the condo had that she hadn't heard before. Whirrs and thuds and strange little grindings right before the heat came on...the nice normal sounds she'd never bothered to notice before.

As normal as the ticking of a clock.

Or the sound of a key in a lock.

"Stop it."

Tess took her own advice and walked back to her desk. Sliding the semi-organized pages into a manila folder, she filed it as it. It didn't really matter, it was just a secondary copy, but still, she would never have considered doing that at the office and the little transgression made her smile. Vince would have been furious if he knew, but Vince would be furious if he knew she was working from home.

Vince had a very strong opinion of telecommuters—he hated the idea. If a person didn't actually *go* to a job, it wasn't really working. Tess hadn't known how strongly he felt until they were driving back from a dinner with Robby and Chuck. *"Goddamned lazy bastards, that's all they are. Slobs who want to sit around in their underwear all day and think they're better than everyone else because they get to work from home. Shit. That's what's wrong with this damn country…people don't care about anyone but themselves."* The dinner had been to celebrate Robby's new "home office."

If she hadn't known her husband so well, Tess would have thought Vince wasn't as angry about the state of the country as he was jealous of not being able to do the same thing.

But she did know him, all too well.

Robby had helped her make the decision…more or less. When they got back to the condo, Tess told what happened at the market and how she thought Vince had followed to the office and he told *her*, with his usual calm and sensitivity, that she could either telecommute or quit and come live with him and Chuck.

Two options, one choice.

But it was *her* decision.

And her fault, if Vince ever found out.

There was another soft thump from somewhere downstairs or from the next condo and, *this time*, Tess ignored it in favor of the blinking message on her computer screen.

ETA MAC-3 REPORT?

Tess clinked SEND and typed:

sent

O'DONNELL FILE?

She lifted the next manila envelope off the stack in her IN box—a gray plastic desk tray she'd bought at STAPLES—and laid it down next to the keyboard. In the six weeks she'd been *"home* working" the routine had become very simple. One day a week, her choice, she went to the office to pick up files—and catch up on the gossip—and drop off the last batch.

The only drawback was the files she was being given. For the most part they were complicated, monstrous, usually dealing with estates and survivor's rights, and were obviously something no one else wanted to tackle.

about to ocr and scan to word, give me a couple hours to see what's up

...and stop SHOUTING!

A moment later a new message appeared:

Sorry

**

Tess was sitting back drinking coffee and watching the pages feed through the optical character scan program when the phone rang. Cup in hand and feeling very comfortable, she took a deep breath and put the phone to her ear. Her supervisor had gotten into the habit of kibitzing with her from time to time, especially if the file she was about to work on was even more of a logistical nightmare.

"Peter, it's only been thirty-five minutes."

She heard a sharp intake of breath.

"Peter?"

"No. It's me. Who's Peter?"

Vince.

"I asked you a question."

The phone suddenly went slippery in her hand, forcing Tess to grip it tighter until she could feel the blood throbbing in her fingers.

"Tess...? Look, I—I know I'm not supposed to call, but... I just wanted to... Oh hell, Tess, I miss you and...and it's none of my business who Peter is."

She closed her eyes so she could pretend she wasn't there. "Peter's my supervisor."

"Oh, he's the one I talked to then when I called your office. So, you're working from home now, huh?"

Tess opened her eyes. *He knows I'm home or he would have called the office.* "No...I—I did some work over the weekend and it was easier to fax it in from—"

"Don't lie to me, Tess; you know how much I fucking hate it when you lie."

The phone slammed back onto its cradle and Tess stared at it as if it'd done it all by itself. When it rang again a moment later, she had no choice but to pick it up.

"That wasn't very bright, Tess." His voice was soft, almost indifferent, as if he were talking to a stranger. "But you never were, were you? I guess this Peter guy must like stupid women."

Hang up. Hang up now and don't answer it again. "Peter's my supervisor and that's all. I—Vince, leave me alone. Please. You're not supposed to call me."

"Stupider and stupider." He chuckled and her body tried to fold in on itself, to disappear into nothing. *Why didn't time disappear again?* "I can do anything I want."

HANG UP!

"I'm going to call the police!"

She set the phone down very carefully sat staring at it as if it were a coiled snake ready to strike...waiting for it to ring again. It was a bluff; of course, she had no intention of calling the police. But Vince didn't know that. Vince didn't call back.

Tess slowly released the tension along her arms just enough to reach for the silent phone. She'd called Robby...just to talk, just to hear a safe voice, a sane voice, a—

In place of a dial tone she heard him laugh.

"You can't call out until I hang up, Tess." He stopped laughing. "Jesus Christ, you really *are* one fucking stupid bitch. Now...open the door."

Tess dropped the phone as she stood up and turned toward the front of the house.

He's here.

CHAPTER 5
JUNE 10th

Something had happened to her, but she couldn't remember what it was.

It had to have been something bad, she knew that much, because when time took pity on her and let her wake up, it was always in the same place—a hospital room. The faces changed, though; sometimes it was Robby, sometimes a doctor or nurse…but never Vince.

She felt asleep most of the time, even when she "woke up" to find herself floundering in the middle of a conversation and the other person was waiting for her to answer with something reasonable, something connected to whatever had been said.

Robby told her not to worry about it, that she'd be fine.

When time slowed enough for Tess to catch up, six weeks had passed.

Bits of memory came back, but not much. She remembered opening the front door and Vince coming in and she remembered how angry he was about her having changed the locks and then…

She remembered screaming and feeling Robby hold her hand and tell her she was okay, that everything was okay… Vince couldn't hurt her anymore.

She was safe, because Vince….

Was in jail. Where else would he be? Even if she did let him into the house—she remembered somebody, one of the faces in the hospital, asking her that—he'd violated the restraining order. She remembered a lot of questions and even some of her answers, but not much more. For all she knew she'd been sworn in and given testimony…or that could have just been from a show she'd watched on the wall-mounted television across from her bed.

But Robby wouldn't lie and he'd said Vince couldn't hurt her anymore.

She was safe.

Tess nodded and exhaled, trying to keep her smile from shrinking any farther while Robby bobbed and weaved behind the tiny digital camera in his hands.

He wanted another picture.

Six weeks and thirty-four hours and she was standing with her arms wrapped around the carton of groceries Robby had handed her *"just for the picture."* Six weeks and thirty-four hours and she was trying to smile and not squint while looking up at the millhouse. Six weeks and thirty-four hours and so much had happened...

...that she couldn't remember.

"Did I tell you Chuck already has a couple interested in the condo?"

Tess lost the smile but kept the squint. He had mentioned it, a couple of times already, and Tess either pretended she hadn't heard or changed the subject. She knew why Robby kept pushing, and loved him for it. He wouldn't even let her go back there when she left the hospital. *"Too many bad memories."* Not all the memories had been bad and Tess had wanted to tell him that...wanted to tell him there'd been good memories and sweet ones she'd treasure for the rest of her life, but didn't because she knew he wouldn't listen. Not now.

It didn't have to happen this way. If I'd been a better wife...if I'd loved him more, I could have stopped it. It's my fault.

She couldn't sell the condo. It wasn't hers to sell; it belonged to Vince. He'd never forgive her.

"Robby, I was thinking—"

He shook his head. "Nope, no thinking allowed. Besides we already settled this at the hospital."

We did? "But..."

"Settled, now smile like you're happy to be here."

She didn't have to act. She'd been watching the march of moving men and painters and gardeners and contractors from the balcony of Robby's office in the "Main House." That had been as close as he and Chuck had allowed her to get. They wanted the millhouse to be perfect before they handed her the keys.

It had been the longest week of her life...if it had only been one week...and now that she was standing here, only a few yards away, how could she not be happy? Within reason, of course. *Vince probably wasn't enjoying himself at all, but...*

Tess heard the camera click and blinked to find the millhouse eclipsing the setting sun. It was engulfed in a fiery corona that turned the roof shingles copper and softened the gray stone walls with a wash of honey. The windows were set in Brick-red frames, the glass shining like ice. The front door and porch supports matched the windows; the stoop matched the stone walls. Twin brass lamps done in a Colonial style braced the front door.

It was as if a small piece of autumn had been misplaced atop a summer hill.

And autumn had always been her favorite time of year.

She'd met Vince in autumn. Their baby would have been born in autumn.

Tess looked down at the carton in her arms and couldn't remember why she was carrying it.

"Great!" She winced as the flash went off. Robby was standing in the middle of the footbridge. "Very subtle, very poignant. Now look up and say horseshit."

Tess stared at the camera. "Horseshit."

He winked at her as he backed off the bridge and up the graveled incline to the porch. "You're a natural. Okay, one more."

"Enough."

"Come on."

"No, really. I'm...tired."

Tess gauged the effectiveness of her pout by how quickly Robby came tearing back down the walk and across the bridge to take the carton from her. She gave it a ten.

"I'm sorry, baby, I wasn't thinking. But I just thought you might like a visual record of today. The first day of the rest of your...yadda, yadda, yadda. Here, take the camera."

She did and took his picture.

"Hey!"

Tess made a face. "You're a natural."

Stepping aside, he nodded his head. "Well, what you waiting for? I'm not going to carry you across, my hands are full."

Her heart was pounding a little harder when walked across the footbridge. And stopped to listen to the millrace as it tumbled over rocks beneath her feet. She would hear it for as long as she stay, it was part of her now as much as it was a part of the millhouse.

Robby cleared his throat behind her. "Plan to stand there all evening or do you actually think you might open the friggin' door? You're right, this *is* heavy. Move!"

The gravel shifted under her feet, making a new sound for her to keep as she ran up the slope to the rain porch. Tess paused once more, brushing her fingers along the shining brass escutcheon plate before she wrapped them around the colonial-styled door latch and opened the door.

The difference between the real twilight outside and the artificial twilight within the thick-walled house was just enough to cause momentary blindness and anyone else would have stopped and waited for their eyes to adjust. Tess didn't, trusting some until-that-moment unused inner sense to guide her as she plowed through the gloom. She managed three steps before her right toe came into swift and solid contact with a large and unforgiving object.

"Ow!"

The pain helped clear her vision.

Bracing herself against the entryway wall, Tess rubbed her injured foot and glared down at the sealed moving box marked *"Misc. /kitchen."* There were more boxes of various sizes along one side of the shotgun hallway that led to the back door and one, medium-sized, at the bottom of the narrow staircase labeled *"bathroom."*

Robby came in and took her elbow. "Break anything?"

"No." She lowered her foot to the floor and wiggled her toes more to convince herself than her brother.

"Well, this is what you get for wearing sandals."

Vince had said the same thing.

Tess nodded but kept her eyes on the boxes. This was all that was left of the life she'd had with Vince. When Tess finally had to accept that no amount of pleading or begging or little sister guilt she could lever against her brother would change his mind about letting her go back to the condo, she'd sat down and made a list of the things she needed.

Wanted.

Deserved.

And hadn't been able to think of one thing.

Vince's things—his books, his DVDs and CDs, his clothes, the art pieces that were insured, all of the jewelry—had gone into similar, well-marked cartons that now sat in the climate controlled storage unit she rented.

Waiting for him.

Robby and Chuck had decided for her.

"You're right."

"No, I'm not," he said. "It's summer. You can go barefoot if you want to…but I wouldn't. Ticks, spiders, snakes, sharp rocks…you're in the country now, girl. And we did volunteer to put all this away for you."

They did. "I know, but you two have already done enough."

"Never. Besides the movers did all the really hard work. But you have our number if you decide we'd like some help. So..." He walked away so she'd have to look up. "What do you think about your color scheme?"

My *color scheme?*

Tess followed him into what the floor plans Robby showed her was called the "Keeping Room." To the right of the entranceway, the room had been divided into a dining room, directly off the entrance, with a galley-styled kitchen along the back wall. A fireplace, big enough to roast the meanest wicked witch almost filled the wall opposite from where she stood, gaping like a tourist.

It was unbelievable.

Robby was still talking when Tess blinked time back into being.

"...houses were supposed to have white walls and I was hoping you'd agree with me. Okay, I'll admit it; I was floored when you showed me the colors you picked out. I mean, we must have brought a hundred paint sample cards, but you knew exactly what you wanted. Sight unseen as it was."

Tess smiled. *Samples? Brought over where? What's he talking about?*

"Yeah, I know exactly what you're thinking—Mr. Ultra modern had a concern about color. But, as much as I hate to admit I might be wrong when it comes to style...I have to admit it's gorgeous. Especially in here."

He walked to the middle of he room, the carton of groceries still in his arms, and turned. "*Valley Hills.* And you have your *Manhattan Mist* in the living room, other side of the entrance, *Pensive Sky* and *Porpoise* upstairs. Pure white trim all around, as contrast. Goes really beautifully with the yellow pine floors don't you think?"

Tess could hardly catch her breath, it was so beautiful, but when she did a scent of something musty and sweet moved through the air toward her.

After-shave?

"What are you wearing?"

Robby looked down at his polo shirt and jeans. "I beg your pardon?"

"No, I meant your after-shave."

"Cologne, baby... *Cool Water*, why?" He lifted one arm and sniffed. "Are you saying I need a shower?"

"No, I just..." Tess took a deep breath. Whatever the scent was that she smelled was gone. "It must have just been the paint. And it's...beautiful, Robby. Thank you."

"Hey, don't thank me, you picked out the colors. I just paid for it. Here, let me put this down and you can give me a big hug of gratitude."

Robby deposited the carton on the white farm table Vince had given her for their first anniversary to replace the old dinette set he'd had since college.

"My grandmother always said the dining room table is like the heart of the home...this is our heart."

Tess ran into her brother's arm, burying her face into his neck and hugging him until he groaned. It hadn't been his cologne she'd smelled.

"Uncle! Aunt! Okay, enough gratitude before you break a rib." Robby pushed her away gently, but held her at arm's length for a moment before letting her go. "Welcome home, baby. Go...explore."

Shoving the carton out of the way, Robby pulled out one of the chairs and sat down while Tess kept shaking her head in wonder. The table and its four chairs sat to the right of the massive hearth and faced the deep-set window that opened to a view of the millrace and field beyond; the Main House hidden by the angle and line of trees that marked the path. On each side of the window, were built-in cabinets painted white to match the table and the country-styled kitchen cupboards on the opposite wall.

"Wow."

"All I can say is 'thank God for Home Depot.'"

Tess swatted him on her way to the fireplace. It seemed even larger up close.

Two dozen red-and-white "peppermint" carnations filled the cast-iron pot that hung from the end of a long, twisted metal "cooking" bar. Their spicy scent filled the air, but it wasn't what she'd smelled earlier.

She leaned down and inhaled. "Thank you, Robby."

"Thank Chuck when you see him." He'd forgotten his promise about not helping her unpack and was digging through a box marked "Utensils/cooking. "I wanted to get roses."

"I like carnations better."

He shook his head. "And I could never understand that. Are you sure we're related?"

Tess would have stuck out her tongue if he'd been paying attention, but since he wasn't she turned back to the fireplace. The deep sage-green paint was perfect for the room. She was glad she picked it. There was enough gray in the tone to compliment the field-stones that fronted the hearth and made the white pine mantelpiece seem to glow in contrast. Robby had been busier than he let on. Along with two new brass candlesticks—complete with gray tapers—the mantel was crowded with framed photographs.

They were photos she hadn't seen in years. Family shots. The two of them as children; alone, together and with their parents. Christmases, birthdays, picnics in the back yard. Small occasions and bigger ones: Tess in a cap and gown, Robby with long hair and sunglasses holding a VOTE FOR DUKAKIS sign. A small gilt oval frame held a sepia-toned image of their grandparents as newlyweds, a more modern frame held their parents...hippies with flowers in their hair.

Tess touched the glass that had protected them for so long. She could almost remember her parents, but they were so young in the photo they looked like strangers. Robby walked across the room and put an arm around her waist.

"I found it years ago when Grandpa died, but there was never the *right* place to show them off, so I just stuck them in a box. I think they look pretty well right here, don't you?"

Tess nodded until she was sure her voice wouldn't break. "Yeah, they do."

"So, tell me how much you love this fireplace."

"Beyond words."

"Thought so. And you know you can actually cook in it, if you ever want to."

Vince had always wanted a big fireplace.

"Maybe *S'mores* this winter."

"Oh God…yes! But for everyday stuff, I think you'd better use the stove. It's propane, so it will take a little getting used to, but once you figure it out you'll love it. We do…well, Chuck does and since he's the chef, I value his opinion. Everything else is electric. You are also hooked up with phone and cable even though it almost took an act of God to get it out here. You should have heard the colorful language when they realized how much wire they had to lay…oh, and I won't even tell you what happened when they saw the millrace, but it's all up and running. We tried it last night. Same with DSL. I had it and the FAX line installed in the room directly above the kitchen. Oh, gotta show this, it's great."

Robby got up and walked to the middle of the room, then pointed to a small, lattice covered circle in the ceiling. "It's covered right now, but in the winter, if you've been baking or have a fire going in here, all you have to do is take off the lid and the heat vents right up into the room upstairs. That's the office, by the way. We had to narrow both of the upstairs rooms a bit when we redid the bathroom and built a bedroom closet for you, but this room—" He jabbed his finger up and down. "—is smaller because it has the access to the attic, so I thought it made more sense to make that the office. By the way, the attic's huge, goes the full length of the house and is fully insolated. It's pretty narrow because of the pitch of the roof...so if you want to put in a bowling alley, just let us know."

Tess smiled at the covered grating. "Was that your idea?"

"No, that was original...pretty clever these founding fathers, huh?" He pointed to the corner units. "But those we put in, as well as the bookcase and window seat in the living room. Walls are solid and about two feet thick and it's a lot smaller than... what you're probably used to."

"But I have an attic."

"Yes, you have an attic, and a basement crawlspace that you get to through a trapdoor in the closet under the stairs."

"Wow." She linked her arm in his. "Show me the rest of the...*my* house."

They both understood the significance of what she'd said but neither of them mentioned it, although Robby did squeeze her hand gently. "Okay, but just remember what I said about it being small."

"Cozy," she corrected.

"Spoken like someone who's been hanging around a real estate agent way too long. Chuck will be so pleased."

They walked arm and arm, with only occasional detours around the piles of moving boxes, into what on the blueprints had been called the "parlor."   And it fit; the room seemed much too *cozy* for a living room, much smaller than the dining room/kitchen.

But that wasn't right. The millhouse was a standard Federal design, which meant the rooms—unless redesigned to accommodate modern conveniences, such as indoor plumbing and closet—were designed to be mirror images of each other. Maybe it was just the way the room was laid out.

Instead of cabinets on either side of the front window, there was a window seat—covered with boxes—the stretched the full length of the wall; and twin floor-to-ceiling bookcases flanked the fireplace, the kitchen's identical and equally massive twin.

It was the furniture.

Tess walked across the edge of a brand new gray-blue and white braided rug, rubbing the goosebumps off her arms.

"You bought new furniture?"

Leaning against the doorframe, Robby folded his arms across his chest and shrugged. "Housewarming gift."

"But you *gave* me the house."

"You should have read the fine print—furniture included. Besides, the stuff in the condo was too big. We might have been able to get part of your sectional in...if we sawed it in half and took out the window to get it in. Besides, new house, new furniture, new start."

"Did you put it storage?"

A guarded looked crossed his face as he shook his head. "No, honey, we sold it, remember? Money's in your account."

Tess nodded, pretending she knew what he was talking about, and looked at her new furniture. *Vince will be so mad.*

"I told you this place was small."

A dove-gray sofa sat beneath the back window, an off-white chenille throw draped over one arm. A birch coffee table sat in front of the sofa, a matching end table with the Tiffany "Dragonfly" lamp that Robby had given them one Christmas and that Vince hated and made her put away, brightened the corner between the sofa and wall. An overstuffed, mushroom-colored chair and ottoman sat at an angle to the left of the fireplace—perfect for cuddling up in on cold winter nights—and faced the plasma television that hovered over the low entertainment unit like some celestial guardian.

Robby's smile wasn't very convincing when she finally was able to look back at him.

"Okay, so it doesn't fit the period, but we got a deal. Buy three, get one free.

There was very little she could say that he would accept. "Thank you, Robby, for everything."

"Shush. Here, let me get this." Without moving from the doorway, Robby reached out and flipped a color-coordinate switch. Tess jumped when the ceiling mounted track lights snapped on. She hadn't realized how dark the room...the house had become.

"Is it that late already?"

Robby glanced at his wristwatch. "No, it's just past six, but the shadows can fall pretty quickly around here. But if you think it's dark now, just wait until fall." He did something and the lights got brighter. "Dimmers. Like?"

Tess walked over and pushed his hand away, then lowered the light to a soft creamy glow. "Better."

"You're not going to be nervous about living here are you?" He suddenly looked very concerned. "Being so far from the main house and all."

Tess looked to see if he was joking.

"Far? Your place is right outside. Besides, what's there to be afraid of? You said Vince can't hurt me."

The same look flickered across Robby's face and was gone. "That's right. He can't hurt you."

"Okay, shall we go up—"

A floorboard creaked overhead, followed by a hollow thud.

"What was that?"

"What was what?"

Another thump echoed down through the plaster. Tess pointed toward the ceiling. "That."

"That?" Robby gave it a casual glance and shrugged. "Oh, that's probably just the ghost."

Tess' heart skipped a beat. She'd forgotten about that. "The miller."

Robby pantomimed wrapping a rope around his neck hanging himself and a loud thud echoed down the stairs. He looked up.

"Oops, sorry. Suicides can be so sensitive. And I think he's still a little unhappy with us."

"Why?"

"Chuck says it happens all the time when you start working on one of these old places. Even minor things can stir up things and we did a lot more than that to get this place in shape."

As if the statement were its cue, a series of distinct creaks sounded overhead. *Footsteps.* Tess leaned around the doorway and looked up the narrow staircase to the second floor. It was already dark at the top and there was the faintest rustling as if something was moving up there in the darkness.

A new set of goosebumps rose across her skin. She wasn't scared, but that didn't keep her from jumping when Robby tapped her on the shoulder.

"Sorry." He leaned close, whispering in her ear. "I think he knows we're here."

Tess saw the switch-plate for the stair light on the wall, but didn't touch it. "You did hear that, didn't you?"

"Oh yeah, I heard it."

Taking Robby's hand, they slowly began to climb the stairs. "What's his name?"

"Chuck probably knows, but *we* haven't been properly introduced."

Tess stopped halfway up the stairs and felt a tickle in her stomach. She wasn't scared, not really. *Well, maybe a little.* "Hello? Is someone up there?"

Nothing, then—

"Yes, O restless spirit of the night, give us a sign of your presence."

"Robby, stop it!"

"Hey, I'm only trying to help. Yo, ghost! I'm talkin' t'ya."

Something hit the staircase wall hard enough to make them both jump. Tess managed to grab onto the railing as Robby elbowed by her up the stairs.

"Okay, *that* wasn't funny." A hollow echoed followed him and Tess followed that as light the color of cotton spilled into the narrow upstairs landing. "Remind me to explain the subtleties between a joke and —"

Robby was standing in what Tess decided had to be her bedroom, his hand still pressed against the wall switch.

"Oh, my God, Robby...it's beautiful."

The bedroom was filled with family antiques. Then Amish "Compass Rose" quilt she remembered having tea-parties on when she was little, bed, hung on the wall above the antique brass bed that had been their grandparents'. A large cut-glass bowl the color of grapes and filled with pale lavender roses— from Robby, of course—sat on the antique rosewood dresser that, according to family legend, had come from Scotland by Clipper ship in the early 1700s.

It was strange that she could remember that and not what happened after Vince....

"I—I can't believe you did this."

"Yeah, well..." He seemed distracted. "You know what they say, sometimes old is better than new. But, um, there's a brand new mattress and box spring on that bed, in case you wondered."

"And no moving boxes."

"Closet." Putting a finger up to his lips, Robby tiptoed across the room and yanked open the door next to the dresser and opposite the bed. "Ah-huh."

Even from the doorway Tess tell how big the closet was. It was huge...even with the boxes.

"Do you always yell at ghosts?" she asked when he closed the door.

"What? Oh, wait, I know. He's probably in the office. Come on. Shh, let's scare him this time."

Hand-in-hand, they tiptoed the ten feet from bedroom to office. Just past the landing, Robby pointed to the bathroom and Tess nodded. It seemed small and murky in the half-light that found its way in through the small window, but was overall pretty standard—vanity sink, toilet and a full tub and shower.

Robby stopped just short of the office door and pulled her close. "Listen."

For a moment Tess didn't hear anything but the quiet, then she picked it up—the soft rhythmic creaking of someone walking back and forth across room.

"We got him now!"

Robby dragged her into the room, shouting—*"Ah HAH!"*—as he hit the lights. The room blinked into being and Tess took an involuntary step back. Aside from the stacks of book cartons and file boxes she alone would need to sort through and put away, the room was exactly as she remembered it.

I was working on a file and Vince called and...

But that was all she remembered.

"It's all here."

"What? Oh...yeah—it's only office stuff, nothing important."

Robby left her in the doorway walked to a small door directly opposite. When he opened it Tess saw the first few steps of the attic stairs. "BOO!"

Tess jumped and wondered if her brother had lost his mind. "What are you doing?"

"Nothing." He closed the door and turned around. The light made him look pale. "Hmm? What? Oh, right...office furniture. Yeah, I kept your set because a computer workstation isn't like a couch or bed...it's more personal because, and..."

creak

They looked up, but only Robby continued to talk. "Okay, you win...you scared the sh—you scared us, so you can come down."

He had lost his mind. "Robby?"

He ignored her.

"Seriously, come on, I said you won. All-the, all-the outs in free!"

"Robby, who are you talking to?"

"Chuck." He took a deep breath and gave her a *you're-going-to-be-mad-at-me* look. "Okay, here it is, we knew how much you wanted to have a haunted house, so... It was all Chuck's idea. But I sort of told him to hide up here and make some noise, so you'd think—"

Tess pretended to be mad.

"And Chuck agreed to it?"

"What did Chuck agree to?"

They *both* jumped when Chuck walked in from the hallway.

"Where..." Robby asked, "...were you?"

Chuck looked confused. "A client called and I had to run back to the house for some papers. Oh, right." He looked at Tess. "Boo. I'm sorry, but I thought I could be back before you finished the tour."

"So, that wasn't you walking up and down."

"No. Oh wow, did something happen?"

Tess looked at Robby who looked at Chuck, who looked back at Tess, who smiled as she gave Chuck a hug.

"Not much, my ghost was just saying hello. And thank you for everything, including the carnations."

"You're welcome...and you really heard the ghost?"

Before Tess could answer, Robby came between them and grabbed one arm apiece and pushed them out of the room.

"Yeah, well, *our* ghost can probably beat up *your* ghost." His voice beat them down the stairs. "Frank was killed...your guy is a suicide and everyone knows the ghost of a murder victim is much stronger than the ghost of a suicide."

"Says who?" Tess wanted to know.

Robby let go of her arm at the top of the stairs and went down first. "I don't want to talk about it anymore."

"He's right," Chuck said. "It might upset your ghost."

Robby shook his head and left them at the top of the stairs. "Okay, we're planning to take you out to dinner to celebrate your first night in your new—"

"Haunted," she added happily.

He turned and looked up at her for a moment before continuing to the front door, Chuck following close behind, trying not to laugh.

"—home. You feel up to it or shall I send over beer and pizza for you and the ghost?"

"I would love to go out. Give me a few minutes to change?"

Robby glanced past her. "Your clothes, at least the ones not inside boxes, are still at our place. Unless, of course, you don't mind changing in front of a strange dead man."

Tess hurried down the stairs and, after making a detour to get her purse out of the grocery carton and running a hand quickly through her hair, out the door. "Ready."

"Glad you see it my way. Oh, and before I forget." Robby reached into the back pocket of his jeans and pulled out a key. "For you, madam. It works both the front and back door and the deadbolt. We have a spare up at the house, but considering how much Frank likes keys, try not to lose this one."

Tess had her keyring in hand and was already slipping it on. "I won't."

"Okay, lock up. And make sure you lock the door every time you go out, even if it's just over to our place. And keep the doors locked when you're here. We're not that far away, but you're still pretty isolated out here."

Tess had already gotten into the habit of locking the doors when she was home. *Not that it had mattered....*

Before she locked the door, with Robby standing there watching, Tess reached in and turned on the porch lights.

"Don't worry, Robby, I'll be fine."

Chuck was waiting for them on the other side of the footbridge. "So where shall it be, my beloved ones?"

"Any good haunted restaurants nearby?" Tess asked and Chuck lit up like a Christmas tree.

"I've heard of this place not that far from here…supposed to be super haunted and I've wanted to go there for ages, but…" He rolled his eyes toward Robby and Tess had to bite the inside of her cheek to keep from laughing. "We just haven't gotten over there yet."

"Then let's go. What do you say, brother of mine?"

Robby looked at her and smiled and glared at Chuck. "Do they have a bar?"

"One of the best in town, I've heard."

"Good. Then I know what I'll be having."

Before she followed Robby across the footbridge, Tess stopped and looked back at the millhouse. It was so perfect, so peaceful, and so safe.

I wonder what Vince is doing?
**

Vince stood in what had been his bedroom and felt every muscle in his body tremble. He'd never felt anything like that before—the creeping, crawling, shudder beneath otherwise motionless flesh—but he'd never been this angry before.

No…this went far beyond anger. It wasn't even rage or… or… He couldn't think what it was; there were no words to describe it.

Vince clenched his fists and felt the shock race up into his shoulders.

What did she do?

It seemed more difficult than it normally did, but Vince finally managed to take a step, and then another and another until he walked out of the bedroom and into the office loft. A wave of vertigo hit him when he looked over the railing into the dark living room below and that was another *new* sensation, but at least he knew what to call it. The dizziness passed in an instant, but he still gripped the banister because it was easier to pretend it was her neck. Spread out pristine and virginal in the soft afternoon light, the living room mocked him.

Empty, just like the rest of the condo. Not a fucking stick of furniture, not even marks on the carpet to show where they'd been. The wall-to-wall had been steam-cleaned to perfection.

He didn't need—or want—to check the kitchen or dining room or garage to see if she'd missed anything, left something behind. Even the air had a *vacant* feel to it. Vince unlocked his knees and sat down on the top stair. She left and took everything, *everything* with her.

Where the fuck is she?

Some women's shelter? "Is that where you went?" *Yeah, I bet they told you to do this, didn't they?* "God, you'd better be in some shelter." *Yeah, you're too stupid to have come up with this by yourself.* "If you're with that Peter guy..." *But did they happen to mention that none of this stuff belonged to you?* "I bet they didn't, did they, those new friends of yours. No, they wouldn't because they don't care. They probably said you had a *right* to do this, to take and sell everything because your husband was... was..." *What the hell happened?* "Doesn't matter, because you didn't have a right. NONE! You stupid fucking bitch. God, when I get my hands on you, you're going to pay and I don't give a fucking care what the cops do to me afterwards! It's justified." *I'll fucking kill—*

A key fumbled into the front door lock and Vince stopped trembling.

He was getting to his feet, hands clenched into fists— *Surprise, honey*—when the door opened and a strange woman, followed by a young Asian couple, walked in.

He vaulted backwards and dropped, going belly low across the loft carpet until he reached the bedroom. He could hear them talking, soft, low tones that told him he hadn't been seen. And that was good. Tess was his, but strangers....

Strangers?

What were strangers doing in *his* home?

For one awful moment Vince wondered if he had somehow wandered into the wrong condo. He'd done that once, a few weeks after he moved into the complex. He was carrying groceries in from the carport and left the back door open. As did his next door neighbor and he walked right in.

It was a mistake, an honest one, and if the fucking brat hadn't suddenly started screaming it would have been okay. Jesus, you would have thought he'd stuck a knife in the kid. But he'd been quick that time, too. Beat the hell out of there and was back inside *his* condo with the door shut and locked before the mother's *"WHAT'S WRONG?"* finished ringing in his ears.

Vince had never made that mistake again. He thought, but...

Wait a minute.

Pushing himself to his knees, he lifted a hand and ran his thumb across a small depression in the wall next to the door. It happened six months before, when Tess' elbow cracked into the plaster. He hadn't pushed her that hard, but she was always so damned clumsy... He'd done most of the repair himself—a little spackle, some sanding and touch-up paint and it looked good as new—but he'd never been able to do much about the dent unless he wanted to replace the drywall. And he didn't want to go *that* far.

Vince pressed his thumb against the dent—*this is my place*—as voices drifted up to him through the still air.

"—floor plan from the dining room to the living room, and the kitchen has a lovely little eating area. All the appliances are included in the selling price."

Selling price?

Vince slumped back against the wall.

"The seller's very motivated and they're letting this place go for a song. If you're really interested I could ask about a ninety day escrow..."

She can't sell this...it's in my name. What the hell— Robby and his fucking boyfriend... Jesus, I don't care what they told her, she can't do this. It's not legal!

"Okay, then—" The woman's voice echoed. "I'll just let you two look around down here and then I'll show you the upstairs. Take your time. When you're ready I'll take you out back and show you the carport and patio..."

Patio, right. That had to be the six-foot-by-seven slab of concrete between the carport and back door—a perfect place to stretch out after a hard day's work if you didn't mind breathing in exhaust fumes. *Some pitch you got there, lady.*

Vince would have laughed except for two things: they would have heard him and...it was *his* patio they were talking about.

You're going to pay for this, Tess...God, how you're going to pay.
**

Tess met Chuck's gaze over the top of Robby's head. They'd been doing pretty well until Robby took a lungful of warm night air...and more or less melted across one of the architecturally beautiful—but remarkably uncomfortable— stone benches that acted as a visual barrier between patio and pool. Tess nodded and Chuck smiled. Without having to speak a word, they'd both come up with the same, perfectly reasonable thought: haul Robby onto one of the padded chaise lounges and leave him there to sleep it off.

It had only been a momentary thought, but Robby woke up before they could implement their plan...which, Tess decided, was probably for the best.

Robby lay flat on the bench and smiled up at the night sky. When his eyes shifted to her, the smile widened.

"So...you *really* like it?"

Tess couldn't remember how many times he'd asked that same question, but not remembering, in this case, had nothing to do with actual time slipping away. Holding onto Chuck's arm for balance, she bent down and kissed her brother's forehead. "No, Robby, I don't like it...I *love* it."

He closed his eyes with a sigh.

"Good. And you know we'll help you unpack, right? Just gotta call."

"Yes, Robby."

"We really will," Chuck added as if to verify the sincerity of the intoxicated offer. "Believe me, I wouldn't mind. They scheduled me to work the phones all week. Boring."

Tess squeezed his arm and nodded. "I'll think about it."

"And—"

They both looked down at Robby.

"I want to get you a new computer."

He'd mentioned this a few times as well and Tess was too tired, and maybe a little too drunk, to be gracious about it.

"No, Robby. No new computer. "

"But I can set you up with a whole new system that's beyond state of th' art."

"No."

He laced his hands behind his head and opened his eyes. "O-kay, understood. I know how you feel. I still think about Bessie sometimes."

Chuck frowned. "Bessie?"

Oh, no. "Don't!" Tess begged, but she was too slow.

"I never *told* you about *Bessie*? Oh, my beloved." Robby somehow managed to get to his feet without falling over and threw his arms around Chuck's shoulders. "She was my first... a beautiful thing, so compact, so responsive...well, after I jacked around with her. I was only fifteen, but she taught me so many things."

Chuck turned to Tess. "Should I be worried?"

"Oh, my sweet little HP-150. You know, I still have her in, all boxed away."

Chuck nodded. "I'm worried."

"She was only a couple years old when I got her, but still a looker. MS-DOS, Intel 8088 with 8MHz...man, I thought I'd died and gone to Heaven. And I boosted her from 256KB to 640. Oh, the times we had. She was my baby."

Robby kissed Chuck and gave Tess an ear-to-ear grin. "But I can't wait for you to meet Caliban...he does everything but make coffee and I could probably program him to do that if —"

"Don't you dare!" Chuck tightened his grip when Robby started to slide and rolled his eyes at Tess "And if you're wise you won't let him anywhere *near* your computer. I walked into the house one night last month and suddenly the lights started flashing in perfect sync to *The Ride of the Valkyries*...which, as it so happened, was blasting from the stereo."

"Hey, it took me hours to program that, but you just sold a house and I wanted to be supportive."

"You almost supported me into the cardiac arrest unit." Chuck straightened Robby into a semi-vertical position and aimed him for the back door. "But I have to admit it is a pretty cool system...especially when I need to use it. Okay, you wait here. Let me get him inside and I'll walk you home."

Tess shook her head. She'd only had two glasses of red wine. "I'm fine."

"You'll fall in the river and drown." Robby turned so quickly he almost tumbled Chuck to the ground. "Stay here tonight. You still have stuff...toothbrush and—"

"And no. I bought another toothbrush I want to sleep in my...own bed tonight." It felt so strange saying that. "Besides, as you once pointed out to me, dear brother, the *river* runs along the *front* of the house. If I fall into anything it will be the millrace...and that's only a couple of feet deep."

"People have drowned in less water."

"But I won't." Giving them each a quick kiss, Tess crossed the patio and onto the white-stone path outlined by a string of solar-lights. She'd have to be seriously drunk to wander into the millrace. "Good-night, gentlemen."

"We don't have all the lights in yet," Chuck called after her. "It'll be too dark to—"

Opening her purse, Tess pulled out her keyring—with its brand new, shiny key—and squeezed the tiny LED flashlight that served as a key-fob. A bright white circle a foot wide appeared on the paving stones next to her.

"Always be prepared." She flashed it toward the patio and waved. "Sleep well."

"Sure you don't want me to walk you?"

"Sure. 'Night."

"Okay, but call us when you get there."

Tess promised with a thumb's up and followed the light-dotted pathway behind the curtain of trees.

Call when you get there, as if she were going hundreds of miles away through unknown and uncertain territory. It was sweet, the way Robby still worried about her, but what could happen to her?

Vince. Vince could happen.

Tess stopped in the relative darkness between two pools of light, listening to the sound of the millrace move through the night shadows. She could hear herself breathe, but the other sounds, the wind, the whirring cry of crickets from the field beyond the trees were muffled, wrapped in cotton.

—You changed the locks, you fucking bitch. This is my house, I paid for it...you had no right to do this. NOW OPEN THIS GODDAMN DOOR!—

Tess whirled, the flashlight cutting a slice of darkness from the trees. The path behind her was empty.

—Did you really think you could keep me out of my home, bitch?
—

—And look how brave it is....—

Tess looked down at her hand, running her thumb across the top of the flashlight. It wasn't right, she'd been holding something else…something cold and hard and….

—Oh, I'm scared. I'm so scared.—

Her cell phone, she'd been holding her cell phone and talking to Robby when Vince broke in…or did she let him in? But she remembered someone shouting and….

If Vince wasn't in jail, it meant he got away.

And it was only a matter of time before he found her again.

He's not here.

Yet.

Tess was suddenly very sorry that she hadn't waited for Chuck to walk her "home."

The flashlight-beam bounced wildly as she ran, sweeping across the path to the field to the millrace and back again, and frightening the field crickets into momentary silence. The porch lights shown like twin beacons through the night and she kept her eyes focused on them.

He's not in jail…he's not in jail…he's not—

Tess only realized she'd left the path and reached the footbridge when she heard the hollow thump of her sandals against the wood. Panting, suddenly embarrassed because she knew Robby or Chuck or both of them were probably watching from the office balcony the same way she'd watched them work on the millhouse.

"He's not here," she told herself, but only half believed as she forced herself to walk, one slow step at a time, until she reached the porch. "He's *not* here."

She missed the keyhole only twice and pretended her hand shook from running. Pushing the door open, she reached inside and felt along the wall until her fingers found the dual light switch. One toggle was already in the UP position, the one for the porch lights, so she flipped its mate and exhaled when the entrance hall filled with light.

There was nothing to be afraid of now...but there never really had been. She'd scared herself...made up a bogeyman and gave it Vince's face. He was right about her, she *was* stupid.

Tess walked back to the front of the porch and pulled her cell phone out of her purse.

Chuck answered on the first ring.

"He's out for the count, but I'll tell him you called. Can you see me?"

She looked out over the night-dappled field to the house and saw him, a man-shape in the upper back window. She waved as an answered.

"I'll watch until you're inside. Everything okay over there?"

"Seems to be." Tess waved again and walked into the house, closing—and locking—the door behind her. "Thanks for waiting up."

"My pleasure. Brunch at eleven, remember. May angels guard you and bring you rest. 'Night, sweetie."

Tess closed the phone and leaned back against the door. The millhouse was quiet, peaceful, safe.

Smiling, she took a deep breath.

"Hi, honey...I'm home."
**

He waited until the light downstairs was extinguished and another appeared in the room above before stepping from the shadow of the trees. He'd watched while she came from the brightness of the house to the stones of the path, and thought himself safe. She wouldn't know he was there, but then she'd started running he'd felt his belly tighten.

She'd seen or heard or he'd done something to let his presence be known and for one moment he thought their eyes met...

But then she ran past his hiding place without another glance and a prayer of thanks had almost come to his lips.

At times he was still amazed by his own foolishness. A prayer, from his lips...not even he was that impudent. But if he had, and she'd heard it wouldn't have changed anything.

For either of them.

CHAPTER 6
JUNE 11th

"There aren't any curtains."

Robby looked at her over the top of his Mimosa. "Excuse me?"

"In the millhouse...none of the windows have curtains."

Somehow, in all the excitement of moving in, Tess hadn't noticed their absence until bright and way too early that morning. Curled onto the right-edge of the mattress, she'd been awakened to a face full of blinding light.

Disoriented, and just slightly hung over, she'd shielded her eyes as best she could and sat up and glanced around the room —only wondering for a half-second where she was. The room was quiet. The door and windows were closed and the thick walls insulated her from outside sounds. Tess had no idea what time it was, the clock radio was still packed away somewhere and she didn't feel like blind-patting the bedside table for her watch and then trying to read the teeny-tiny numbers; but it *felt* early...*much* too early to be up and semi-awake.

Especially with sunlight pouring in through the *curtainless* window. There was nothing she could do but get up, make coffee...once she found the coffee maker...and start to unpack.

It hadn't been the best morning she could remember, but it certainly hadn't been one of the worst.

"*We* don't have curtains." Robby took a sip and shrugged. "You're out in the middle of the woods, baby, who do you think is going to see you?"

"*You* can see me from the house."

"Only with binoculars, and we use those strictly for bird watching. Seriously, you have us in front, and we'll promise not to sneak peeks in your direction—" He crossed his heart. "—unless we're really bored. And you have the creek and forest behind you, so...."

"I though I saw someone over there this morning."

Robby didn't seem all that bothered until she added. "At first I thought it was Vince."

The cut-glass champagne flute caught the sunlight and made tiny rainbows across the white linen tablecloth as he lowered it.

"But you know it couldn't have been Vince."

No, I don't. "Sure."

Robby reached across the table and took her hand. "It *wasn't* Vince."

"I know, but...I *thought* I saw someone across the stream back, in the trees, looking at the house. I was making coffee and it was only a quick glance, but it looked like—" *Vince. It looked like Vince.* "I guess it could have been a deer."

"Or a hiker." Chuck said, pouring more coffee into Tess' cup. "There are lots of great hiking trails over there. The park entrance is a couple of miles down the road on the other side of the pike, so I guess we sort of forget this isn't our own private forest."

Robby held up his empty flute in surrender. "Okay, okay, point made...I'll come over later and take measurements and then we'll go shopping."

Tess refilled his glass from the pitcher next to her. "Thank you."

"Thank *you*. There were a lot of looky-loos during the renovation, and, this guy may have been one of them. He probably didn't know anyone was living in the millhouse and you caught him snooping. Can't say I blame him, though. Chuck's been over on that side of the creek a couple times with his sketch pad." Robby waited until Chuck wandered back to the kitchen then suddenly leaned forward, crooking his finger at her to do the same. "Don't tell him I told you, but he's painting a picture of the millhouse for you. He wanted to have it finished before you arrived...hung over the mantle in the living room but got busy with a multi-million dollar condo development in Center City, so it'll be awhile. Just leave that spot blank."

He winked and sat back. Tess remained leaning forward over the remains of her four-cheese, turkey-bacon and cremini mushroom omelet (in hollandaise sauce).

"Why's he painting the *back* of the millhouse?" she whispered.

"He said he likes the way it looks through the trees, with the river below." Robby shrugged. "Artists."

"What about artists?"

Tess leaned back quickly, feeling the beginnings of a blush deepen along her cheeks. She felt they way she had when a teacher caught her talking in class.

Robby came to her rescue. As usual.

"Tess was just blathering on about how *beautiful* everything is...including the food, so I told her all because of your artistic nature." He blew a kiss. "Thanks, love."

"Yes, thank you. It was fantastic."

Chuck bowed over the platter he was carrying. "You are both too kind, but I will graciously accept such honest praise. Okay, so who's ready for poached pears in brandy sauce?"

Tess looked at her brother and whimpered as Chuck began playing musical plates—removing the empties so he could replace them with desert bowls.

"Please tell me you don't do this *every* Sunday." Tess begged.

She was about to refuse, citing imminent internal combustion, when the savory aroma of warm pears and brandy inexplicably made her mouth water.

"No, this is more a 'special occasion' or 'any time I don't have to show houses on Sundays' brunch."

"Which *does* make it a special occasion," Robby said, digging into his pear, "considering this is the first time in, what, three months that you haven't had to show a house on Sunday?"

"He tends to exaggerate," Chuck told Tess, "have you ever noticed that?"

"Only since I was born."

"You poor thing, it must have been hell for you."

Tess pouted. "It was."

"Ah, excuse me…" Robby tapped a spoon against the side of his coffee cup. "I'm still in the room."

Chuck walked around to the back of Robby's chair and kissed the top of his head. "Sorry…were we being bad?"

"Horrible.

Tess smiled around a spoonful of pear. She'd enjoyed listening to their gentle, safe bickering. *Vince would never have apologized…or joked like that.*

"You said there are hiking trails across the stream?" she asked. "Well, I'm going to need a hike after this."

Chuck's eyes lit up.

"Great! We can show her our graveyard."

Tess' spoon stopped halfway to its second scoop and she turned to look out the dining room windows. From where she sat at the long mahogany table she could see the expanse of the flagstone patio leading and a corner of the pool. Beyond was the field and farther still, the millhouse warming itself in the morning sun.

"You have a graveyard?" she asked.

"Well, it's not really ours," Chuck grinned as he picked up his coffee cup. "*Officially* it belongs to the State of

Pennsylvania Parks Department, but we helped clean it up after last winter's storms and put up a new fence."

Tess looked at her brother who emphatically shook his head. "Not me. Remember, Chuck's part of the 'Hysterical' society."

"Historical," Chuck corrected. "It's a great bunch of people. Robby's met them. And they were thrilled when they found out where we lived. I've found out so much about this place..." He lowered his voice, leaning toward Tess. "That's how we found out about Frank's untimely demise. We've even hosted a couple meetings—"

"Him." Robby pointed his spoon at Chuck. "I hide in my office with the doors locked."

Chucked ignored him. "You should come to the next meeting. It's really interesting. I was going to do more research on the millhouse for, you know, put together a folder and everything, but it got busy at work and..." He gave Robby a quick look before turning his attention back to her. "But I think you'd have more fun finding out the history of the millhouse yourself."

"And the ghost?"

"Oh, God, yes. We have records of all the local hauntings." Chucked pushed his empty plate aside and leaned forward on his elbows. "Speaking of which...did anything happen last night?"

Tess shook her head.

"If it did it happened while I was asleep. Sorry."

He seemed so disappointed.

"Well, maybe he's just shy. Give him some time to get used to you and I'm sure he'll introduce himself."

"Well, until he does, enjoy the peace and quiet especially if your ghost is as light on his feet as our dear Frankie. Okay then..." Robby pushed back from the table and stood up. "So...are we going hiking or curtain shopping first?"

"Shopping?" Chuck beamed up at them.

And it was decided.

**

He ran his fingers across the buttonwood's rough bark, a habit he'd had since childhood whenever he was frustrated with himself. It was a careless motion for an equally careless man.

She'd seen him.

The day had only begun and he'd thought himself safe, had assumed that she'd still be asleep. And been wrong. For all that he knew and all that had happened, he should have realized how terribly unpredictable women were.

Victoria had taught him that lesson.

From that time to this morning...he should have remembered that one irrevocable fact.

And yet, the woman had seen him.

Balling his hand into a fist, he struck out at the tree as hard as he could. Where once it would have jarred his shoulder in its socket and broken the skin across his knuckles; perhaps even had shaken the bright summer leaves on the boughs, there was not even a shiver through the furrowed trunk and he turned and stalked away. Above him the leaves moved by the caprice of the wind.

He kept the trees between himself and the creek, as a barrier between himself and the millhouse until he'd reached the ruins of the stone dam. Another of his habits had always been to stride to the very edge of the crumbling embankment, to test himself against the fear as he stood watching the churning rush of water.

He could remember when the flood breached the dam and the sounds that the water made tumbling over the rupture was like a war. The sounds were softer now; the rocks and jagged sheaves of mortar wore smooth. Time and the patient creek had worn them into whispers.

Time and patience can work magic.

He nudged a fallen twig into an eddy and watched the water snatch it away.

Time and patience…one he had in abundance, the other had never been his.

**

"Did I ever tell you how exasperating you can be?"

"Every day when we were growing up."

"Well, you've gotten worse."

Tess blew her brother a raspberry.

"Children!" Chuck warned, clapping his hands twice. "Behave. Don't make me separate you."

Tess and Robby blew him a raspberry. Chuck sighed and turned puppy-dog eyes at Tess.

"Is that the thanks I get for agreeing with you on blinds over curtains?"

"You're right." Tess left Robby holding the headrail —"Hey!"—and rushed as quickly as she could through the obstacle course of still-unpacked moving cartons, scattered tools and mini-blind boxes, to give him a hug. "Thank you… and I apologize for the raspberry."

Chuck hugged her back while Robby made a great show of obviously ignoring them.

"*You're* forgiven. And you were absolutely right, curtains would have closed in the windows and make the rooms look even smaller. Blinds and a valance will really add the right finishing touch."

The right side of the headrail dipped off its mark as Robby turned to glare at them.

"Speaking of finishing… This is just the first room, we have six more pairs of mini-blinds and valances to put up; except for the bathroom that…if I remember correctly… *doesn't* get mini-blinds but *does* get a half-curtain with the valance." He turned back to the window and shoved the headrail back into position. "And they say we're picky about window treatments. Will one of you *please* screw this thing in!"

Tess grabbed a Philip's head screwdriver on the way back. "Just be glad I didn't want different colors in each room."

Robby fit a screw into the hole Chuck had made with the electric drill and took the screwdriver from her. "I would have killed you and buried you were no one would ever find you."

Vince told her the same thing, but Tess laughed because she knew her brother was only joking.

With Robby's near constant grumbling, and only two mishaps with the drill, they managed to get all the mini-blinds and curtain rods up by the time it started to get dark. The valances and bathroom café-curtain were still in their individual hermetically sealed wrappers, waiting to be ironed.

The evening of the second day at the millhouse and they were sitting outside on the dining room chairs, watching the shadows gather across the creek and drinking lemonade.

"We need to get you some patio furniture." Chuck had turned his chair around and was straddling it, arms crossed over the top. "Or at least a picnic table so you can sit out here with your laptop."

"And a patio."

They looked down at the semi-level terrace of rock and grass.

"Not sure if we could get a concrete truck out here, but we might be able to lay down paving stones."

"I like it this way," Tess said. "If I want a real patio, I'll come over to your place. But a picnic table would be nice."

"Okay," Chuck said, "I'll pick up one of those kits at Home Depot as a housewarming gift."

Tess was about to take a sip and quickly lowered the glass. The ice tinkled softly. "No, you won't. You've already given me too many, including the house."

"Who said this is a gift?" Robby asked. "We expect rent."

"Oh..." She felt her face go crimson. "Um, of course. We were paying—"

"A dollar a week."

He was joking again.

"Be serious, Robby. I have a job, I can pay rent."

He thought a minute then looked at Chuck. "What do you think?"

Chuck stood up, hands raised. "Oh no, I try never to come between siblings. Besides, I have to head back to the house. You two fight it out, but try to come to some decision within the next half-hour. We have that thing to go to tonight."

Robby groaned.

"A thing?" Tess asked.

"Oh, yeah. Whoopee. It's a real estate *thing*," he explained and nodded as Chuck carried his chair into the house. "Okay, I'll be up in a few minutes. Don't use all the hot water."

Tess waved goodbye then leaned forward and put her hand on her brother's knee. "I would like to pay rent, Robby. It would make me feel...better."

"A buck or nothing. Take it or leave it."

"You drive a hard bargain, *Bobby*."

Childhood nickname that he hated.

"Only because I love you, *Tee-tee*."

Tess retreated. Childhood nicknames, like childhood diseases, are easier to survive when you're young.

"Okay, you win."   Going inside, Tess grabbed her checkbook out of his purse and wrote a check for two hundred dollars. He'd yell, but she felt better. She fluttered it to air dry and handed it to him, but didn't give him a chance to yell. "A dollar a week, two hundred weeks paid in advance."

"Jesus...that's, what, a couple year's worth?"

"At least. So...do you really think the mini-blinds look good in there?"

"Yes, especially now that they're up. I've got a couple of conference calls in the morning and afternoon, but I can come later and help."

"To hang valances? Robby, I'm not completely helpless, you know."

"Didn't say you were. But they need to be ironed before you hang them and I don't remember moving in an ironing board. I can bring ours over."

Tess shook her head. "I have an iron...it was in the box with the rice steamer and slow cooker."

"Good place for it."

"*And* I have the kitchen table. All I have to do is put down a towel and use that as an ironing board. I did it all the time in college."

"You had a kitchen table? Wow, my dorm room was so small I could hardly fit in the trapeze."

"Stop," Tess said and when he did it took her a moment to remember what she was going to say. *Vince never stopped.* "Be serious for a minute, okay?"

"Good idea." He leaned forward, trapping her hand beneath his. His skin was cold. "Can we talk about Vince?"

Tess looked down at her free hand and wondered where she'd put her glass. Did she have a glass? Yes, of course she did...Robby did and so did Chuck. Robby still had his and Chuck took his into the kitchen. She saw it in the sink when she went in to...

"No."

"We should."

"I don't want to talk about—" The rest of the words caught in her throat.

He's here...

Tess jerked her hand free and stood up, staring at the dark shape emerging from the shadows across the creek.

He's here.

"Tess?"

The deer stepped out of the trees and froze.

"Tess! What's the matter?"

The animal fled in terror of her brother's voice.

It's not him. She blinked and felt the breeze move against her face.

"I—" *I though I saw him, Robby. I thought I saw Vince...* She took a deep breath and felt her lungs tremble. "There was a yellow-jacket on your glass."

Robby got up so fast he knocked over his chair. Both of them were allergic to wasp bites.

"It's...it flew away."

"I'm going to add 'Bug-Zapper' to Chuck's list. God, I hate wasps." He checked his glass carefully then handed it to her and picked up his chair. "Think I scratched it, but I'm pretty sure we have glossy white paint in the garage. I'll bring you some tomorrow."

Robby grabbed both chairs and headed for the house. Tess set his glass next to Chuck's and hers in the sink.

"All trash?" He yelled from the hallway. Tess walked out the kitchen exit into the hall and saw him nodding at the two over-stuffed and sealed black garbage bags in the entrance hall.

"Uh-huh, but I didn't know where to take them."

"The garbage cans are in the garage, pick-up on Mondays and Thursdays. I'll—" Robby looked at her for a moment as if he wanted to say something besides— "take them this time. I would like to talk to you about—stuff. Okay...guess I should go."

Tess was glad he didn't say anything else. She didn't want to talk about Vince...not yet and not with Robby.

"You should, you have that thing to go to."

"Right."

He sighed so heavily Tess didn't hear the latch snap when she opened the door.

"You love parties," she reminded him, then pushed him out onto the porch when he sighed again. "

"Parties, yes...this is going to be a *thing*. Hey, that's an idea...go unpack a party dress and come with us. Chuck won't mind and I'd really love to have someone to talk to who doesn't cream their jeans over low interest rates."

"Robby!" Tess backed up and put the door between them. "Besides, I wouldn't even know where to start looking for a dress. Or shoes...or pantyhose for that matter. Besides, I have ironing to do." She wiggled her fingers. "Bye-bye. Have fun."

"Fine, enjoy your ironing, but I hope you know you're condemning me to a night spent with people who can't talk about anything but amortization and quitclaim deeds."

Tess waited until he'd clomped over the footbridge, trash bags swinging, before closing the door; then walked into the Keeping Room. The box containing the iron (and rice maker) sat on the raised hearth...waiting for her.

She made a quick U-turn.

"Robby?"

He was already a few yards away, just short of the trees.

"Change your mind about coming? Please."

"No...I just wanted to know where that cemetery is. I might take a walk over there later."

"Now? He looked up at the sky. "Kind of late for a hike, isn't it?" Robby lifted his hand to look at his watch, the trash bag swinging like a pendulum. "Whoa, it is late; Chuck's going to kill me."

He began crab-stepping down the path as Tess stepped out to the edge of the rain porch and looked up. The sky directly above her was still bright, although it was fading to the color of a bruise behind the Main House, and there were more shadows. One in the shape of the millhouse stretched out across the footbridge and race, stretching toward the edge of the field.

Robby waved a trash bag at her as he reached the tree line.

"Wait until tomorrow and I'll take you on a personal tour."

"Is it far?"

"Only about a quarter-mile that way." He waved vaguely downstream of the millhouse. "Once you get across the creek it's easy, the path is well marked, but unless you want to drive around to the park entrance...which will be closed in about a half-hour…you have to cross what's left of an old dam. It's not hard once you've done it, but…" He looked up into the darkening sky and shrugged. Tess could hear the trash bags rustle against his legs.

"Okay, get the message." Tess nodded and gave him a thumbs-up. "It'll be too dark to see."

"And you're going to do it anyway, aren't you?"

Tess leaned against one of the porch stanchions and tapped her wrist. "You're late."

"You always were the fearless one of the family." Shaking his head, Robby waved and began a slow backwards jog. "Okay, but if you do get to the cemetery don't bring anything home. We have enough ghosts around here already."

Tess watched until he disappeared behind the trees. *"You always were the fearless one of the family."* She'd almost forgotten that.   Her poor aunt and uncle—a month wouldn't go by without a trip to the Emergency Room. If there was a tree to climb, a Frisbees that needed to be gotten down from a roof or a hill that every other kid in the neighborhood knew was too steep to bike down…she was right there, scaring everyone—but herself—silly.

The first time Vince had to take her to the Emergency Room—*"She said she fell down the stairs."*—the X-ray technician had made some comment about the old fractures and Vince laughed.

"She's always been clumsy, my poor baby."

Vince always did have a way with words.

Tess walked back into the house rubbing her arms as though the warm, muggy evening had suddenly grown cold. Back against the door for a moment, she listened to the millhouse settling in for the night—hushed, quiet sounds— then, as quietly as she could, twisted the deadbolt shut and walked down the hall to the back door. The ironing could wait.

Shadows met her at the door and welcomed her in. Evening had come to the back of the millhouse and mist filled the narrow creek-bed like a ghost flood, spilling out over the step banks in silent waves. The twilight sky, the bits and pieces of it Tess could see through the summer thick leaves, was still bright, but there was more orange and red tinting the edges of the clouds.

Tess closed and locked the door. She *had* been fearless once.

When had it changed?

When she met Vince? No, that was too easy an answer and not really an honest one. She'd stopped because it was easier not to be. Being fearless meant you were brave, and brave meant you were strong...and Vince had proven that she was neither.

She was 23 when they met, she starting her first year of Art History, he just finishing up his MBA. It'd been a spring social—an event Tess wouldn't have normally gone to, but her dorm mates had decided she needed to "get out," so they hid her textbooks and physically dragged her there. It wasn't as if she had no social life...she'd dated a few boys, but not seriously. She knew what she wanted her life to be, to teach Art History, and went after it—fearlessly.

It'd been the same, at first, with Vince. He was tall and good-looking and much closer to the demarcation line that separated childhood and the adult world than she was. Tess couldn't keep her eyes off him, it was the way he moved through the crowd of beer-drinking *kids* that caught and kept her attention, but there was something about Vince her dorm mates didn't like. They could never say *what* it was, but that didn't stop them from taking every opportunity to try and get her to stop dating him.

"Does he ever ask you what you want to do?"

"He treats you like his own personal property."

"He's always hanging around...like he doesn't trust you or something."

"He doesn't listen."

"He always has to have the last word."
"What's that on your arm?"
Tess decided they were jealous.

She'd fallen in love with him and he loved her, but she'd stopped being fearless so when he suggested they elope the day after he graduated she accepted without hesitation. He didn't like to be kept waiting, especially by her. It was decided she'd quit school—teaching Art History really was a silly idea, she'd never make money that way—and take the first job she could get to help support them until he found the perfect position.

And they were happy…for a while. But she never took his feelings into consideration. He wasn't the kind of man who wanted his wife to support him, but she never thought of that. Didn't she know what it did to him when she handed over her paycheck every other week? Didn't she care how that made him feel?

But even when he found the right job—*"You think we need the piddling amount you bring in? You don't think I make enough, is that it?*—she kept working.

Because it gave him something to yell at her about.

A mosquito buzzed near her face and Tess slapped at it, hitting her cheek hard enough to make her blink. *I deserved that, Vince wouldn't have done that. He loved me.*

Then.

Tess walked back into the house, turning on all the downstairs lights and the one at the top of the stairs, before she began digging through the box for the iron. She couldn't remember the first time she wondered if Vince still loved her, but it really didn't matter.

People change.

Sometimes.

**

"God damned fog!"

Vince stopped walking and did a slow 360. Yeah, that helped. Now he knew *exactly* where he was. Lost.

"God damned BITCH!"

He yelled it into the fog, because it was, after all, her fault and hers alone. If she hadn't *stolen* the condo out from under him, he wouldn't be…wherever the hell he was looking for her. But, shit, that seemed to be the way his life had been going lately. She'd do something—press charges, get him arrested, try to kill him, sell his condo—and he'd have to go looking for her to make things right. Damn, it felt like he'd been doing *that* since he married her—*no, let's get the details right, Vince, boy, you didn't just marry her, you took pity on her.* Yeah, exactly. Her life wouldn't have been shit without him…and now *his* was shit because of her.

He should have killed her when she pulled that knife, but —

Something moved through the mist behind him and Vince spun on the balls of his feet, hands up, ready for anything. And came face-to-face with nothing.

"Calm down, son, it's just fog."

But hell, he couldn't even remember where he parked the —

Car. Where the hell did he park the car? He knew he had to have driven to wherever the hell he was because this didn't look like the condo's VISTORS PARKING LOT. Vince looked down at his feet and saw dirt and rocks.

Definitely not a parking lot. *So where the hell am I?* His mind went blank.

He remembered being in the condo—*'Think you can lock me out, bitch?'*—and the look on her face when she fell—*God, that was so sweet*—and her grabbing something—*'I'm so scared.'*—then watching the Real Estate bitch talk about his patio, then…

Here.

Wherever here was.

"DAMMIT!" The fog seemed to dampen his shout down to a whisper. She must have hit him, yeah, caught him a good one because he remembered falling... *Right*...face-first on the kitchen floor after she... *Shit!* Yeah, hit him hard enough to give him a concussion and scramble his brains. *Fucking bitch!* She was going to pay for that when he found her, no question about it. She'd pay. *With interest.*

The anger cleared his head and he smiled. Vince still had no idea where *he* was, but he suddenly knew where she'd go; the only place she could go.

"Roberto."

Which meant, even though he wasn't completely sure where he left the car, or where exactly he was, he wasn't lost. Tess had run to her brother's *expensive* house in the woods...so that meant he had to be part of those same woods. Vince congratulated himself. It was only the fog that had him turned around, that and the concussion.

Bitch.

Vince batted at the fog directly in front of him and it parted to reveal something large and dark. For a moment it almost looked like a man and he stepped back, but then the fog reclaimed it, dissolving it into nothing. There was still nothing a few minutes later when Vince took a step forward. If it was anything, it had to have been a deer because there was nothing in front of him but fog, trees and more fog and trees.

She was a deer, too...always running away.

"I guess that could have been my fault," he told the fog and trees and deer, if it was still around. "The world's hard; it chews people up and spits them out. I was trying to teach her that, but I let her get away with too much. I was too easy on her. And this is what happened. I failed her, but that won't happen again."

Vince smiled as the fog closed around him.

It would definitely not happen again. And, as soon as he found, her he'd put things right.

The *hard* way.

CHAPTER 7
JUNE 12th

The mini-blinds worked perfectly, shutting out the rising sun...and it didn't make one bit of difference.

Something woke her up.

Curled onto the far right-hand edge of the mattress, even though she had the entire bed to stretch out, Tess stared at the empty moving boxes she'd stacked beneath the window.

And waited.

She'd been sound asleep; then suddenly and completely awake with only a vague impression of... *something*.

In the condo there was always at least one set of neighbors, and usually more, which she could blame. Lathe-and-plaster did not ideal soundproofing make. Alarms set loud enough to stun small animals and endless sessions of slamming doors woke them up more often than the pre-set station on Vince's clock radio.

But she wasn't at the condo, she was here, alone behind thick solid stone walls in what amounted to the middle of the woods.

Tess blinked the dryness out of her eyes and looked at the new digital clock next to her side of the bed—*all* of it was her bed now, but even after all these weeks her body still refused to trespass on what had been his side. It was just after five, the blind-covered rectangle that was the window, just barely brighter than the walls that surrounded it.

A bead of sweat formed along Tess' hairline and rolled down the side of her forehead. She'd kept the windows closed against the humid night air, but now the rising sun was defeating the millhouse's natural insulation.

Maybe that's what woke her up, or maybe her internal Timekeeper went haywire and forgot she didn't have to get up for work. Although she couldn't remember *when* she called, Tess remembered speaking to Peter, her shift supervisor, and being fully prepared to hear that the company was very sorry, but they'd have to let her go. In fact, she'd been the one who brought it up.

"I know I've missed a lot of work lately, so I understand if..."

But Peter stopped her before she could finish and told her that he'd already spoken to their employer about her.

"Mr. Mayrdal is more than happy to have you continue working from home...whenever you feel up to it. You still have a couple week's worth of sick-leave you haven't used up, so use them in good health —" Ha, ha. *"—and send me an e-mail when you're ready and I'll put you back on the clock."*

That'd just been a little over a week ago.

Hadn't it?

Ten minutes had passed since according to the clock. It was still so early, but she was awake now.

Pushing her legs out from beneath the thin cotton sheet, Vince couldn't sleep unless he was covered; Tess stretched and tugged the front of her nightshirt down across the tops of her thighs.

A thump echoed softly from somewhere in the silent house. Tess let her toes play with the carpet's texture as she looked toward the open bedroom door and felt something like a tiny chill creep along her belly. She'd closed it before getting into bed, Vince never left the bedroom door open.

"It was you, wasn't it?" she asked to the dark hall. "You closed the door."

A soft thump answered her and that was how it started.

Tess soon discovered that talking to a ghost was much like talking to a cat—both generally ignored you, never answered, but always had little ways of letting you know they were there...

Like waking someone up at 'O-You've-Got-To-Be-Joking'-thirty. It was as easy as that, and *much* saner than if she were just talking to herself.

"Well, if it was," she said, "I wished you'd learn to tell time. I'm on...vacation, so I don't have to get up this early. But you did, didn't you?"

Nodding, Tess smoothed down the front of her nightshirt as she stood and felt a blush start at the back of her neck. "You probably had to get up before dawn to start the mill, didn't you? But let's make a deal, okay? You don't get me up this early again and I won't—" *How exactly do you threaten a ghost?* "—I won't paint the house bright pink. How's that?"

There was no answering thump this time, but Tess was sure a bargain had been struck. Yawning as she walked to the window, she leaned over the boxes and opened the blinds.

The sky above the main house was the color of lavender jade, banded with thin wisps of rose-gold clouds. The sun was a diamond chip peeking out from an ebony setting.

Tess shoved a box aside with her foot and sat on the wide recess ledge, shivering only for a second when the plaster's chill worked its way through the thin cotton. She couldn't remember the last time she'd watched a sunrise...or if she ever did. Probably not. She was the night owl, Vince the morning lark.

Vince.

"What are you doing? Jesus Christ, do you expect me *to make breakfast?"*

She jumped up and took a step, the muscles in her legs trembling.

"What *am* I doing?" Tess ran a shaky hand through her sleep-tangled hair. "He's not here." Then louder, her voice echoing through the empty rooms. "I didn't mean you. I mean...*him*. Vince. My husband. But don't worry, he won't be moving in. He—he's...

"Vince is away, so you don't have to worry about him. It's just you and me."

Until he finds me.

"Okay then, I guess I might as well start the day since you were so kind to wake me up."

Tess walked around the bed to the west-facing window and pulled up the blinds. The woods were still dark, the creek a deep shadow, and only a few pale tendrils of mist moved through the silhouette grove...but she stood there for a moment and watched the shadows where she'd seen the—*man* —deer the day before.

Deciding against turning on a light—if either Robby or Chuck were up and happened to see it, there'd be a phone call to ask if anything was wrong—Tess found underwear, shorts and a tank top by feel alone. She couldn't swear to the color of anything—the dawn light gave everything, even her skin, a grayish-pink tone—but it didn't matter all that much. Vince never liked her in vivid colors, preferring her in soft baby tones, so there was a limited chance her outfit would be too mismatched.

Besides, there wouldn't be anyone to see her or complain.

Except the ghost.

And Tess didn't think he'd care; or, if he did, she was sure he wouldn't say anything.

The perfect man. Not like Vince.

"I didn't mean that. It was my fault, I should have tried harder, he wouldn't have—"

A sigh echoed through the still air.

That wasn't me.

Up to that moment, despite the fact that she'd just been talking to him and had teased Robby about him really being there...Tess hadn't believed there really was a ghost. It'd been a game, make-believe.

"You really are here, aren't you?"

He didn't answer, he didn't need to. It was still like having a cat, but now she knew she wasn't just talking to thin air.

"Okay." Tess took a deep breath. "I'm going to take a shower now. New rules; the bathroom's off limits."

That only seemed reasonable; even though it was...*had* been his house. Besides, he had the rest of the house to haunt; one small room for her wasn't too much to ask.

The outside light was brighter when she reached the bedroom door.

She reached out and ran her hand across of front of the door. "You opened this, didn't you? I'd rather keep it closed at night, if you don't mind. And remember what I said about the bathroom being off limits. A lady has to have some privacy, you know."

Vince never believed that, but maybe the ghost would.

**

Vince leaned against the trunk of a dripping tree, wiping his face against the windbreaker's sleeve. It was more out of frustration than perspiration and gave him a something to do besides stumbling around in circles while he waited for the sun to burn off the fog.

Sometime during the long, uneventful night, finding the car had taken precedence over finding his wife. Not that it mattered. Then, sometime *later*, all he wanted to find was a path through the mist-shrouded brush.

He was 3 for 0.

Then he heard the first bird call and the world began to crawl reluctantly into view. If there'd ever been a path, he'd wandered off it miles and hours ago.

Vince pushed away from the tree and stopped. He knew from his Boy Scout days—*youngest Eagle Scout in Montgomery County*—that as soon as the sun got high enough, he could use the shadows to fix east and west and then follow them out, straight as an arrow. The only problem was that without a map or visual point of reference—*or knowing where exactly the hell he was*—he could walk right past an entire town and not know it.

If there'd been a town nearby.

Leave it to Tess' brother to buy a house in the middle of a fucking state park.

Of course, since it was a state park, all he had to do was find a nice sunny spot and wait until someone came along. Anyone would do, a ranger or fishermen or day-hiker or tree-hugger, and then he could ask for directions back to the parking lot...or main entrance...or wherever the hell it was he'd parked the damn car.

That's all he had to do. Just wait. A little while longer.

"Goddammit."

Dawn broke with agonizing slowness, but little by little the fog gave way and Vince found himself—in the middle of the fucking woods. He kicked at a fallen branch, missed, and wished for the umpteenth time that she was there. His little wifey. There was nothing like one-on-one contact with living flesh for tension-relieving satisfaction.

God, he missed her.

Closing his eyes, Vince rolled his head to work out the kinks and was pleased by the absence of the muffled *snap-crackle*-and *pop* that usually accompanied that. It was a good sign, meant that regardless of the shit he'd been through—*that she'd put him through*—he was still loose and ready. *More than ready.* As soon as he found her—*he had to be close, dammit*—and took care of a little unfinished business, he could be on his way to parts unknown to the police and his parole officer.

And no one could blame him this time for what he was going to do, even if they did find her body.

Which wasn't going to happen until he was a long, *long* ways away.

Vince let his muscles relax and when he opened his eyes, he watched the last tendrils of fog sink into the ground as the sun punched holes in the tree's leafy armor.

What do you know? It was going to be a nice day after all.

**

By nine o'clock the house was filled with sunlight and the warm smell of coffee. The number of boxes had diminished in equal proportion to the number of trash bags stacked on the front porch; and the Keeping Room, bathroom, and *half* the bedroom were already noticeably larger. The boxes in the living room would be saved as an "evening project"—something to do instead of simply vegging out in front of the TV.

And that only left the office, AKA: "The Disaster Zone."

"Oh, boy."

In the condo, because her "office" had been consigned to the narrow but adequate landing, she'd been very circumspect about what was necessary to "get by." Her desk, computer and printer took up one wall; the twin file cabinets, another. That was all she needed, so that was all the room she took. She left the rest of the landing alone and kept her back to the bookcases filled with Vince's books, the leather chair and ottoman that had taken him and two of his friends to get up the stairs, and the sweater he'd left across the chair back.

Living with a real ghost wasn't hard after that.

But sitting there musing over the past, or present, wasn't going to get things put away. *Darn it.*

Tess set her mug down on the Bio-Hazard mouse pad she got as a "Secret Santa" gift and turned her desk chair in a semi-circle, trying, as she had for the last twenty minutes, to decide where to start. Robby and Chuck had set the room up in a rough "L-shape," but it worked and she liked it, so that, at least, was done.

Maybe.

Her desk faced the front window, which, now that there she had blinds that could be lowered against the morning sun, was fine. *Check.* The printer stand was to the right of the desk, the two small file cabinets from the condo to her left. *Good, works.*   A trio of maple bookcases—massive and sturdy compared to the clear lacquered, open-backed ones Vince chose—lined the wall to her right. *Crap.* Computer boxes, file boxes, and boxes marked "office (?) supplies" were stacked beneath the back window opposite.

Tess exhaled slowly and swiveled her chair to the right. And the pile of boxes already designated "storage" "winter clothes" and "?" that would go directly to the attic when she felt up to starting the marathon relay again.

A rolled area rug, still in the mover's plastic sleeve, held the attic door open.

Tess reached back for her mug, then turned and sat looking at the door. Unlike her bedroom, the ghost apparently wanted *this* door closed.

At first she thought the floor must be warped or the door hung at a slight angle so it would close automatically. That made sense, until she tested the theory by pushing the door open and waiting to see how long it took to close.

It didn't.

Until she turned her back.

"And Robby called me exasperating."

The rolled rug suddenly lost its balance and fell backwards, which should have been impossible; but impossible or not, it did and Tess jumped. Warm coffee splattered the front of her shirt and when she looked at the attic door it was closed.

"Fine," she said, "have it your way. I'm going to change so...do whatever it is you want."

When she came back, the attic door was open.

Tess picked up a box of winter clothes and carried it up. "Thank you." By lunchtime, she'd moved all the boxes that needed to go to the attic, connect the computer—explaining the intricacies of the electronic age to the ghost as she went—and answered three e-mails from Robby.

"He's worried about me," she told the ghost, "but I'm okay. I just wish he wouldn't talk about selling the condo. It belongs to Vince...my husband and he's going to... He won't be happy when he finds out what I did. Vince loved that condo."

A soft beep pulled her attention back to the screen and its undulating flying letter. Another message. Tess yawned and leaned back in the desk chair, stretching her arms above her head. Besides the three messages from her brother, there'd been thirty-eight others, twenty of which were spam and she deleted without reading. Of the eighteen left, minus two more from Chuck—one inviting her over for "drinks on the veranda" after work and the second with a link the historical society's web-site—three were from co-workers who missed her: *"Miss you! "Take it easy." "You're in our prayers..."*

Nice.

And the rest were about work: *"Sorry to bother you, but—" "Know you're taking some personal time, but—" "Hate to ask, but —"*

The newest e-mail was of that variety.

"Hi Tess, know you don't need to think about work right now, and I wouldn't normally think about asking under the circumstance, but—"

Tess wanted to write back, *"Hey, it's only a divorce, no big deal—people get them all the time..."* But she couldn't, of course, because it was a big deal, to her...and undoubtedly to Vince, wherever he was.

"Did you really think you can keep me out of my home, bitch?"
He's here.

On her feet without realizing she'd even stood up, Tess heard the chair collide with the wall as she whirled around. Heart pounding, hands clasped against her mouth to stop any scream that might come; she faced the empty room and felt her knees tremble against the strain of holding her up. For a moment, only a moment she thought she saw him standing at the door....

There was no one in the room besides her. And the ghost.

The air moved through Tess' fingers in a ragged, but steady rush followed by an even more ragged giggle. Shaking her head, she retrieved her chair and sat down.

"Oh...God, don't mind me," she said out loud, "I'm just having...a...some sort of breakdown, I guess. Bet you never thought you'd be living with a crazy person, did you?"

Tess didn't wait to hear if she got an answer. Scooting the chair closer, she watched the screen for the words her fingers tapped out.

<what's the problem?>
<systems crash—you have backup of j.reese file?>
<hard or electronic?>
<electrons will do <g>>

Tess opened the desk's upper right drawer for the "office" pin-drive. Another few automatic keystrokes and the file was off on its journey across the electronic superhighway.

<there you go—good luck>
<bless you, my child>
<anything else?>
<shouldn't be—thanks—sympathies>

Sympathies? Just for moving? God, what would they have done if she told them? But told them what—about Vince? Losing the baby? The real reason behind the bruises? What happened the last time in the condo when Vince...

"What do you plan on doing with that..."

Tess stood up without knocking anything over and walked out of the office.

"I need a break," she called back over her shoulder and heard her echo through the empty rooms. "If anyone wants me, I'll be...exploring history."

The afternoon felt warm against her face as she headed downstream and hoped the remains of the old dam Robby told her about would be easier to find than the rutted path along the stream was proving to be.

**

He heard her before he saw her and stepped back into the trees when she passed.

Her face was red from exertion and her hair damp from the summer's moist heat, had begun to curl at the ends. *She should wear it down;* he thought when she, as if having heard his thoughts, purposely rebelled against them and wound her hair into a loose braid that she bound with a dark band. The tiny act of defiance bothered him, and he forced a smile at his own audacity. He'd been alone too long, with only his memories and sins to keep him company. A woman had every right to wear her hair as she chose.

It shamed him that he'd forgotten that as he stood and watched her move among the gravestones like some misplaced specter, pausing now and again to read a carved inscription or to touch a weathered angel. She stopped most often at the smaller, those of children, and each time he'd feel his belly tighten.

When, at last, she stopped before one particular stone and bent down to trace the epitaph that had been written decades before she'd been born, he walked back into the woods and disappeared.

She didn't belong there, but neither did he.

**

The cemetery was as lovely as Chuck said, but it was smaller than she thought it would be. When she and Robby had been growing up, their aunt and uncle had loved nothing better than to pile all the kids into the car and drive out to Laurel Hill Cemetery—Philadelphia's own flamboyant Victorian *"requiescat in pace"*—for impromptu picnics among the elegant sculpture gardens and mansion-like sepulchers.

That was a cemetery.

Their parents were buried in a far less elegant necropolis, but even that modest suburban "memorial park" was well over ten acres.

This...tiny collection of grave would have been hard pressed to qualify as a churchyard. If there'd been a church anywhere in the vicinity.

Alone and secluded, Tess counted fifty headstones within the weathered split-rail fence. The most *recent* burials had been in 1904, a family of five—mother, father and three children under the age of ten—from influenza. Most of the stones were from the 1800's although she found a few so weathered they appeared blank, but all were upright and neat and the summer weeds—for the most part—pulled around their base...either the work of the Park Rangers of Chuck's beloved Historical Society.

She might have to consider joining.

Tess studied the grave in front of her

Hannah Johnson Wade

Beloved wife of—

and listened to the constant interweaving of birdsong and the wind through the trees. The little cemetery was quiet, peaceful...perfect. She took a deep breath of the warm woods smell, and then continued along the first row of stones—getting to know the neighbors.

Samuel Whitney Mathers

2nd November - 7th November 1883

Sleep, little one, sleep

Forever in our hearts

Only five days old.

Tess bent down to touch the worn carving beneath the epitaph—a lamb she thought—then let her hand fall to the wilted bouquet of Black-eyed Susans someone—*probably from the Historical Society*—had left. A similar bouquet, this one tied with a bit of sun-bleached ribbon, lay on the grave to the right of the child's.

Victoria Whitney Mathers
2nd March 1864 – 9th November 1883
Grief took her too soon away.
Loving mother of Samuel
Beloved wife of—

The baby's mother.

Tess twisted on the balls of her feet, steadying herself against the child's grave to face the mother. *'Grief took her too soon away...'* Wasn't that what mothers were supposed to do—die of grief when they lost a child?

Standing, Tess pressed her arms against her belly and walked to the next grave. It belonged to another woman—*beloved wife, died of fever in her forty-second year.* Hmm. So where was the *beloved* husband and *loving* father? On the other side of his son? No, the baby's grave was the last one in the row.

That was odd.

Tess turned and walked past the fever victim and squinted at the next headstone. It looked much older than the three previous, the epitaph all but worn smooth. Bending closer, Tess could just make out the final date—*1721.* Not daddy.

Now it was a mystery.

She'd seen enough cemeteries to know that sometimes family members weren't buried together—mother and child go first, father years later...or father remarries and is buried with his new family—but, given the period his family died in, he had be to here somewhere. Travel wasn't as common a thing to do the 1800s or as simple a thing to do.

Sell a house, move, start your life over.

It wasn't that easy.

Or maybe it was.

Tess came to the end of the row—*still no Mr. Mathers*—then retraced her steps and started at the beginning.

Patience Unity Doyle
Beloved aunt of—
Ely
Ripple
Miller
Then, finally
Augustus Mathers
1793 – 22nd day of December 1860
Elsbeth
Wife of Augustus
3rd day of April 1805 – 24th day of May 1858
Grandparents of little Samuel. To the right:
Daughter
Margaret
14th day of January 1810
and the left:
Son
Samuel Grant Mathers
4th day of August 1811 – 31st day of July 1863
Wife of Samuel
Gretchen
3rd day of September 1814 – 31st day of September 1866

Daughter Emily
4th day of August 1830 – 9th day of February 1891

Son Martin – 18th day of June 1833

Tess tapped fingers against the top of her leg in frustration. The dates were wrong even if the name wasn't. This *Samuel* died two year before the infant *Samuel's* mother was even born. There may have been a family connection between the two, but the child's father was still missing.

There was a smaller stone, laid flat into the ground next to the mother's grave with just the initials *R.M.* carved on it.

Another child, possibly stillborn, but given a name, of sorts, and a final resting-place because it was part of the family.

Unlike baby Samuel's father apparently.

Maybe he had died somewhere else—*had there been a war around that time?*—or maybe he'd been...a whaler and lost at sea. Or maybe Samuel's daddy had been the black sheep of the Mathers' family and—

He's here.

Tess scraped both knees as she fell forward, then ground dirt into the abraded skin when she twisted and *saw* him—*Vince*—move through the line of wind-stirred trees directly behind her. If it was Vince, all he had to do was step out and take her. She couldn't move, couldn't get enough air into her lungs to do more than keep from passing out. It was as if she'd suddenly turned to stone...one more among the graves of the forgotten.

But she was screaming, inside her head, when he pushed aside the branches and stepped into the sunlight.

"Hey, Tee-tee."

Her body and mind reconnected the moment she was on her feet and running toward the sound, toward her name, her life flowing back into her with each step. Robby wasn't prepared to be body-checked. The air left his lungs in a loud whoosh.

"*UGHH!*" It took some doing, but he finally was able to snake a hand down between them and push her away. "Yeah, good to see you, too...you can let *go* now. What was that all about?"

Tess was panting and fighting the urge to look back toward the trees. "You scared me."

Robby held her at arm's length while he caught his breath. "Obviously. I called, but you don't have your cell phone with you, do you?"

Tess' hand went to the pocket of her shorts and felt nothing but denim. It was then she noticed the sky. Time had slipped again. The sun was low, the color of the light changing.

"I…lost track of time."

"Yeah, it happens…especially here. I can't tell you how many times I've had to come drag Chuck out of here before it got dark. When I stopped by the millhouse and found you not t'home, I figured you'd be here. Nice, isn't it?"

The trees were mostly shadows now. If Vince was there, she wouldn't be able to see him.

"Yeah. Chuck invited me for drinks. Is the offer still good?"

"Always. So, wanna race back?"

"No." Tess took her brother's hand and tried not to grip it too hard. "You lead, I'll follow."

**

Vince followed them from the little cemetery and watched, from the other side of the creek, as she picked her way across the broken dam. He kept watching, the smile grown hard on his lips, as brother and sister climbed the bank to the millhouse together.

She should have known she'd never get away.

Not from him…her loving husband.

Got'cha.

CHAPTER 8
June 16th

The rest of the week passed in blessed tedium.

It had only taken a few days, but with Robby and Chuck's help, she'd finally finished unpacking, putting away, throwing out (boxes), filling up (trash bags), hanging pictures, and started the processes of learning to live alone.

With ghost.

There were still a few things she had to get used to. Sometimes the attic door refused to stay open and the bedroom door refused to stay shut, but time stayed with her and she congratulated herself on every dull, repetitive, and safe project she accomplished.

But it wasn't enough and when she e-mailed her supervisor and told him to put her back in e-harness that coming Monday or she'd go crazy, Peter thought she was joking and sent a smiley face.

Then promised to send over a new batch of files first thing Monday morning.

Great. Perfect. Wonderful.

Now all she needed to do was get through the weekend.

The days had been easy—there was always something she could find to do—but when the light began to soften and the windows facing the creek filled with a mellow glow, Tess noticed she couldn't seem to stay focused on anything for more than a minute or two. Her hands would suddenly forget how to work a twist-tie, or she'd walk into a room and forget why she'd come into it. Then, without any reason for it, she'd think about what happened at the small cemetery, even though nothing *had* happened except Robby showing up and scaring her.

There'd been no reason for her to think Vince was within a hundred miles of her...he wasn't stupid, he wouldn't have just shown up, she knew that, but...

It was just a feeling she'd had that Vince was watching her.

Just a feeling.

Like the one she was having right now.

He's here.

Tess turned off the kitchen faucet and held onto the front of the sink to keep from running to make sure the front and back doors were locked even though she knew they were. She hadn't gone outside that day, hadn't even unlocked or opened either door since yesterday afternoon...no, not even yesterday...she hadn't been outside in at least two days. There was no reason to, but she'd planned on taking the last few bags of trash out today...yes, she had planned to do that, but...

Time had gotten away from her again and now it was too late.

He's here.

On tiptoes, leaning forward over the sink until her forehead almost touched the window glass, Tess looked across the shadowed creek to the woods beyond and saw exactly what she expected to see. Nothing, because Vince *wasn't* stupid. If he was out there—*he was, he is, he's here*—he'd be very careful to keep out of sight.

"He should be, he knows I'll call the police if I see him." Even though she'd whispered it and had only the ghost as witness, Tess felt her stomach tighten against the lie. She knew she wouldn't be able to. Worse yet, Vince knew the same thing. Even the last time she hadn't been capable of calling the police.

"And look how brave it is. Oh...I'm scared. I'm so scared."

She closed her eyes and pushed away from the window.

"He's playing with me." This time her voice was a little louder and a whole lot shakier. "Vince likes to play games. He knows I can't tell Robby without sounding—" *Crazy.* "—paranoid. God, maybe I am. Vince wouldn't come here, not after—"

It was like cutting into a loaf of fresh bread....

A cramp doubled her over as her stomach emptied itself in a stream of bile the color of Key Limes. It was almost a repeat performance of the night she told him about the baby. When the cramp subsided, Tess reached up and turned on the faucet and washed out the sink. Vince knew her so well. If he did anything overt, like letting her see him, it wouldn't be as much fun.

For him.

"I didn't even call the police...Robby did," she explained to the dark that was gathering in the corners of the house. "He said...Robby said it wasn't my fault, but it was. If I hadn't... Robby said—"

"Tess, there was nothing else you could do. He would have killed you."

"What did I do?" Tess scooped up a handful of cool water and rinsed out her mouth. "Why can't he leave me alone?"

It couldn't have been anything but her imagination, but as she stood there in the dark, she felt a light pressure encase her wet hand, as if someone was holding it.

And it felt nice.

Even if she was crazy.

**

Vince nudged a twig off the crumbling slab of concrete with the toe of his shoe and watched the water snatch it away. The twig took the rapids directly below the dam easily, dipping and swirling, but each time it went under—however briefly— Vince clenched his hands and felt something like a electric shock jump along his spine. It was only after it disappeared into the shadows beyond the rapids that Vince made himself look straight down at the water.

Funneled through the broken sections of the dam, the normally placid Wissahickon hissed and spat like some wounded feral beast. A miniature comber, invisible in the dark except for a brief flash of white foam, broke against a jagged edge and splattered the concrete at his feet. Vince turned and ran back to the bank, the soles of his shoes grating against deteriorating cement and stranded debris.

What the hell was going on?

He'd never been afraid of water. He lived in Eastern Pennsylvania, for God's sake...you couldn't go two blocks, even in the heart of Philadelphia, without coming across water is some form or another—a stream, a river, ponds, pools...he'd never gave it a second thought. *Until now.*

His dad made sure Vince knew how to swim almost before he could walk and he loved it. Swam like a fish as a kid, took every diving and swimming team medal his high school had to offer... even took a couple of kayaking lessons last summer, and mastered the infamous "roll" the first time he tried it. *There was no fucking reason he should be standing there, sweating bullets at the thought of crossing a goddamned stream he could probably jump across if he got a good enough start.*

"Shit."

He'd seen her do it, cross the dam, her and that brother of hers...and *that* bothered him. His little wifey, who hadn't been able to do more than sit on her ass and watch him jog, had suddenly become a regular outdoorswoman—hiking through the woods, exploring cemeteries, jumping from one broken section of the dam to another like some fucking gazelle.

She'd changed and he didn't like it.

But the water had been lower then...like now. In the days between the creek had run high and fast, rising to cover the dam at one point and smoothing out the rapids. Vince had watched from the safety of the trees—pacing back and forth like a caged animal, anger building because he couldn't get to her.

And now that he could....

Vince walked back to a fallen log, high on the bank, and sat down. His legs felt like jelly and he was shaking so hard his eyes wouldn't focus. It made the ground in front of him look like it was covered with Mexican jumping beans. *Jesus, what's the matter with me?* Leaning forward, he pressed his elbows against his knees and stared at one tiny patch of mud near his left shoe until the world settled down.

There was only one explanation for it—he was sick, caught some damn bug while he was traipsing around the woods looking for her. Of course, the concussion she gave him probably helped...lowered his resistance. If she'd simply behaved like a loving wife the last time he wouldn't have had to come after her. Hell, he might have even forgiven her.

It was a long shot, he had to admit that, but stranger things had happened.

And maybe he'd tell her that—right before he snapped her neck.

Vince sat up and smiled. It was surprising how a single thought could change a man's entire outlook, but suddenly the shakes were gone and he felt like he could walk across fire, let alone some cruddy stream.

Standing, he rolled his shoulders and made his way through the deep shadows to the water's edge. The dam was for sissies; he'd just stroll on across and use the mud to mess up her nice little—

There was a flicker of movement to his left and Vince turned right into a haymaker.

There was more surprise than pain, but the suddenness and force behind the attack knocked him off balance and onto his ass. It was too dark to see his attacker beyond a body shape—a big man, almost as big as him—but sitting there guessing who it might be wasn't an option. Vince got to his feet, fists raised, and a second blow to the ear dropped him to his knees.

He slid back and his left foot went ankle deep into a churning backwash. A jolt of pain unlike anything he'd ever felt on or off the gridiron ricocheted through every nerve ending in his body and filling his mind with....

A sound like a scream filled his head and for a moment the world disappeared. But it was only for a moment, and the next he was up on his feet, putting everything he had into a solid right hook.

His right hand could already feel the warm yielding flesh giving way to the solid, hard, *momentary* resistance of bone. He swung with everything he had and hit—

Nothing but thin air.

The momentum of his punch carried him a quarter-turn, but he shifted his weight to the balls of his feet and dropped one shoulder. His left arm cocked into the ready position, but the target was missing.

Vince straightened but didn't drop his guard—not again— and first checked the tree-line and then the bank in both directions.

He was alone.

"Fucking bastard!"

His assailant was fast, but not overly quiet. When something skittered away quickly through the brush to his left, Vince was after it like a shot.

"Think you can get away from me? Come here!"

If he'd said that to Tess, she would have already been crawling to him on her hands and knees, whimpering and contrite—but, unfortunately, that tactic only seemed to work on wives. Cursing, Vince tucked his arms in closer to his side and sprinted as fast as the terrain and growing darkness would allow. The guy might have known the woods, but the brief glimpses Vince got of him showed a dark, solidly built, *compact* silhouette a good deal shorter than he was. It was the typical *"little man"* syndrome, he thought, blindside a *real* man and run away. *Probably some fucking tree-hugger showing off for his limp-dick buddies.*

"ASSHOLE!"

There were other skitterings and mad-dashes, smaller animals running for cover, as the man took a sudden hard right and plunged down the crumbling bank toward the creek. Vince was right on his tail.

Literally.

Vince's feet slid on the muddy bank as the six-point buck plunged into the stream and swam for the other side. For a split instant he had a choice—fall back into brush, bramble and rock...or go face first into three or four inches of water. No contest.

His left elbow struck the ground first, his spine a close second. More or less flat on his back, Vince watched the deer, white flag of its tail flying, scramble nimbly up the opposite bank in a wave of foam and disappear around the side of the millhouse.

She was standing in the window, surrounded by light... looking right at him.

"Tess."

Her hands were pressed against her mouth, like she was trying to hold back a scream and seeing her like that— frightened—brought back every wonderful moment they'd ever shared together. He missed her, he wanted her, and he'd *get* her...but not yet. And especially not when he was flat on his back. Having her see him like that was...wrong. He'd come to her walking tall, shoulders back...fists ready.

Soon, baby, soon.

Keeping his head down, Vince stood up and turned his back to her. Smiling, he slipped his hands into the pocket of his jeans and slowly walked up the bank and into the trees. He could feel her eyes on him—a tiny prickling like spider legs along the back of his neck. When he'd gone far enough that he knew the shadows covered him, Vince turned and carefully made his way back to the stream along a different route; just close enough so he could see her.

She was still in the window, hands still against her mouth —frozen in time. He knew she'd stay like that for the rest of the night unless something happened to make her move: a phone call, a knock on the door…a stone through a window. Something to startle her into motion. He'd trained her so very well.

Reaching into the pocket of his windbreaker, Vince pulled the cell phone into his hand. She'd done so many things wrong, his little wifey, and he'd make sure she knew it.

**

He's here. Vince is really here.

Tess slowly levered herself back from the window but it didn't matter…she'd seen him.

And he'd seen her.

At first there'd only been the deer. She'd notice the small herd—a buck and three does—a few days earlier, coming down to the stream at twilight to drink and she'd made it a point to watch for them since. Usually the does appeared first; moving cautiously, ears pricked for the slightest sound, muscles tense, ready to run. Tess knew how they felt. The buck only came down to the water after his harem had begun to drink, after they'd proven it was safe.

Tonight the buck was alone, exploding from the trees in a leap that carried him over the bank and into the middle of the creek. Tess had leaned back over the sink, standing on tiptoes to get closer to the window, watching as another deer stumbled and fell down the embankment.

Except it wasn't a deer.

"Vince."

He'd found her.

Just like she knew he would.

Despite Robby's assurances, there'd never been a doubt in her mind that he'd find her. Vince wasn't the kind of man who gave up easily—if he wanted to get her, he would, and there was nothing anyone could do to stop him. Not now.

And this time he'd kill her.

She had no doubts about that, either.

Tess had felt herself go numb as he—*Vince*—stood up, but instead of acknowledging that he'd seen her—or she him—he turned around and walked back into the woods.

"Vince!"

Her call echoed through the otherwise silent rooms, but he never turned around. Tess pressed her hands over her mouth and backed away from the window until she was standing in the middle of the room.

It's him.

Then why hadn't he turned around?

Of course it's him, who else could it be? She knew him, knew his walk and the way his body moved...he was even wearing the same windbreaker and jeans he'd had on at the condo, but...

Why didn't he turn around?

As the outside light continued to fade, the kitchen light turned the window glass into a mirror reflecting back a transparent image of her—a new ghost to haunt the millhouse.

"It had to be him. You saw him, didn't you?" she whispered behind clenched fingers. "The man out there, across the stream...you saw him. It was my husband...I mean, I think it was."

Moving at an angle that erased her reflection from the glass, Tess crossed the room and turned off the light. At the same moment the Keeping Room darkened, the evening outside the window brightened enough for her to see the woods on the opposite side of the stream. The man—*Vince*— was gone, the woods empty.

It had to be Vince, but—*the man walked away*—he wouldn't have done that...not after he'd—*found me*—come all this way.

If it had been Vince he would have waved or shouted or— *walked in the front door.*

Tess kept looking at the window as she backed out of the room.

It wasn't Vince. Vince would have already been there unless...

"He's playing with me."

It all made sense. He knew her so well. All he had to do was let her see him and walk away and he knew—*oh God*—she'd stand there wonder and worry and try to make up her mind if really was him. She'd stand there and time would slip away while he crossed the stream and came for her. He knew it. He knew her.

And *she* knew there was nothing she could do to save herself.

"NO! NOT THIS TIME!"

Tess screamed hoping he'd hear and ran into the hall. *Not this time, not this time, not this time—* The cadence of her words matched the pounding of her feet on the stairs. *Not this time, not this time, not this t—* Her foot slipped on the top stair, twisting out from under her. There wasn't time to grab the handrail.

Tess felt her stomach drop in the rush of motion as she pitched forward and, just before she squeezed her eyes shut, watched the stairs telescoping up toward her. Any moment she'd feel the impact, hear the dull thud of her body against the yellow pine floorboards, the sharp crack as her neck broke.

An arm caught her around the waist and held her.

Tess opened her eyes with a gasp. She was standing on the bottom stair.

There was nothing around her waist, but as she looked she felt it...an invisible force pull her gently down until was sitting, her back against the wall, knees toward the open banister, and then the sensation was gone.

But she could still feel the chill against the front of her shirt.

One of the entryway floorboards creaked as if he were backing away, leaving her alone now that she was safe. Tess followed the sound with her eyes.

"Thank you."

Another creak, softer than the first, answered her.

"We really should really come up with a system...one knock for yes, two for no?" Tess took a deep breath and hunched over her arms, then started to rock, very slowly, back and forth. It seemed to help. "Or maybe I could just leave out Scrabble letters and you could—"

Her cell phone rang.

Tess stopped moving, talking, breathing...nothing was more important at that moment than listening to the computerized tones of *The Entertainer*. The tune, Robby's pre-programmed gift, drifted out from the kitchen where she'd left the phone and filled the downstairs. It played through once and cut off before Voice Mail could pick it up.

It was Vince. He hated leaving messages.

When *The Entertainer* began again Tess braced her hands against both sides of the narrow staircase and stood up.

"He'll keep calling until I answer and then he'll...." She stepped from the staircase to the entranceway's yellow pine, eyes fixed on the doorway leading to the kitchen. "I have to; you can't save me from him. He's—"

Three sharp knocks sounded against the front door.

—*here*.

The Entertainer ended as she reached for the doorknob and a feeling almost like peace settled over her. He'd taken pity on her and decided to put her out of her misery sooner rather than later.

He still loved her enough to do that.

Tess took a deep breath and opened the door.

"I didn't think this place was that big...where were you?"

Robby leaned on one elbow against the doorframe, his eyebrow raised in mock wonder. Tess gripped the doorknob to keep from falling.

"See, *this* is why people need landlines and answering machines...that annoying little red light is a great incentive to *answer your phone!*"

"*You* called me?"

"Yeah...why? You expecting someone else?"

"No! I mean..." *I can't tell him. Not yet...not until I'm sure.* "I —I was upstairs. In the attic. I didn't hear it."

Tess could always tell when her big brother didn't believe her, and this was one of those times. Wrinkles creased the smooth skin between his eyes as pushed away from the door.

"What's wrong?" he asked.

"Nothing. Tired."

He slipped his cell phone into a pocket then reached out and took her by the shoulders. When they were younger, he'd do the same thing when he caught her in a fib.

"Tired I believe, and I'll even accept you didn't hear the phone...but you're shaking and as pale as a ghost."

Tess had to bite the inside of her cheek to keep from telling him what...besides seeing Vince...happened. *"Funny you should mention 'ghost', Robby...mine just saved me."* She didn't know if he'd believe her or not, but it was too private a thing to share, even with him.

"I almost fell down the stairs, that's all."

His grasp tightened. "What do you mean that's *all?* What happened? Did you catch your foot on something?"

No, he caught me. "I...did hear the phone and just came down the stairs too quickly. I'm okay. I promise."

She crossed her heart with a big X. That part, the part about her being okay, was real, at least. He grimaced, looking past her to the stairs. "I'm so sorry, honey. I'll just knock next time."

Now she felt a little guilty.

"So...you called me?"

"Oh, right." The hint of a smile came back on her brother's lip. "Grab a sweater and some bug spray...we're going on a picnic."

She glanced toward the back door. She couldn't go outside, he was there. "Now? But it's so...late."

"No, it's not and don't worry, I have bug spray. The Hysterical Society is having some sort of reenactment whatever at the old Lodge House this weekend and tonight's their kick-off concert for members and their guests."

"I don't... I really don't feel up to it, Robby."

"Sure you do." Robby moved her to one side and headed for the kitchen. "Lights, lights...where's that—ah!"

"Robby, I really don't feel like it."

She heard cupboard doors opening and closing. By the time Tess shut—and locked—the door and went into the kitchen, Robby was shoulder deep in the pantry.

"The catsup and mustard are in the refrigerator."

He shuddered without turning around. "Heaven forefend! We're strictly gourmet picnickers...thanks to Chuck we're going to be eating along the highest portion of the hog, but I forgot to get paper plates and cups and if you don't have any we're going to have to use the fine china and crystal. Please tell me you have some."

Tess pointed to the half cabinet above the stove. "I got them for... I don't know why, I guess they were on sale, but I never used them. I must have just put them in a drawer and forgot about them. They're still sealed."

"Perfect." Robby pulled out the shrink-wrapped stack of bright red plastic plates and matching hot-cold cups. Tess hadn't forgotten them; she'd hidden them from Vince. When he told her *they* were hosting the office Christmas buffet, he never told her what color plates to buy, so she picked red. Because, she thought, Vince liked red. He did, but not in plastic-ware. She'd realized her mistake the moment she walked into the conference room and handed them to him. Later, when they got home, Vince explained why green would have been a better choice.

"Can't you do anything right? I told you I already ordered a red tablecloth and poinsettias... Jesus, it looked like a blood bath in there. What were you trying to do, make me look incompetent? My boss puts me in charge because he trusts me, and you ruin it. You stupid —"

Tess moved away from the memory of what followed. "I don't have any napkins. Sorry."

Robby was leaning forward, reading the label on a can of soup. "It's a picnic; we can go crazy and use paper towels if we have to. You like lentil soup?" He closed the cupboard with a shrug and turned around. "You're a lifesaver and red is the perfect picnic color. So, I'll take these, you grab the bug spray, house-keys, not too sure you'll need a sweater but you will need shoes. Git 'em and let's git goin'."

Tess stopped him before he could grab her purse off the back of the dining room chair. "Robby, please...I *really* don't want to go out tonight."

"Why? What happened, Tess...and I don't mean you almost falling down the stairs. Something else happened, didn't it?"

"I..." She couldn't stop herself from glancing toward the window. "I—I thought I saw—" *Vince.* "—a man was standing on the other side of the stream looking at the house. Again."

Robby handed her the plates and cups and went to the window.

"Don't...he might still—"

"It's okay, baby." Cupping his hands against the light, Robby leaned over the sink and looked out into the night. "No one there now. Are you sure you saw someone?"

"Yes. I... It scared me."

"Hell, it would probably scare me." Straightening, Robby lowered the blinds. "Forget what I said earlier and keep these closed when you have the lights on, okay? Now, it's probably just another hiker," he said as he came back to her side, "but, there'll be a couple Park Rangers at the 'do' tonight, and I'll mention it."

"No, it's okay—" *Vince would see their uniforms and think they're the police.* "I...it was nothing."

"Nothing, yeah, right...I can tell by the look on your face it was nothing. Besides, the rangers will probably love to have something to do besides directing tourists and leading nature walks."

"Robby—"

"End of discussion. Now, give me those and go put on some shoes." He scooped the plastic-ware out of her hands and shouldered her toward the stairs. "I mean it...move or the champagne will go warm."

"Okay, you big bully." Maybe it would be okay...Vince wouldn't try anything with people around. Tess was halfway up the stairs when she stopped to look at him over her shoulder. "Did you say Champagne? For a picnic?"

"What did you expect, *lite beer?* Please, go get whatever it is you're going to get."

Tess was almost at the top stair when Robby came up behind her, his hand against the small of her back, to steady her.

"I'm okay, you know."

"Did I say you weren't?"

Tess reached the landing and turned around. Her brother was still standing at the bottom of the stairs, his hand full of red plastic-ware.

"You forget something?"

"No...yes, are we going to hike or drive? I'll need to put on sneakers if we're going over the dam."

Robby shook his head. "With the amount of food Chuck's packed, we're driving so wear whatever's comfortable. Oh...do you want me to grab your cell phone? It's on the kitchen table."

"No," Tess shook her head and walked into her bedroom. "Leave it. If anyone wants me they can call back."

**

He watched her and, at first, thought she was just being coy—playing a well rehearsed part for the growing number of men who'd found reasons throughout the night to be close to her. His own mother had been that way, an accomplished master of drawing men to her side; but the more he watched, the less sure he was that it was an act. As unlikely as it was, she seemed genuinely surprised by the attention she was given and equally troubled by it.

It was her brother who strove to keep her the flame to draw out the moths. An unattached man could not pass within a few feet of the bench where they sat that her brother wouldn't call out to introduce her.

He'd counted ten times it had happened and ten times she met the newcomer's eyes just long enough to be polite. Still, it angered him. It was not a brother's duty to barter his sister as if she were a spring lamb.

When the music began again, he walked closer to where she sat. Night had fallen and there were too many others for her to notice him, but still he was careful to keep either darkness or the crowd always between them.

There was time enough before she saw him.

When the music began again, he watched from his new vantage-point as her brother leaned over and said something. She shook her head and took a sip from the red cup in her hand. Her brother spoke again, pointing to the spot on the wide lawn where men and women were pairing off for the Virginia Reel. This time, along with another—more vehement shake of her head—she turned away from him.

He should leave her be.

But he didn't.

Finishing his own drink, her brother took the cup from her and pulled her to her feet. Half-running, half-stumbling he dragged her to the woman's line and left her.

Blowing a kiss, her brother turned and motioned another man who, smiling and eager, to take his place opposite her.

"Robby!"

Her shout hovered above the music for a moment, but there was no anger in it. Her voice was light, the objection only for show.

So at last the truth came out. If she hadn't wanted to be there, taking the stranger's hands and allowing his arm to find her waist, she would have walked away.

Instead, he did.

**

When he found his brother-in-law's car in the parking lot, Vince made sure he never wandered far enough away that he couldn't, at a moment's notice, turn and find it again.

He still wasn't 100% sure of where he was, in comparative distance to the Millhouse, but the two-lane road just beyond the parking lot gave him hope. It'd be easy now, he'd watch to see which way they turned onto the road and that would give him the direction. It couldn't be more than a couple miles. Even if it meant he'd wear down the treads on a perfectly good pair of running shoes, it was still better then trying to forge the stream.

Just the thought of all that rushing, bubbling water made him queasy.

"So stop thinking about it." *Good advice.*

Above the sound of tin whistles and violins, Vince heard the slow, steady cadence of footsteps on gravel and moved away from the cars. He didn't think it'd be Tess—the last time he looked, she was having *way* too much fun doing an Irish jig or something—but it was always a good idea to keep as low a profile as possible. All it'd take was some paranoid bimbo to see a "stranger" hanging around the parking lot and every cop and Park Ranger in the borough would descend upon the area like Sitting Bull on Custer.

From between the branches of a conveniently planted pine, Vince watched an elderly couple make their slow and steady progress to a Lexus that was still wearing Dealer's plates.

Some people have all the luck. Jesus, just look at them. Brand fucking new luxury car and they probably won't live long enough to take it in for its first tune up. Shit! They're so old the only thing they should have bought was a his-and-hers burial plot.

The longer Vince watched the old fart and frau, the angrier he got. It wasn't fair, nothing in his life had been, but once he settled things with Tess that would all change.

For the better.

CHAPTER 9
June 17th
1:30 A.M.

Vince aimed a vicious kick at an anchored Park Department "trash receptacle" and missed by a mile. Already off balance, the miscalculation of velocity plus trajectory minus mass sent him stumbling to the left.

It was not the result he had hoped for.

"FUCKING GODDAMNED MOTHER-FUCKER ASSHOLE SON OF A BITCH SHIT!"

The small forest creatures that had been investigating the area since the party broke up beat a hasty, scampering retreat. The deer did exactly the opposite—they froze, muscles locking tight—and stared at him with round, liquid eyes.

Just like Tess.

"BITCH!"

This was her fault, too. She'd seen him by the water only a couple of hours earlier so she knew he'd be waiting for her. All she had to do was leave the party and come to him. That's all. Was that too much for a man to ask of his wife? Hell no.

But did she?

"Shit."

He'd stayed with the cars as long as he could, but after a while he had to see what was taking her so long. And he wished to God he hadn't. One after another, all a man had to do was hold out his hand and she'd take it. Dancing, talking, laughing, flirting with any man who'd give her as much as a smile. She was like some goddamned spider, trapping every available man who got close enough.

It'd been hard to watch her *whore* herself like that, but Vince forced himself because he was still her husband, Goddammit. They'd made a promise to God to love, honor and *obey*…until death they did part and he'd been prepared to see that she kept her part of that bargain. And would have, if it hadn't been for that cop…or Park Ranger or whatever the hell the guy was.

Vince hadn't been there two minutes, imagining the look on her face when he tapped her on the shoulder and asked her to dance, when he noticed the man watching him from the edge of the crowd. He, the watcher, was just far enough back from the strings of white lights that bordered the picnic grounds so Vince couldn't get a good look at him.

The guy hadn't been one of Tess' numerous partners, which meant he was either some pussy-whipped jerk who was there only because his wife or girlfriend had dragged him along, or he was gay. The fact that he seemed to be wearing a costume made Vince think the latter was the most probable reason he'd stayed on the sidelines and, normally, that would have been the end of it. But there'd been something about the man that kept drawing Vince's attention back to him.

His eyes.

They were dark and hard and unblinking. And they made Vince's skin crawl.

For a good five, ten minutes the man's gaze never moved, never verged a fraction of an inch—it held Vince as effectively as a pin holding a mounted butterfly and that was getting to him. Not a lot, he wouldn't let anything…or any*one* get to him *a lot*, but unless there was a modicum of admiration in it, he didn't like being watched that closely. It cramped his style.

He was just about ready to push his way through the crowd and work out the particular cramp when the man stepped back—

"Yeah, you'd *better* think twice about giving me the stink eye, you fu—"

—and suddenly was standing at Vince's side.

"You look like you have a problem, friend."

Vince moved back so quickly that it was all he could do to keep upright while the man just stood there, watching. There still wasn't enough light for Vince to get a good enough look at him, but even without it he could tell the man wearing a costume…and that just made him pathetic.

And nothing to worry about.

Vince hiked his own jeans up and smirked, then let his eyes do a slow roll over the linen shirt and pants, held up thick suspenders—*no belt, no belt knife*—and tucked into knee-high boots that made Vince's feet sweat just looking at them.

It was the kind of look that always made Tess wither, but the man just stood there and gave it back. Vince knew he could take him; they were about the same size, weight, age…maybe a few more inches of muscle along the guy's shoulders and arms, but…

The timing wasn't right.

If he started anything with the jerk in the costume now, Vince would blow any chance he'd hope of surprise. And there were just too many witnesses. Stepping back, Vince raised his hands in the universally accepted "no trouble here, boss" gesture, smiled and headed back to the parking lot as if that had been his objective all alone.

When he reached the lot, he turned and half expected to find the man right behind him…and was disappointed. More or less. The jerk in the costume wasn't anywhere in sight, but Vince could feel him out there in the darkness, somewhere, watching, and jumped—ready to fight—every time a twig snapped.

And that's how he missed them.

If he hadn't been so preoccupied waiting for the man to do something stupid, he would have seen Tess get into her brother's car and drive off. But he didn't...one minute it was there, parked between a Volkswagen NAB and some nondescript overprice "Save the World" hybrid, the next minute, the space was empty.

He could, he supposed, pretend he'd had a bit too much of the free beer and hard cider and ask to be driven "home," meaning her brother's place. Unfortunately, the way his luck had been running lately, he'd either ask someone who knew Robby or a Park Ranger ...or the jerk in the costume would show up again and make things so much more complicated than they needed to be.

No, wasn't worth it.

He'd already spent a night in the woods, what was one more? Especially, once he got back with his sweet little wifey, she'd be the one who'd suffer for it.

Yeah.

In the morning he'd try to find another way across the stream that didn't actually involve going over water, but for right now, it made very little sense to do anything but find a nice, secluded spot and hunker down for the rest of the night. The moon was almost set and even though his eyes had grown accustomed to the murky half tones, he knew the minute he stepped into the woods he'd lose all sense of direction. He *thought* the road was just up the gravel drive to his left, but he wasn't sure. The woods were just too fucking big and empty.

He found what he was looking for a few yards away from the lot. Hidden behind a stand of windbreak cedars, the fallen tree looked comfortable enough, if he didn't actually try stretching out on it. Tucking himself into a comfortable looking crotch between trunk and limb, Vince leaned back and let his mind wander to more pleasant things.

"It'll have to quick," he told himself. "Can't take the chance to stick around too long. Make it look like an accident...yeah. Snap her neck and throw her down the stairs...drown her...yeah, drag her ass outside and hold her under. That'd be good...naw, keep it inside. Suicide. Perfect."

Nobody would raise an eyebrow about that. Everyone knew she was crazy...a woman who'd accuse her own husband of abuse would have to be.

A dark shape glided silently along his periphery and he jumped. Vince's first thought was that it was the man come back to find him, but when, after a brief pause, the shape moved on, he sat up and flung a stone after it.

"Fucking deer. You know what I'm going to do? After I take care of my wife I'm coming back here with a gun and blow your fucking heads off! You hear me?"

It felt good to be in control again.

Rolling his shoulders Vince laid sat back and looked up at the twinkling stars. He felt like a kid on Christmas Eve.

The hard part was waiting for morning so he could play with his new toy.

**

He stood in the doorway, watching her sleep.

The moonlight had found a small chink in the window's cover and flowed onto her face, deepening the lines that had formed between her eyes. She was dreaming, but her dream was not a pleasant one and it reminded him of another bad dream he'd watched form across a different face.

So long ago.

That dream had ended badly because he'd been unaware of how deeply some wounds went even after the scar had seemingly healed. It was his fault. He had only been aware of his own nightmare and not the dreamer.

But it wouldn't happen again, not to this one.

Moving through the shadows he reached her bedside and leaned down, his lips all but touching the curls of hair that lay against her cheek.

"Rest easy," he whispered, "you're safe. I'll protect thee."
**

11:20 A.M.

"For me? Oh, you shouldn't have."

Chuck, dressed in the highest fashion allowable for an 1850's "Gentleman" farmer, was reaching for the wildflowers Tess was carrying when Robby smacked his hand away.

"We didn't." Robby was dressed in pressed chinos, sandals and the most garish fuchsia-and-lime green Hawaiian print shirt he apparently could find. He told her it was so *no one* at the event would mistake him for another reenactor. "See, this is what comes from spoiling a man. I bring him flowers so often he thinks every bouquet is for him."

But it didn't stop him from taking one of the miniature field daisies and threading it through the top buttonhole of Chuck's collarless gingham work shirt.

"Thank you." Chuck winked at Tess over Robby's shoulder.

"Well, play your cards right and you may have roses waiting when you get home tonight."

They kissed and Tess felt a surge of envy raced through her like a cold wind. *I wished someone loved me like that.* It came unexpected and quick, like one of Vince's surprise "love taps"—and almost achieved the same result. Tess staggered back a step and turned, pressing a fist to her stomach as she gulped down mouthfuls of the thick, warm air.

The bouquet of wildflowers, their stems crushed, shivered in her hand.

What am I thinking...Vince loved me—loves me. If I'd just been a better wife he wouldn't have had to do... Vince couldn't help it. He loves me and I love him...."

No, I don't.

"Oops, looks like we're embarrassing someone."

Tess blinked and felt the corners of her smile quiver.

"No, you didn't."

Robby slipped on a pair of sunglasses, completing his "tourist" look, as he walked over to Tess and kissed the top of her head. "Love you, too, sweetheart."

"Thought so." Tess gave him a one-armed hug, hiding the broken flowers at her side. "So, what's on the schedule?"

"Let me check." Chuck reached into a back pocket and pulled out a folded brochure.

"You mean you don't know?" Robby tossed an arm over Tess' shoulder, staggering when he looked at the items listed. "There can't be *that* many things going on today."

Chuck gave him a look that would have melted concrete. "Spoken like a Double-E major, but this just happens to be *the* historical event of the county and we're expecting a couple hundred people a day. Let's see...besides the on-going events like spinning, weaving, story-telling, the blacksmith shop...Oh, yeah this is great. Today there's a sheep shearing demonstration at one, Dutch over baking at two and I'm doing the..."

"Oh God, please tell me you're not going to demonstrate how to sex chickens."

Tess really hadn't meant to laugh.

"See what I mean," Chuck told her when she finally stopped giggling. "He's so mean. No, I'm leading the kitchen garden and medicinal herbs tour in about five minutes...and you, dearest man, are coming along to take pictures." He stuck the brochure back into his pocket and straightened his collar. "I just wish you were wearing better shoes, after the garden we hit the trail into the woods. But don't worry...I'll point out the poison ivy."

Robby backed toward the parking lot, using Tess as a shield. "I'd better go home and change."

"Nice try, but you're not going anywhere. You'll be fine as long as you pay attention. To me. Got your camera?"

If Robby hadn't stopped to pat down every pocket in his shirt and pants, he might have gotten away. "No. Funniest thing, I must have forgotten it. I'll just run back and—"

Chuck held out his hand. A small digital camera lay in his palm.

Robby was trapped and he knew it. "That's not very 1900's."

"1870 to 1887," Chuck corrected, "and it's okay since *you'll* be taking the pictures. Shall we away?" He linked arms with Robby and began dragging him toward the Lodge House. "You coming with us? It'll be fun."

Tess shook her head and lifted the flowers just quick enough to add credit to her excuse. "I'll catch up with you two later, I have to deliver these."

"She's fallen in love with your little cemetery," Robby said and motioned for her away. "Quick, save yourself before he has you out in the fields picking corn."

"That's tomorrow at three;" Chuck nodded happily, "followed by a Shucking Bee and bonfire. If you're really interested in the cemetery, I can put you in touch with someone from the Society. We're always looking for volunteers."

"Don't do her any favors."

Wrapping an arm around Chuck's neck, Robby swung him into a headlock and took the lead. It was all in fun and both of them were laughing as they stumbled against each other. It wasn't anything like the way Vince treated her.

"What do you mean 'don't do her any favors'?" Chuck wanted to know, loudly. "These are a great bunch of people. You just wait, you'll see. Oh, and I told the group you'd be our official photographer, so get a lot of pictures. Tess! Meet you back at the refreshment tent in about an hour, okay? It's on the front lawn of the Lodge House."

"Right next to the quaint and totally historic 'port-a-potties'," Robby added.

"You know, you really are terrible."

"But you love me for it."

"I do not."

"Oh, yes, you do."

"No...seriously..."

They went off arguing like the old married couple they were, and Tess hurried away in the opposite direction before the cold wind found her again.

**

She hadn't really believed Chuck about the event's popularity; if she had she would have brought nicer flowers.

A group of about twenty people all appropriately dressed for the humid summer heat in shorts, tee shirts and halter-tops were scattered among the gravestones, listening to a woman in long sleeves and full sweeping skirt. The wilted calico bonnet, securely tied under her chin, acted like a megaphone.

"...ther and child, unfortunately all too common. With one doctor for an area that covered many miles, midwives were generally the only help an expectant mother could hope for. If it was a difficult birth, or if the new mother contracted what was known as 'birthing fever,' there was very little anyone could do. Now, you'll notice this gravestone holds the remains of several children, evidence of the many epidemics..."

Tess turned and walked into the shadow of the trees to wait for the group to leave. It wasn't much cooler—if anything the thick canopy of interwoven branches seemed to make the air heavier and harder to breathe—but the farther back she got, the less she was able to hear about dead children, so that was some compensation at least.

A dozen or so trees back into the woods and the only thing she couldn't hear besides her own steps was a constant soft drip of moisture falling from the leaves like a false and constant rain. Buttercups and violets still bloomed in the deeper, wetter hollows and Tess picked some to add to the bouquet. Birdsong filled the humid air and squirrels scolded her from branches as she passed...it was all so peaceful she continued walking even after her calf muscles told her the ground had begun a gradual upward slope.

She was panting by the time she reached the bluff that overlooked a narrow ravine. Water seeped from a small opening in the rock face opposite, trickling down to form a tiny stream dotted with wild geraniums.

Tess followed a wide and well-marked animal path down to the water. It was icy against her cupped hands and Robby would have had a fit if he knew she'd drank it, but it was sweet and clear and the best tasting water she'd ever had. If she got sick, she got sick...she probably deserved to after what she'd done.

'—*I'm scared, I'm so scared*—'

Tess gasped as the cold water hit her face.

The sharp, spicy scent of geraniums filled the air as she turned and noticed it.

At first Tess thought it was a mile-maker set alongside some forgotten path. Set at one end of the ravine, the moss-covered marker was ticker and wider than others she'd seen and rose from a pile of equally mossy rocks. If it was a mile marker it was a very ominous one. Instead of the usual green-on-white numbers that indicated how many miles it was to the next reference point, the marker had only one word carved into its surface:

LOST

Great.

Tess looked back over her shoulder, just to make sure she could still find the animal trail and the way out, then stood up and walked to the pile of stones...stopping when she realized what it was.

It was a grave...very old, very hidden, and very much alone.

Tess let the bouquet's weight pull her hand to her side.

But why bury someone out in the middle of the woods when there was the cemetery was just a few hundred yards away? Maybe it wasn't an actual grave, but simply a remembrance to all those who had been lost and never found. That made more sense and would explain why it looked like a real grave. River stones, weathered, dotted with lichen or moss, ranging in size from a man's head to fist, covered the "body" of the grave. Tess couldn't hear the steam, so unless there was another source of water nearby, it must have been very hard carrying the stones up from the Wissahickon, especially through the trees.

Something was carved into the stone below LOST.

Tess stood up and stepped over the wild geraniums, then began picking her way through the brush. If there'd ever been a path it had grown over long ago; probably so long ago not even Chuck's Historical Society knew about it. Using a narrow branch as a lever, Tess pulled herself onto the mound of rocks and looked down.

It was a grave, but LOST was neither a family name nor a memorial. It was a judgement.

HE ABANDONED ALL
WHEN HE ABANDONED GOD

"Did you bring those for him?"

The stones beneath her feet probably hadn't moved since the day they were laid on the grave, but they shifted and ground against one another as she turned to look at the man on the bluff above her.

It's not Vince.

He had to be part of the reenactment, another of the costumed volunteers...perhaps even someone she'd met the night before. Tess didn't recognize him, but he did look familiar. He was tall, maybe even as tall as Vince, and a bit older...forty, if that. He had lines around his eyes and bracketing his wide mouth, and there was some gray sprinkled throughout his longish black hair. His eyes were gray—*He has gray eyes...I've never seen that color before. It's like fog*—and set deep beneath thick brows.

And he kept those eyes locked onto hers as he treaded his way down the rise toward her.

Tess dropped her gaze to the costume he wore.

It resembled Chuck's in that it represented a laborer of some sort, but there the similarities ended. Chuck had gone to great lengths to make sure his outfit was both stylish, keeping within the time period standard, and fastidiously clean whereas the man's clothing looked well worn and well used. Both knees of the flat-front, buttoned canvas trousers were shiny and, although there weren't any obvious patches on the linen shirt he wore, sleeves rolled loosely to the elbow, Tess noticed that a button was missing and the banded collar frayed along the top edge.

He's not married or his wife would have mended that.

She cleared her throat, as if she'd said the thought out loud, and stared at his boots when he stopped at the pile of rocks. They were scuffed and dull, the heels worn along the outer edge. He must have been a volunteer for a long time.

Tess stepped down from the rocks and briefly let herself wonder why he didn't offer a hand to help.

"The flowers are lovely," he said, then looked back along the way she'd come, "but you'd best save them for those back there. He doesn't deserve anyone's pity, least of all yours."

"Why me least of all?" It was an odd thing to say and the man seemed to realize that at almost the same time she did.

"I'm sorry; it's just that your flowers will be wasted here with no one to see them."

"I didn't pick them for the tourists."

Tess laid the bouquet at the base of the tombstone. There was a name carved beneath the condemning epitaph, caked with dried mud and almost completely hidden by the pile of stones, but still visible. Tess reached toward it, intending to push the stones away when the man grabbed her hand.

"No!"

The skin of his palm was hard and cold, but it was only the suddenness of the touch and sound of his voice that made her jerk back. He let go almost as soon as he'd touched her but Tess could still feel his fingers against her wrist.

"I'm sorry. I didn't mean any harm." He backed away, putting more than just the grave between them. "There are snakes here, Copperheads. Sometimes they seek out the wet places between the stones. I—thought only to protect you. "

Tess smiled and fought down the urge to rub her wrist.

"Thank you. I'm glad you told me... I *really* don't like snakes."

He smiled and the lines on his cheeks and around his eyes deepened. "Nor I."

His smile continued until she asked, "So, this is a real grave?" Then it vanished so quickly Tess wondered if she'd only imagined it ever being there.

"It is."

Tess waited for him to continue with the history. On the drive over, Chuck had treated them to a sneak preview of his tour lecture. Each volunteer, he said, had been given a "part" to play during the weekend along with an historically accurate script to memorize; but the man standing in front of her just stood there, silent. Maybe he'd forgotten his lines.

"Who was he?" Tess smiled, hoping he'd take the cue. "I mean, it's sort of a harsh epitaph, isn't it? About 'abandoning God' and all?"

"Harsh? Yes, I suppose it is, but them who buried him thought it a just and deserved one." The man's eyes met hers only for a moment before they returned to the grave. "He's a suicide, unfit to lay in peace among good Christian souls...but being Christian, they had no choice but to bury him. They laid him here within sight of the Paradise he would forever be denied..."

Tess turned around. "Within sight?"

The man made a small laughing sound.

"As the crow flies," he explained. "It was thought that suicides don't rest easy in their graves, so they left him here to walk the woods."

Tess rubbed at the sudden goosebumps on her arms; she still liked ghost stories even if she lived with one. "Who was he?"

"A foolish man."

Tess waited for him to continue and listened to a full minute of trickling stream, birdsong and the falling drops of counterfeit rain. "You said he killed himself?"

"Yes."

"Then this is the miller's grave, isn't it?" Tess didn't wait to see what his reaction would be. "My brother and his partner—you probably already met Chuck, he's one of the volunteers—bought the property across the stream and he told me the story when I first saw it. I'm...renting the millhouse from them. The miller's ghost still haunts it, did you know that?"

"Yes. Have you seen him?"

"No, but I've heard him."

"And it doesn't bother you...to be living with a spirit?"

Tess shook her head. "I like having him around."

And she liked that the man simply nodded. Volunteer or not, and even though he probably knew the story better than she did, he would have had every right to look at her as if she were crazy or start backing away.

Leaf shadows drifted across the man's face when he walked past her to the opposite end of the ravine and stopped. "If you're ready, perhaps you'll allow me to show you back to the festivities?"

"I'm ready. Thank you..." Tess looked at the front of the man's faded work shirt where his black-on-gold Historical Society Volunteer badge/nametag should have been. Chuck was very proud of his. "I think you lost your nametag, Mr..."

"My name's Thomas."

"Thomas." *It suits him.* "I'm Tess...Warren."

He reached up and tugged a lock of hair above his forehead. It was an old-fashioned gesture and very charming. "How do you do you, Tess Warren?"

"Mrs." The correction came so quickly she hardly felt it on her tongue. "I'm... I'm married."

But only until the divorce is final and that will be in...in... I can't... That will be in....

He tugged his forelock again. "How do you do, *Mrs.* Warren?"

Tess felt a rush of blood into her cheeks and started babbling.

"Chuck, my brother's partner, who I mentioned earlier, the volunteer..." *Good God.* She took a deep breath and forced the words to come slower. "He's playing a farmer. What are you supposed to be, Thomas?"

"I'm the miller. Shall we away?"

He backed into the shadows to let her pass.

Vince would never have done that.

**

"Bitch."

It was so natural a thing for him to say about her he didn't even have to think about it. But this time he said the word so softly, almost as if it were a blessing.

Besides, shouting it at the top of his lungs wouldn't have mattered. She was too far away and *much* too busy flirting... with the jerk in the costume from the night before.

Vince shoved his hands deeper into the windbreaker's pockets and watched them join the group of tourists gathered at the small cemetery. He had never wanted to admit it to himself, but some part of him had always known what she was: a cockteasing, round-heeled slut. Why else would she have hopped into his bed the first time he asked?

He should have known he couldn't change her, but hell, he had tried. Because that's what a man does, he tries no matter how hard it is or how long it takes…he tries. But it didn't work. He knew that the moment his back was turned—no, correction, the moment *after* she called the cops on him the first time and had his ass tucked safely behind bars—she was out wagging her tail at the first available dog she could find. *Probably the jerk in the costume…yeah. That's why he challenged me last night…he knew who I was…she told him.*

"Shit."

God, he'd been so naïve thinking he could change her; but when you're young you think everything's possible. Then age comes a'knocking with the realization that you wasted a good chunk of your life on nothing, and it's a little hard to take. A leopard still had its spots and a bitch is still a bitch regardless of the fancy collar and all the manners you tried to beat into it.

He should have put her out of her misery long ago.

A laugh, unmistakably hers, drifted into the air and Vince watched her reach toward *the jerk* in the costume only to watch it fall short when the man moved away. That said something for the jerk, but the very fact that she'd *wanted* to touch another man turned Vince's stomach.

It wasn't even the fact that Tess was cheating on him, it was that she was being so Goddamned *public* about it. More than one head had turned to stare at them—*his* wife and *her* new lover—as they wandered through the graves.

It was almost as if she knew he was there, watching, and didn't give a shit. He couldn't believe it and *that's* what made him whisper instead of shout.

Vince hunched his shoulders and kept his head down as he walked to the edge of the cemetery and joined the crowd gathered around a woman in a long dress and bonnet. Tess and the man were at the opposite end, talking softly—the man pointing to one of the graves, Tess nodding, her eyes never leaving the man's face…completely absorbed.

She'd never looked at him that way, not once in all the time they'd been together.

He should have killed her at the condo when he had the chance.

He'd had time, opportunity and even a defensible justification if it came to that. Yeah, he broke the restraining order, but he could always say she called him...from a pay phone, no records...yeah, that's what he would have said, but shit—*she pulled the fucking knife on me!* Yeah, I should have....

Why didn't I?

When the crowd began drifting away, Vince went with them...but only as far as the trees that bordered the cemetery grounds. When the group of people continued on to the Lodge House its historical displays and funnel cakes, he sidestepped back into the trees where he could watch her and her lover boy.

There was another tour group coming, this time following an old man dressed as an 19th Century undertaker in funereal black and carrying a cheesy plastic wreath.

Jesus, don't these people have lives?

**

"You've not put down the flowers yet," he reminded her, gently and for the third time.

Tess looked at the bouquet of violets she'd picked on the way back from the miller's grave and then at the tour group walking toward her. She remembered meeting the old man dressed as an undertaker the night before and returned his smile and tried to hide the bouquet behind her back.

It didn't work.

Someone took her picture of her as she stood there, flowers in hand and red of face. Vince would have been so embarrassed. Tess could almost hear him calling her an attention-hungry—

"Bitch."

She turned and looked toward the trees.

"Is something wrong, Mrs. Warren?"

"I just thought..." She blinked, forcing a smile. "No, sorry. Nothing."

"But you've changed your mind about the flowers?" Thomas pointedly nodded toward the bouquet.

Tess moved as far away from the old docent and his tourists as the small cemetery would allow and dropped her voice to a whisper. "They just look so...miserable."

He laughed and Tess felt a small flutter race through her belly. Vince had a nice laugh, when he wanted it to be—soft and gentle—but most of the time, when he was laughing at her, it was another sound entirely. Thomas' laugh was deep and mellow...and if they'd been standing anywhere except a cemetery, Tess would have started cracking jokes just to keep him laughing.

"I doubt that the dead care what the flowers they receive look like," he said, "but if you'd rather not."

"No, I brought them for the...for here. Excuse me."

Before her courage failed entirely, Tess took a deep breath and walked back to the graves of the miller's wife and child. A murmured "Oh, how nice," caught her ear and she turned to see the wide smile and gleaming false teeth of the pantomime undertaker.

"That was a lovely gesture, my dear," the old man said, before turning back to his group. "As you can see, the dead are never forgotten here."

More digital cameras and/or cell phones went off. Tess smiled, waved and hurried back to Thomas' side.

"May I ask why you picked those two graves?"

"I guess it's because they're here and...he's out there."

His gray eyes moved from her face to the stones. "That was very kind of you."

Her own eyes began to burn as he watched her.

"How did they—" She was about to ask how they died, when Robby's voice shattered the moment.

"TESS!"

Tess, Thomas, the volunteer undertaker and his entire group of tourists turned to see Robby, Hawaiian shirttails flying, charging down the path toward them.

"You have to save me—he wants me to milk a goat!"

She couldn't tell if Thomas had joined the eruption of laughter that statement caused or not...but Robby didn't seem to mind and continued barreling toward her as fast as his sandals would carry him.

"My brother."

"Ah," Thomas said. "I see the resemblance...in the eyes."

Tess took a deep breath. "I'd better go."

"You probably should. Milking goats is difficult at best."

"Will you be here all day? I mean, I'd like to come back and talk to you...about the miller and his family."

Tess hoped it hadn't sounded as desperate to him as it had to her.

"I'll be here."

Robby pounced on her the moment she walked out of the cemetery's gate. "I'm serious; can you see me milking a goat? No, neither can I, but Chuck thought it would be so much fun he signed me up for the Goat-Milking contest. I'm afraid to ask what First Prize is!"

Laughter followed in their wake.

"I told him there was no way I was going to do that unless I got hip-boots and rubber gloves, but he thinks I'm joking. You have to help me talk to him, okay? Good, I knew you'd understand. Oh, and you'll never guess who I saw wandering around taking pictures with his kid...that director you like so much, you know the one who does those *good* psychological ghost stories. Maybe you can talk him into milking the freaking goat in my place. Oh, God, what am I saying—Chuck's probably doing that right now! Come on!"

If Tess had been able to get a word in sideways, she still wouldn't have known what to say to that.

**

Vince watched them run past and bit the inside of his cheek to keep the curse bottled up where it was safe. For the moment. *Her first,* he promised himself, *then her fucking brother.*

**

He watched as she climbed the stairs, singing a song he'd never heard before, but one that sounded almost like the lullabies he'd heard mothers sing to their babes. As Victoria had sung to their son as she held him that last time.

He remembered the sound of her voice…hushed all but to silence and remembered also that she'd had a lusty voice when they first married, a sweet voice that lifted into song without care from morn 'till eventide, heedless of whom should hear.

He hadn't realized until that moment how much he'd missed the sound of a woman's voice raised in song. It wasn't Victoria's voice, but it was as sweet.

She stopped singing at the top of the stairs and looked back.

"I saw your grave today…and left you some flowers. I hope you don't mind but I left flowers for your wife and child, too. Goodnight."

He waited until he was sure she was asleep before ascending the stairs. A fear of closed doors had grown in Victoria while she was carrying Samuel. And, after his death, she had made him promise upon his soul never to lock her away before closed doors.

It had been part of the madness growing within her. Whatever it was she'd feared he never discovered, and even now, with both her and the child turned to dust, he could not break his pledge.

Listening to the sound of the woman's soft breathing, he slowly opened the door.

CHAPTER 10
JUNE 20th

Tess never expected to see him again.

Thomas.

Why would she?

Robby's terror at the thought of milking a goat, even though he'd done surprisingly well for a "city kid", had kept Tess by his side shouting encouragement, for almost an hour. Then there was lunch, followed by Chuck's garden tour. By the time the three of them got back to the Lodge House, it was late afternoon and the evening's festivities—music followed by ghost stories on the front lawn—were just getting underway.

And she was stuck.

There'd been no reason for her to leave at that point. Robby and Chuck expected her to sit with them and listen to ghost stories...and she couldn't very well tell them she'd rather listen to Thomas talk about the miller. Then she'd have to tell them where she met Thomas and...

It'd been easier just to stay were she was, sitting on a blanket-covered hay bale between her brother and his partner and listen to an old campfire story that she'd first heard when she was a Brownie Girl Scout.

Tess hadn't realized she'd been searching the lantern-lit faces of the crowd for him until Robby jokingly asked who she was looking for. She'd planned to say *'no one'* but what she answered surprised her and hardened her brother's face.

"Vince."

"But you know he can't hurt you anymore. You know that, don't you, Tess?"

She knew nothing of the sort, but nodded and shushed him with a finger to her lips. Robby hadn't looked any more convinced than she felt and pulled her close, holding her like that until the story ended as if she were a frightened child. It'd been a little embarrassing, but comforting nonetheless, and Tess was glad—at that point—that Thomas wasn't at the campfire.

Or at the hot cider stand they went to afterward.

Or the funnel-cake booth because Robby suddenly had a craving.

Or wandering around the parking lot trying to find his car.

Tess didn't see Thomas again that night and early Sunday morning, a few hours before dawn; God took pity on her. It started to rain.

Softly at first, the rain turned into a steady downpour a few minutes before 5a.m. while Tess, propped up against her pillow and with her legs drawn up to her chest, listened. She hadn't slept for more than a few minutes throughout the night, dozing off now and again only to jerk back into full consciousness covered in sweat…remembering only that it had been Thomas' face she'd seen in the darkness behind her closed lids.

Not Vince.

When Chuck called at 9, telling her the day's reenactment had been canceled, Tess pretended to yawn and hoped she didn't sound as disappointed as she felt. Unless she took Chuck up on his offer and joined the Historical Society, she'd never see him again—Thomas—and that was probably for the best.

Especially now.

He was back.

But when a day passed and then another and another, Tess began to wonder if the man she'd seen at the water's edge was Vince at all. If he were there, close enough to have let her see him, he would have done *something* by now. Called or just come to the door and knocked.

"You think you can keep me out, bitch?"

No, if it had been Vince he would have taken her by now.

So, maybe it was Thomas she saw. He played the miller in the reenactment, it only made sense he'd be interested in the building.

It'd made *perfect* sense.

The rain stopped on Tuesday and that night Tess didn't dream at all. Wednesday she woke with to a severe bout of cabin fever.

Heat mist curled around Tess' legs as she walked toward the broken dam. The ground was the consistency of slurry and tugged at the soles of her running shoes with each step. If she hadn't needed to get out she would have turned back and spent the rest of the morning going over the files she'd been e-mailed…like the good drone she was supposed to be.

And maybe she should have. By the time Tess reached the crossing, she was sweating and out of breath and was covered with mud from the ankles down. If there'd been a dry place to sit, she would have taken it…instead, she leaned back against a tree and watched a red-and-white picnic cooler go sailing by. The usually placid Wissahickon had become a surging, boiling torrent of mud-brown water that had swallowed the broken dam and overflowed its banks by more than a foot.

"God."

"I've seen it worse."

Tess never expected to see him again, but there he was.

Thomas.

He stood on the opposite bank, still in costume and character, watching her watch the water. Tess knew he had to be shouting for her to hear him over the sound of the rapids, but there was no strain to his voice. It was almost as if he was standing next to her, whispering.

"I've seen it so high it looked like God had scooped the sea up in His hands and carried it here just to show it could be done." Thomas touched his forehead as he had the first time they met. "Good morning, Mrs. Warren."

Tess nodded back, giving herself the excuse that her voice wouldn't carry if she answered, then cupped her hands around her mouth. "Call me Tess...please."

He smiled and shifted his weight from one foot to the other. His boots, unlike her sneakers, were remarkably mud-free. *It must be dryer over there.*

"Good morning, Tess. Were you planning to cross to bring more flowers?"

The last was said with a smile as Tess stepped away from the tree. "I was thinking about it. Or maybe I should just plant seeds, there seems to be enough water."

When he laughed Tess lowered her hands and spoke just a little louder than normal. If she could hear something as soft as laughter, she was sure he could hear her.

"I guess the cemetery's pretty muddy."

"It is that."

"And his grave...the miller's? Is it all right?"

"Stones don't change."

That would have been a natural place to end the conversation. She could wave and walk away, and that would be the end of it.

"Too bad about the event."

Thomas cocked his head to one side. "The event?"

"Being rained out."

"Oh...yes. Too bad."

"But you're still in costume.

His smile became contagious. "I always wear this."

"Oh. Oh, I'm sorry; I thought you were just another volunteer with the Historical Society. I didn't realize you worked for the Parks Department."

"That's all right. Look." He pointed upstream and Tess gasped as a six-foot fence rail sailed between them.

"Oh, my God...I didn't think the storm was *that* bad. I mean, the millrace rose, a little, but I didn't even think to check the creek. I'm glad the rain stopped."

"So am I, but you needn't worry, Mrs....Tess. The millhouse has never been flooded, you'll be safe."

Robby had told her the same thing when he first showed it to her, somehow, it sounded more...*certain* coming from Thomas.

"Thank you." *Turn around and go home.* "But I wish the water wasn't so high."

"It will go down soon."

She nodded. "Have you seen the millhouse since the restoration?" *What am I doing?* "My brother and his partner did a beautiful job."

"I'm sure they did."

"Would you—" *Don't!* "—like to see it?"

"Very much."

Tess felt her heart beating in time to the one word repeating itself in her mind: *stupid...stupid...stupid...stupid...*

"You could drive over. After work, I mean. If you like. I work at home, so...I'm always there." She pointed back toward the millhouse as if he didn't know where it was. "So anytime you'd like to see it..."

"Would now be convenient?"

Now?

"Sure, that'd be fine." Tess took a deep breath and started back along the path. Thomas did the same on the opposite bank, matching her steps. "I'll meet you at the millhouse then. You can park in the driveway of the main house...you know where that is, right?"

"I do, but I know another place to cross upstream and I'd rather do that." He nodded his head once to the left. "I'll show you, if you like."

Graceful as a cat in the sun, he stretched out his long legs and climbed back up through the trees, walking upstream before she could answer. Tess watched him weave in and out of the shadows until he got to a small rise and turned around, smiling.

Vince had never done that. When he walked away, usually angry over something she'd done to embarrass him; he never turned around or waited for her to catch up. He didn't have to; he knew she'd be there, following, ready for whatever he decided to do next.

Tess put her hand over the sudden constriction in her throat.

"Are you alright?"

"What? Oh, yes, I'm fine. I was just thinking about something. Sorry."

Thomas turned and walked back along the path until he was opposite her.

"I should be the one apologizing." His voice soft, but she could still hear him above the roar of the water. "My manners have become somewhat lax over the years. I presumed too much. You must have things to do. Another time, perhaps."

With a nod he turned to go and she stopped him.

"No, now is fine. Really, I have nothing that urgent to do." Tess laughed at her own inability to fabricate so much as a white lie. "Please, I'd love to show you the millhouse."

This time, when they walked their separate paths upstream, Thomas matched her step for step; slowing when she did, but never speeding up to pass her. It was only when he paused to look at the millhouse that Tess recognized him. Thomas was the man she'd seen her first day there, the man in the shadows on the opposite bank.

So it stood to reason he'd been the man she'd seen the following the deer.

Thank God.

"It was you, wasn't it?"

Thomas' brows raised in question.

"I saw you that day, looking at the millhouse." Tess wasn't sure because of the misty light playing across his face, but she thought she saw him blush. "It was you, wasn't it?"

"Yes. I often come to look at it. I apologize again for my transgression into you privacy. I meant no harm."

"No, it's all right; I just thought you were—"

He nodded and lifted one hand in a careless wave. "It's not much farther."

And Tess did her best not to smile when she noticed a sudden ruddiness to his cheeks. Two miles later, the thought of smiling was the farthest thing from her mind.

"*How* much farther?" She was fighting her way through a screen of young willows when he answered.

"We're here."

Finally. "Where?"

A trick of the air and water and trees made it sound like his laugh was right beside her ear. "Straight ahead another few yards, there's a clearing just on the other side of the willows."

A likely story.

Tess push a curl of sweat-sodden hair out of her eyes and, uttering a whispered curse at the heat, humidity and mud, pushed through the willows to a bare mantle of rock. Thomas still looked unreasonably clean and scratch-free on his side of the stream, one boot resting on the bare roots of a huge fallen tree that spanned a rushing waterfall.

The lightning had cored the tree like an apple, burning away the insides and leaving behind a layer of fire-polished bark. It was breathtaking, but what made it even more amazing was that the tree was still alive. Although it had fallen and lost most of its limbs along with its insides, the roots still dug deep into the bank and green leaves that size of her hand crowned the single branch that bowed outward from the trunk to lay against the bank at Tess' feet.

"It's alive?"

"Very much so. Her roots are planted firmly and even the loss of her heartwood could kill her."

"It's sort of a living bridge, then."

His smile finally made it all the way to his eyes. "Yes, exactly.

"No one knows how long she stood or her age." Thomas rested his hand against the rim of the blackened scar. "Her heartwood is gone, but there are old maps going back to the first Woodsmen who tramped this place that describe her. For all anyone knows the lightning that toppled her struck even before the Lenape roamed these woods.

"Can you imagine the sound when she fell? Like thunder a hundred-fold or cannon fire."

Climbing the roots like a ladder, he took hold of the charged ring of bark and stepped into the hollow trunk. A dozen pale yellow butterflies startled by Thomas' invasion of their domain startled into the air. Tess watched his eyes follow their flight.

"By all rights," he said, "she should be dead as stone, but she lives."

"You keep saying 'she'. Why?"

Thomas pointed to the patch of rustling leaves. "Do you see those globes …the things that look like balls on twine, those are the seed pods. This is a grand lady and as long as she lives, the world is an easy place to transverse."

Tess smiled at his choice of words. He was still in character. "You mean, this is an easier way to cross the stream."

"Yes." Thomas nodded, his eyes fixed on her face. "It is easier to cross here."

Tess turned and pretended that the only reason she moved was to brush her hand against the willows.

"But a lot harder to get to."

"At the moment," he conceded, "but it will get easier the more you travel it."

She shook her head. "I'm not so sure, I mean...you must have come over here a lot, before the place was sold, I mean... and it's still overgrown."

"I... The woods soot me more, but the path will open in time."

Tess turned back with the intention of saying something clever. "I'm married."

He smiled.

"I mean I was married...I'm getting a divorce and—" *Shut up, shut up! What's the matter with you? What are you doing?* "I mean...I—I didn't want you to think that I invited you to see the millhouse because—"

Oh God.

"There's no need for you to explain your reasons, Tess. I never thought you anything but a lady."

It was the soppiest, sappiest...sweetest thing anyone had ever said to her and Tess hoped he'd think the sudden blush filling her face was sunburn.

"Uh—" Fortunately a roll of distant thunder saved her from herself and provided a safer topic. Tess stepped back, off the log bridge and looked into the western sky. "More rain?"

His voice sounded as distant as the thunder. "A good chance."

"Well, in that case." Tess took a deep breath and tried to make her voice sound as casual as possible. "If you'd still like to see the millhouse...."

"I would."

Tess watched his eyes darken from fog to twilight as he literally flung himself forward and disappeared within the hollow trunk. The tree was even bigger than she thought. The inside must have either been covered with moss or the rain had softened the wood and made it pliable, because she couldn't hear his steps. A few times the top of his head appeared above the rim of twisted, fire-scored wood and then, just as quickly, slipped back. When he finally burst out as if the Devil himself were chasing him, she yelped in surprise and backed up.

Right into a patch of stinging nettles.

"OW!"

"Tess! What is it?" His face grew a little paler as she stepped toward her. "A snake?"

"No." She pointed down, hobbling away from the plants and sucking air in through her teeth. The back of her right calf felt like it was on.

Thomas looked down and just as quickly looked away.

"I— that is the consequence of going around with bare legs."

Sarcasm? No, he was embarrassed, how...old fashioned. "I suppose."

Thomas stepped closer but didn't so much as offer her the comfort of a pat on the arm. "Do you have any soda ash at the millhouse?"

"Soda...what?"

"Soda ash. My wife...used it for baking."

He's married. Tess hoped he thought the look on her face was from the pain. "Soda ash? Do you mean baking soda?"

"I...believe so. If you have some make a paste of it and apply it to your...to the site. It will help. Go on and I'll follow."

A gentleman would have gone first, holding back branches and lending a hand when needed, but the pain was growing and *he was married.* Tess turned and plowed—gracelessly— back through the willows. Thomas—*the married man*—was right, it was easier to follow the trail she'd made.

He obviously hadn't come this way in a while...*His wife probably wouldn't let him.*

Tess didn't pause when she reached the true path, but limped onward until she the millhouse came into view. He wasn't there when she turned around.

"Thomas?"

There was no answer. *Why are you waiting, he's married.*
And so are you.

Glad that he wasn't there to see her struggle up the rise, Tess limped into the millhouse's shadow and called out, hoping he was close enough to hear her. "Thomas, I'll leave the back door open. Just come in...I'll be in the kitchen."

She only knocked over two spice containers before she found the baking soda.

**

Her voice floated to him on the sluggish wind...but stayed where he was and listened for the other sound he'd heard. There were men who wouldn't have noticed it—town dwellers, deaf to everything but themselves—but to him it was as loud as the sudden snapping of a branch.

Thomas moved slowly back toward the hollow tree...*a living bridge, she'd called it*...and scanned the opposite bank. Nothing moved along the reeds and shrubs that grew there and the narrow deer path was empty. He'd known about the hollow tree—*the heartless tree* they'd called it, himself included—since childhood. It would become a castle, a pirate's ship or whatever fortress their imaginations could conjure...later it was a place he'd take her to sit and steal small affections. It was there he asked her to marry him...and there he came back to when his solitude drove him mad.

A living bridge for the dead.

The sound came again and he tensed. It was not a twig snap or the whisper of a stem pushed aside, no breath was taken but there been something above the rush of water and birdsong. Something.

Thomas stepped into the heartless tree and startled a long-tailed chipmunk into near apoplexy.

He turned away, laughing an apology, and with steady, unhurried stride walked up the embankment to the millhouse.

**

So his name is Thomas. How nice.

Vince waited until he was sure the man—*Thomas*—had walked away, then counted to twenty, and added ten more—*just to make sure*—before stepping out into the sunlight. The guy was still in a fucking costume, for God's sake...but that hadn't stopped her from inviting him over. His little wifey.

Even if he hadn't heard her—*I'll leave the back door open, just come in*—Vince would have known where the man was headed. He figured that out the moment he saw the two of them at the river.

Bitch.

He'd wanted to do something right then and there, take apart her boyfriend while she watched from the other side, screaming and helpless.

No, she wouldn't scream, he'd trained her too well. *Dammit.* Condo walls do not a reliable sound barrier make and she knew that, learned it fast, too. He'd been able to do anything he wanted and the most he'd get out of her was a pathetic little whimpering sound, the kind a dog makes...shit, what kind of sound was that for a man to hear his wife make? It would have been nice to hear her scream, just once.

"No! Get out of here. Leave me alone!"

Vince spun toward the sound of her voice...he would have sworn to God it was her voice, but that wasn't possible. Tess was—waiting for her lover at the millhouse.

Weird. Vince tugged at the collar of his shirt and frowned, then ran a hand through his hair. The concussion must have shaken him up more than he thought.

"You'll pay for this, too, baby. You and your boyfriend."

She could scream there, all right, all she wanted to because there'd be no one to hear her. Vince was looking forward to that, already imagining what it would sound like inside that place of hers. Hell, the sound would probably echo back and forth off those thick stone walls like a ricocheting bullet and never get out.

Cool. That asshole brother of hers would never hear a thing and by the time he wandered over to discover why his loving sister hadn't answered the phone in a day or two, Mr. and Mrs. Warren's only son would be miles away.

"Yeah."

Vince sighed, satisfied, for the moment, and followed the same narrow animal path *Thomas* had taken down to the water. He'd watched the man cross, running like some fucking dog after a bitch in heat and had to force himself not to react., although it would have been nice. Nice? Hell, it would have been perfect...catching up to the guy and tossing his ass into the stream. Of course, there was always the chance he might not have drowned or cracked his head on the rocks, but the force of the water would have carried *Thomas* a good ways downstream and, by the time he climbed back upstream, Tess would be long gone.

Now there was an idea worth thinking about. Vince felt his smile grown Yeah, he didn't have to kill her at the millhouse; no, he could *take* her somewhere, some place quiet and isolated and secluded, where no one would ever find her. Yeah. They could charge him all they wanted, but until they found her body she'd just be *"missing."*

Vince began laughing as he grabbed onto the deadfall's gnarled roots and pulled himself up; pausing for a moment just to take in the size. The tree was fucking huge, the hollow center almost big enough to drive a semi through. Shit, compared to the balancing act it would take to get across the remains of the shattered dam, this was nothing...a walk in the park. He could do it blindfold—

He stepped inside and the world suddenly twisted up inside his gut and backhanded him off the tree and onto the muddy bank. A whirlpool swirled his innards into mush and shot it out his mouth. It wasn't vomit, because there was no taste or raw acid burn on his tongue, but whatever it was, he couldn't get off his hands and knees until it stopped.

Vince hadn't been sick like that in…his life, and that included the time in college when, on a dare, he'd downed twelve shots of peach schnapps in less than a minute.

"Fuck."

When his body finally unlocked, Vince got to his feet gasping for breath. *Jesus, what the hell was going on?* He had to be sick, that was the only explanation. Bending over, he braced his hands against his thighs and breathed deeply until his head cleared.

"Come on, man, shake it off. Just take it nice and easy and get across…then you can have Tess take you to a doctor." He straightened and took a step. *So far, so good.* "Maybe it was something I ate."

Although he couldn't remember exactly when he'd eaten last or what sort of meal it was, it seemed as good an explanation as the concussion.

Wiping an unsteady hand across his lips, Vince took another deep breath and pulled himself back onto the roots. His stomach clenched, but held steady. "Okay, let's go."

He stepped down into the dead tree and a vortex opened. This time, however, he pushed through it, launching himself forward.

"SSSSSSSHHHHHHHHIIIIIIIIITTTTTTT!"

Vince almost made it halfway across when he suddenly found himself falling.

**

Tess stood at the bottom of the stairs and watched Thomas' face as he descended, his hand running lightly over the polished wood of the banister. It was the same look of admiration he'd had since entering the millhouse. At each turn, he nodded his approval of the improvements to the original design and complimented her on her taste.

She didn't mention her only real contribution was in the choice of paint, but accepted the praise with as much humility as she could, under the circumstances, and listened while he described the original millhouse.

"Even long dead," he said, stopping on the bottom step to examine the newel post and finial cap, "wood retains the image of life."

"Like a ghost?"

He laughed softly, but the stairway carried it up into the rafters. "But much more substantial."

"Especially with the miller's ghost." Tess walked into the living room and tried again to imagine it as the "Spinning Room" Thomas described. Before she died, the miller's wife had kept her loom and spinning wheel here...with baskets filled with raw wool to be carded and bundles of dye herbs hanging from the beams. Maybe that's what she smelled that first day...the ghost of long dead herbs.

The millhouse had more than she thought.

"He isn't a nuisance, is he?"

Tess turned to find him in the doorway. "Who? Oh, the ghost? No, he's sweet."

"Sweet." Thomas looked down at his boots. "And how is he...sweet?"

"He just is." Shrugging, she sat down on the couch and scooted to the far side...giving him more than enough room if he wanted to sit down. He remained in the doorway. *Of course he will, he's married.* "He's quiet, although I do hear him walking around sometimes...and he... Oh, he likes to open my bedroom door. I'm not sure why."

"So you won't feel locked in... I imagine."

"Could be. Anyway, I've gotten used to it. My husband didn't—"

"Is your leg better?"

The question came so suddenly it caught Tess off guard. She'd forgotten all about the nettles and the thick paste of baking soda and water she'd troweled on while waiting for

Thomas—he'd taken a different route, he told her when he arrived.

Tess leaned forward and looked down. The backs of both legs were stained white, but there were only a few patches left. Once he left, she'd have to break out the vacuum cleaner.

"Fine. Much better."

"I'm glad. And you're sure you're not afraid...of the ghost, I mean."

Tess stayed on the edge of the cushion and shook her head. "Of course not."

He held her in his eyes a moment longer then crossed the room to the fireplace, ignoring the empty place on the couch next to her.

"I especially like what you've done with this room. It's snug...is that the right word?"

Tess nodded. "Yes, it is snug in here."

He looked like he was about to say something else, but walked across the room to stand in front at the fireplace. "The fire in here was always banked, kept low and constant to dry the herbs. Wild celery, alder, fennel, goldenrod, rosemary and yarrow...colt's foot and buckwheat...dandelion and sunflowers. I remember the... I remember being told this was more a workroom. I prefer it this way."

"Thank you. Is your wife a volunteer? With the historical society, I mean."

Thomas kept his back to her. "No. She died a long ago."

Oh. "I'm sorry."

"You shouldn't be, her misery's ended. I..." He turned and glanced out the window. "You have company coming... and I should be getting back to my duties. Thank you for the tour, Tess. I'll let myself out."

"What?" Tess saw Robby through the window as she hurried after him. "Thomas, wait a minute. I'd like you to meet my brother...he's the one who did most of the—

"Thomas?"

The hallway was empty and the backdoor open by the time she reached the entrance hall; and even though she knew who it was, Tess jumped when her brother knocked.

CHAPTER 11
JUNE 21st
Midnight

He'd watched the man struggle for hours before he was finally able to drag himself from the water, clawing at the rocks and kicking back as if at some unknown enemy. If he'd thought it would have done any good or served a purpose beyond the obvious, he might have told the man exactly what sort of enemy he was fighting.

But it would have done neither, and the man wouldn't have believed him.

Not yet, at any rate, and perhaps never. Considering the man he was.

Still, he would try...for her.

The song of a night bird winging overhead pulled his attention from the man to the millhouse. Save for the porch lamp's soft glow, the house was dark. She'd retired early...a secret smile resting gently against the corners of her mouth as she spoke.

"Thomas is a nice man, don't you think, ghost?"

He remembered her face when she asked that and wondered if *Thomas* really was as nice a man as she thought.

If things were different...

But they weren't and could never be. Not between them.

When the near-drowned man turned to face the night sky, chest pumping needlessly, he turned and melted back into the darkness.

The fool, he thought, *but which of us does that title best fit?*
**

Vince concentrated on breathing and nothing else.

If he had thought of something else, it would have been drowning and he couldn't face that. Not now, not ever…not again.

A bat zigzagged across the patch of black-gray sky directly above him and Vince's eyes trailed it until it disappeared into the dark tree shapes above him. *It's night. Jesus, how long was I in the water.*

He remembered climbing into the hollow tree and taking a step and…falling. That was the strangest part. The tree looked solid and he was pretty damn sure he would have noticed a hole big enough for him to fall through…but there must have been one.

A big fucking one he somehow missed.

Vince's eyes closed for less than a fraction of a second, but it all came back…all of it…and not just the memory of drowning…all the memories he'd ever had in his entire life……

—there's our little boy—

—happy birthday, dear vincent, happy bir—

—hey, batta-batta-batta—

—sure, yeah…whatever…love you—

—and as you can see, gentlemen—

—take thee, teresa, as my—

—what the hell do you think you're doing—

—down here, bitch and open this door right now if—

—what my little wifey wants to do—

—take your shot. Come on…. COME ON—

—oh, I'm scared…I'm so—

Without thinking or remembering anything of his Boy Scout training that stated one should never move an accident victim until their injuries were assessed, Vince found himself not only standing upright, but moving away from the stream with surprising speed and agility. Fuck, what they said was true…his entire life had passed before his eyes but… He wasn't in the water now, he was sitting on dry land and—

He felt fine.

If he was injured, it apparently wasn't anything major.

Vince took a deep breath, held it, and waited for the pain to start. Even if nothing was broken—*please God*—he must have hit a few rocks along the way and, at best, that meant bruises and scrapes.

Something.

Anything.

Nothing.

Exhaling slowly, he cautiously began patting himself down, ready at any moment to pull his hands away if they encountered protruding bone or warm, sticky spots. No, he was fine, there wasn't a mark on him and he must have been out cold for longer than he thought. His clothes and shoes were dry.

Vince found a convenient log and sat down. *Okay, let's think about this.* When he fell—*slipped somehow*—into the stream it'd been morning...now it was night, so that meant he'd probably crawled out of the water hours ago. Hours.

No one saw me? It wasn't possible that no one had walked by him at some point during the day. *This is a fucking state park, for God's sake, it should be crawling with hikers and fishermen and rangers and....*

Vince didn't realize how cold he'd been until the sudden flush replaced the bone-numbing chill. They must have seen him...her and her lover...and left him there to die.

"Shit."

It was the only thing that made sense, but Vince doubted his little wifey had been the mastermind behind the plan, not her...it would take imagination for something like this, and she'd never had any. No, it had to have been the man—*"I saw your husband, but don't worry. He fell in the river and even if he's not dead yet, he will be by morning. All we have to do is wait."*—but she'd gone along with it.

"Fucking bitch, wait until I get my hands on—" Ignoring whatever path there might have been, Vince scrambled up the steep embankment and burst out laughing, not caring who heard him. "Damn me to hell."

His luck was still holding.

The trees were thick and the brush overgrown, but he could still just make out the faintest glimmer of light not more than thirty feet from where he stood. The millhouse.

It was all he could do to keep from running, to keep his steps slow and sure and light, his hands and body loose. Any sort of tension, he knew from experience, would only cause his muscles to fatigue faster when he… needed them.

A dark shape—deer possibly—moved deeper into the shadows next to the millhouse when he reached the back door. Vince ignored it as he wrapped his hand around the knob.

"Hi, honey," he whispered. "I'm home."

**

He's here.

Tess' eyes were already open and staring at the small dark gulf between the mattress and bedside table when she woke up. The room was dark, but no darker than usual and, once her eyes and brain reconnected, held nothing that hadn't been there when she fell asleep. Beyond the shaded window, the night moved to the sounds of the wind in the trees and the tumbling serenade of the millrace.

Inside, the prominent sound was the frantic and muffled beating of her heart echoing through the mattress.

She had no idea how long she'd been asleep or what the actual time was. It felt late and early at the same time, but finding out exactly how late or early would mean moving and that wasn't an option.

As long as she stayed still—curled on her right side, back to the door and regulating each breath's comings and goings with the slow regularity of sleep—she'd be safe. As long as she played dead he wouldn't hurt her.

Vince.

If I scream and Robby hears it...

He'd never get to there in time and Vince was already *here*. Tess didn't need to see him to know he'd be standing in the exact center of the doorway—blocking it so she couldn't escape—filling it with his body, arms and ankles crossed, leaning slightly to one side or the other...comfortable, relaxed...smiling.

"You asleep, wife?"

Tess squeezed her lips together to keep from screaming. He always knew. He'd wait, so patiently, until she began to wonder if he was really there or not and turn over....

"Didn't think so."

A floorboard creaked near the door.

He's here.

Tess felt her body move...but instead of the slow and deliberate tightening of muscles and skin, of hunkering down and trying to make itself as small a target as possible, it bolted from the bed and took her with it. Feet kicked free of entangling sheets and arms raised, hands reaching to tear the blind from the window. Tess followed her body into a crouch and felt her lungs begin to fill with air. It was only then, while her body was occupied, that *she* was able to turn and look over her shoulder.

Vince was little more than a silhouette, a shape within the lighter darkness of the doorway, but she saw him...saw him as clearly as if the room were filled with light. She even saw him smile just before her body resumed control and snapped her head back toward the open window.

"ROBBY! HELP ME! HE'S HERE...VINCE IS *HERE*!"
**

There was nothing sweeter than the sound of her screams.

Vince took a step forward, toward her, then immediately felt himself hauled backwards through the dark. Whoever had him was strong—the hands that gripped his shoulders through the windbreaker felt like a pair of steel vice-grips.

It'd all happened so quickly he didn't have time to react, let alone fight, and that's what he kept telling himself as the stairs slid by beneath his feet. When they reached the end of the stairs, Vince had a momentary sensation of falling from a great height, then they were outside and he was dragged into a thick stand of trees some distance away.

They were close enough to the millhouse that Vince could still hear Tess screaming, but how close was a mystery. And he wasn't given the opportunity to figure it out.

Vince hit the ground, face first, and was held there by the force of a large, thick-soled boot in his small of his back.

"You will stay quiet when I let you up," a deep voice said.

Lifting his face out of the decomposing leaf mulch, Vince spit to clear his mouth even though there seemed to be very little debris clinging to it. He recognized the voice, no way he couldn't. It was the little wifey's boyfriend.

He spit again, this time to get rid of the taste of bile in his mouth.

"Did you hear what I said?"

Vince ignored the question and asked one of his own. "Enjoy fucking my wife, did you?"

The pressure on his back increased until it felt like his spine was going to come out his ribcage. "You do her wrong, *friend*."

"Oh, really?" The words came out as grunts. "Then what were you doing in my house?"

"*Your* house." Vince felt the man's chuckle through his backbone. "The millhouse has nothing to do with you, nor does she." The humor left the man's voice. "You will leave her alone."

"The *hell* I will."

Digging his fingers into the loam, Vince twisted to the right—hoping to offset the man's balance—and let fly with a double handful of debris as he got to his feet. There weren't many times in his life where he found himself bettered, but he never let that stop him from fighting dirty. His dad always joked about never hitting a man when he was down—*"Kick him, that way they stay down."*—and Vince took that philosophy to heart. As he turned, he cocked his right leg, ready to fire; figuring the man would have staggered back, half-blind and brushing at his face. One well placed kick to the groin or knee, whichever presented the clearer target, would put even the burliest contender into a nice *manageable* state.

What he hadn't counted on was finding the man standing up and still, not even breathing hard. If it hadn't been for the whole costume thing, Vince might have really felt intimidated.

The man just stood there until Vince took a step forward. Then all he did was raise one hand like a stopping guard, and Vince's feet ploughed to a halt as if a fence had suddenly gone up in front of him. *What the hell?*

"There are things you need to know," the man said and his voice was as smooth and cold as a sheet of ice.

"Oh, really?" Vince eased his left foot forward just to see if he could. "Like what you're doing with my wife?"

"You no longer have any rights or claims to her, and you *will* leave her alone."

Vince couldn't believe what he was hearing. "What the *fuck*—?"

He would have said a lot more and loud enough to momentarily drown out Tess' screams, if he hadn't heard the sound of footsteps pounding against the ground on the opposite side of the trees. Robby...or his boyfriend...or maybe both of them were coming on a dead run to Tess' rescue.

Again.

Vince mentally stepped down. Tess' boyfriend was obviously crazy...no *normal* man wore a costume when he didn't have to; and one had to deal with crazy people in a different way than normal folk: preferably quickly and from behind without their notice.

"Look, I don't know what she told you, but..."

"Whatever she said, or didn't say, doesn't matter. You're here and you shouldn't be."

"Oh? Where else should I be? She's my wife."

"No, she's not," the man said. "Not anymore."

I'll kill that bitch...I'll make her hurt more than she ever thought possible.

It took every ounce of willpower, but Vince smiled and relaxed his hands, chuckling low in his throat so the sound wouldn't carry. Tess' screams had finally stopped and the night seemed very quiet in their absence.

"Did she tell you we're divorced? Because if she did, she lied to you, pal. We're still married."

The man shook his head. "You still don't understand any of this, do you?"

"No...I think *you're* the one who doesn't understand."

The man lifted his hands, palms toward Vince, but not in surrender. It was a gesture to pacify...as if he were trying to calm a frightened child or hysterical woman. Vince had done the same thing to Tess—after one of their more violent discussions.

"This might be difficult for you to understand, but—"

The man never got a chance to finish.

Intimidation, violence, anger those were the things Vince understand and, partly, respected...but the man was being condescending and that was something no self-respecting man would put up with.

Testosterone is a wonderful thing.

With it coursing through his veins, a man can believe himself invincible regardless of the odds against him; and, in some cases, actually triumph. Vince usually triumphed without any help, so when the testosteronic rush hit the back of his brain it was like a rocket going off. He didn't even think about his next move. Coming in low and fast, he waited for the last possible moment before firing straight from the shoulder with a right hook designed to separate lower jaw from skull.

He could already hear the sound of his fist cutting the air and imagined the *oh-so-satisfying* impact jolt; but the man didn't move or try to protect himself. He just stood there as Vince swung and...

**

"Tess! It's okay, I'm here...I'm here."

The last lungful of air ran out just as Robby's voice echoed up the stairs. Wincing at the raw burning sensation in her throat as she gasped for breath, Tess collapsed against the wall, her strength gone. She hadn't screamed like that since Vince....

"Tess, what happened? What's the matter?" Robby's silhouette filled only half the doorway. "Where are you?"

"B-by the window."

"Okay, close your eyes. I'm going to turn on the overheads."

A soft thumping drifted through the darkness and suddenly the room was filled with light. Shielding her eyes, Tess pulled the nightshirt's hem down over her legs and watched her brother stumble into the room.

If he looked like hell, which he did—wild eyed and tousled hair—Tess could only imagine what she looked like.

"I...woke you up. I'm sorry."

"Doesn't matter." He crossed the room and knelt by her side, scooping her to him. "I was just dozing on the back porch when I heard..." His arms tightened around her. "Jesus, Tess, what the hell happened? Wait—where's the closest phone? I have to call Chuck and let him know you're okay. He's going to call the police if I don't.... You *are* okay, aren't you?"

Tess looked back toward the empty doorway and nodded. "Use the phone in the office. Oh God, Robby...the front door —I must have left it unlocked..."

Robby soothed her into quiet with soft sounds. "It's okay, the door was locked. I used my key."

"Then how did he get in?"

There was a new look of horror on his face. "Oh God, Tess, what happened? Who was it? Who got in?"

"Vince."

**

...hit nothing but air.

Unable to catch himself, Vince staggered past the man like a drunk after a three-day bender. He couldn't figure it out, but it was a clean miss.

"You fucking coward!" Vince yelled, no longer concerned about being heard. "You moved."

The other man shook his head. "No. Let me explain."

"Explain *this!*" Vince sprang into a linebacker's crouch and charged, arms outstretched to grab and hold and pull down. He'd ruptured a kid's spleen in high school with that move and he hadn't even been trying.

This time he was going to try for more than just a spleen.

Vince came in low and fast and—

**

Robby made her get back in bed while he went into the office to call Chuck. Tess had wanted to go with him, suddenly afraid to be left alone, but forced herself to stay curled up in a tight ball against the headboard, wrapped in a blanket even though the room was uncomfortably warm.

Bits and pieces of her brother's side of the conversation drifted through the still air of the hallway.

"—yeah, probably just a nightmare— —yeah, Vince...I know, but that's what she said.— —I know...I *know*, but I have to. She has to— —Yeah, think it's best if I do. Okay...we'll be over for breakfast. Love you, see you in the morning."

Tess pulled the blanket tighter over her shoulders when Robby stopped in the doorway and raised one arm to rest against the frame. Just like Vince.

"We have to call the police, Robby. He's probably still out there, watching the hou—"

He hit the frame with his fist. "Stop it, Tess, Vince isn't here."

"Yes, he is. I saw him."

Robby ran his hand along the side of the door. "Oh, God, Tess."

He walked to the bed and held out his hands and wouldn't sit down until she took them.

"We have to talk, honey. About Vince."

**

—missed again.

Vince looked at his hands. *It wasn't possible.* He made fists just to make sure they were working and felt the bones and sinews slide against one another. He could hear the whisper of his fingertips against the palms of his hands and felt the touch of skin against skin, but....

There was something terribly wrong.

Vince turned and held his hands out toward the other man. "There's no way I could have missed."

"You didn't."

**

"You don't believe me, do you? About Vince being here, I mean."

Robby shook his head. "No, baby. It's not possible."

"But I—" Tess stopped herself. Her voice sounded shrill, hysterical...just like it had at the condo when she...when Robby came after she....

Tess licked her lips. "I know he's not supposed to come anywhere near me, but he was here, Robby, standing in the doorway."

"You saw his face?"

"I—" *Did I?* "I *know* it was him...who else would it be?" *Thomas?* "No, I know what Vince looks like. He must have—if the front door was locked then he must have gotten in through the back. I probably forgot to lock it after..." She looked at her brother's face. "You *don't* believe me."

Robby let go of her hands to cup her face, forcing her eyes to his. "Oh, baby, I'm so sorry. I do believe you *think* you saw Vince, the doctors said that might happen, but it was only a dream. Vince can't ever hurt you again."

"But he was here."

"No. He wasn't."

"But—"

"He's dead, honey. You killed him."

Oh God.

**

She remembered…

**

"I said let me in."

Tess gripped the phone tighter as the knocking started. It was soft at first, but growing steadily louder by the second. *Why doesn't somebody hear it? I can hear their TVs and radios…why doesn't somebody hear this and stop it?*

"Did you hear me?" Pound. Pound. Pound. "Get down here and open this door right now if you know what's good for you."

What's good for me? Do you know what's good for me? God help me.

She couldn't move even when the pounding stopped and another sound came from downstairs—the sound of a key hitting the doorknob. The new sound didn't last very long.

"You changed the locks. You fucking bitch, you changed the locks. This is *my* house, I paid for it. Who the hell do you think you are? OPEN THIS GODDAMNED DOOR!"

A single, loud crash echoed up through the condo. He was slamming his shoulder into the door. Tess remembered the sound from the one and only time she'd ever tried to lock him out of their bedroom.

"It's not rape if we're married, Tess."

It was the memory of what he did that finally made her run. Tess dropped the phone on the stairs, she heard it bounce and fall, shattering when it hit the simulated hardwood flooring. Her cell phone was in her purse; the purse in the kitchen…and the kitchen was just off the living room, less than twenty feet from the front door.

She was almost across when the top hinge splintered away from the frame.

Oh God.

"Open the Goddamned door!" —*snap*— "Do you *hear* me?"

Tess grabbed her purse from the kitchen table and upended it. It was quicker than digging through the layers of debris for the phone she never bothered to put into its designated pocket. *Robby's told me so many times to—*

A loud *crack* thundered through the house.

OhGodOhGodOhGod

"TESS!" His voice sounded closer. Cupping the phone in both hands, she scrolled down the contact list to her brother's number and hit CONNECT.

It was still ringing when Vince walked into the kitchen. He was sweating and his face was flushed as if he'd just come back from jogging. But he wasn't wearing the new jogging suit she'd bought him for Christmas…Tess didn't recognized anything he was wearing. He had on dark jeans and a cheap black lightweight windbreaker over a T-shirt, and wore a Phillies baseball cap pulled low over his eyes. Vince never wore baseball caps, just like he never wore jeans or T-shirts and all their friends knew that. It was the perfect disguise.

"Hi, honey. Did you miss me?"

The blood pounded so loudly in her ears Tess could barely hear Robby's voice whisper from the cell phone. *"Hey, sister mine…what's up?"* But Vince didn't hear it. Tess set the phone on the counter and backed away. He noticed that. And smiled.

"Were you going to call someone?"

"N-no, Vince."

She said his name clearly and distinctly and prayed to God Robby had heard her. And understood.

"No? You weren't even going to call the police like you promised?" He took off the cap and tossed it onto the table as he walked toward her. "You sure?"

"Yes, Vince."

"That's my girl. But why don't we just make sure you're not tempted." Vince whirled and brought his fist down full force. The cell phone sprayed fragments of itself across the kitchen. "There, now everything's back to normal. Well, almost..."

Vince backhanded her across the face, apparently he no longer worried about leaving marks, and Tess crumbled to the floor.

"Did you *really* think you could keep me out of my own home, bitch?"

Tess dragged herself across the kitchen, expecting at any moment to feel his shoe against her back; but he just stood there, watching her. When she reached the far cabinet she made a blind grab for the handle of the uppermost drawer. When a nail broke as she grabbed the decorative bar, the tiny pain barely registered. The laminated wood creaked as she tried to pull herself up, but it supported her just long enough for Vince to stroll across the room and sweep her legs out from under her. The drawer fell with her...its cutlery sounding like broken wind chimes as it scattered.

Vince used the toe of one shoe to turn her over. He was smiling. "Are you done?"

A strange sense of calm came over Tess as she looked up at him. He was going to kill her. Some part of her always knew he would, one day, and today was that day.

"Yes."

"Good. Now, I asked you a question, Tess, and I expect an answer."

She couldn't remember what he'd asked, but it didn't matter. He wouldn't care what answer she'd give him...he was just playing with her, prolonging the moment until he...

Her fingers touched something cold and thin and closed around it. The knife looked so very small when she held it up.

"No more, Vince. Get out of here. Leave me alone!"

He started to laugh as he squatted down next to her.

"It talks." Vince shook his head, still laughing. "And look how brave it is. Oh...I'm scared. I'm so scared."

He hit the cupboard next to her head with the flat of his hand and she cried out before she could stop herself. Vince was smiling when he sat back on his heels.

"My, oh my. First you lock me out and then you pull a knife? What would your lawyer say about that? So, are you going to kill me? Is that it? Is that what my little wifey wants to do? Kill me? *Aw*. Well come, then, take your best shot, you're only gonna get one. So come on, do it, bitch. Come on.... COME ON!"

She looked at him, looked right into his eyes. "All right."

It was like cutting into a loaf of fresh bread. There was very little resistance as she pulled the knife blade across his throat.

Vince made a small, gurgling sound—eyes wide, mouth trying to form the words that spilled down the front of the cheap black windbreaker, his face literally draining of color—and grabbed this throat.

Tess wasn't sure which of them was more surprised when he blinked and toppled backward.

He was dead before he hit the floor.

**

Vince squared his shoulders. "Then what the hell is going on?"

The man cocked his head to one side, as if listening to something Vince couldn't hear.

"What's the last thing you remember before you...came here? The last thing before these woods?"

"I was in my *empty* condo...the bitch is selling—"

"And before that?"

"I..." Vince rubbed his hands against his face trying to squeeze his memory into sharper focus. He was...   "The condo again, with my wife."

The man shook his head.

"She's not your wife," he whispered. "She's your widow."

CHAPTER 12
JUNE 21st
2:34 p.m.

Tess stared at the bronze marker until her eyes blurred and, when she finally looked away, the afterimage floated before her like a pale lavender ghost. It ruined the illusion that they were standing in a park. Most of the carved headstones and monuments were in the older section, here, where they were standing, the graves were flush to the ground...for the most part.

The newer graves, like Vince's, hadn't completely settled yet.

"You okay, honey?"

Tess nodded and watched the fading afterimage bounce across the softly rolling green hills. A red and silver "Happy Birthday" Mylar balloon glinted in the sunlight four rows away.

She didn't believe Robby when he told her...*reminded* her of what she'd done. It wasn't possible, it had to have been a dream—*nightmare*—and she told him that, over and over for most of the night until... Then waited for time to slip away so she could wake up. She was still waiting.

"I— Why aren't I in jail?"

Robby brushed his knuckles gently down her arm. They'd talked about that, too...how there'd been an inquest while she was recovering—another lost segment of her life—and the verdict of justifiable homicide given. She was free...and safe... and a murderess.

And she'd forgotten it.

I killed him. He's here.

Vincent		*Teresa*
1970-2008		*1973-*

—*finis vitae sed non amoris*—

WARREN

She'd forgotten about the "family" plot, too, until she saw it again. Vince had bought them "for her" on their first anniversary. He'd been so proud, showing her their names and dates of birth already inscribed, waiting only to be finished.

"See the inscription? It means 'the end of life is not the end of love'...I'll always love you, Tess. Forever."

Tess backed away. "I don't want to be here."

"Okay, we can go."

"No, I mean—" She pointed to the flat ground next to Vince's grave. "There. I don't want to be buried there."

"Then you won't be...but that's still a long ways off. Don't think about it, okay?"

"Okay." *I killed him.* "How could I have forgotten...doing that?"

"Trauma. The doctors said it was temporary amnesia from the shock, but I think God was giving you a break. I don't know, maybe I shouldn't have told you—"

"No, I'm glad you did." And mostly that was the truth. "I just don't understand...how I could have forgotten it or the trail or—"

"Do you remember it now?"

Tess closed her eyes until the lavender grave marker faded to black. "Yes."

"Good, now you can forget it, okay?"

"Very funny."

"I try."

"But what about last night? I did see him, Robby."

That had been the one thing Robby couldn't explain, but kept trying to. "No, you didn't baby, it was a nightmare…your subconscious playing fast and loose with reality."

"Or guilt."

"You have nothing to feel guilty about, Tess. It was self-defense, pure and simple and some part of you knows that. The rest of you just has to accept it, is all. So…"

Robby tossed an arm over her shoulders and turned both of them toward the car.

"How about we see how the *'other half'* lives and grab a bite to eat at the Philmont Country Club? Sound good?"

Tess' stomach turned at the thought of putting food into it. "Don't you have to work?"

"Work? Me? One of the many, many benefits of being your own boss, my dear little sister, is that I can play hooky whenever I feel like it. Shall we?"

"Sure. Sounds great."

They got within a yard of the roadway when Tess stopped and turned around. His grave was easy to spot, despite the distance. "I should have brought flowers or something."

"Let it go, Tess."

"But he's… He was my husband, Robby."

"Yeah, he was, but he was also a bastard and would have killed you." He turned her around, making her face him and the truth. "You know that. Hell, the police and judge knew that. If you hadn't…fought back I'd be here visiting your grave and that is something I don't like to think about. He wanted to hurt you, there was no other reason why he came to the condo and he might have even gotten away with it."

"But he…loved me, Robby."

Robby pulled her in and rested his chin against the top of her head. "That wasn't love, baby, that was never love and the best thing you can do right now is forget he ever existed."

"You're right…he doesn't because I killed him."

When the tears came he held her and made comforting sounds that only made her cry harder. She couldn't tell him... would *never* tell him the real reason she was crying. They weren't tears of sorrow or remorse or guilt. *He's dead...he's dead...*

It was release.

"It's okay, baby, it's okay. We never have to come back here, baby. It's over."

Over. Thank God.

Tess wiped her eyes against the shoulder of her brother's polo shirt and took a deep breath. It was over, he was dead, Vince was dead....*then who was in my room last night?*

**

"Bullshit."

Vince sat with his back against the blackened trunk of a lighting-struck tree and listened to the sound of churning water in the streambed below. A mist had risen just after sunrise and grew into a thick haze that covered the ground and moved through the trees like...*shit*...restless ghosts.

"She's not your wife. She's your widow. I can't tell you why you're here like this, only that it happens sometimes. But try to accept your death and move on. You have no business among the living... especially her."

Especially her.

Vince had to admit the guy was good—the soft voice and slow movements, the way he kept sidestepping Vince's blows...even the vague hint of sorrow in his manner. Damn, Vince had almost applauded. It'd been first rate community theater quality...but, *fuck me blind*, the plot needed a lot of work. All that *'she's your widow'* bullshit might be fine around the campfire, but come on...telling someone they were dead?

And then expecting them to *believe* it?

"Shit."

It was the most ludicrous attempt to scare someone off that he'd ever heard...although, that didn't explain what happened when he closed the distance and drove his fist into the side of the man's head...only to watch his fist pass completely through and come out the other side.

The man moved, that's all, he was a fast bugger or it'd been a trick of the light...or the shadows or...

"Do you know how you came to be here?"

Of course he knew. He must have driven; it was too far to walk from the condo—

"Do you remember anything about the last time you were with her?"

Shit, what a thing to ask. He remembered everything... colors and tastes and smells and pain and blood and—

"Do you remember how you died?"

Vince's hand moved toward his throat. He *remembered* coming to the condo to straighten things out with her, once and for all...to tell her how much he still loved her and how sorry he was that things had gotten so crazy. He'd been all ready to forgive her...and she'd gone and changed the locks. He *remembered* wanting to break the door down with his bare hands but—

She opened the door...didn't she?

That had made him a little angry—*"You think you can lock me out, bitch?"*—but he might have even forgiven her that, if she hadn't pulled a knife on him.

"Goddamn psycho bit—"

Vince remembered a few more things: pain and grabbing his throat and feeling his lungs deflate and not being able to fill them up or yell for help...and

Dying.

Vince's fingers found what they were searching for. The slit was just above his Adam's Apple, hardly wider than a scratch and maybe two inches long. It was surprising how little pressure it took to slide a finger through the opening and feel the ridges at the back of his throat.

OhGodohshitdamn

Vince wiped his hand off against the leg of his jeans and waited for his stomach to stop twisting. He didn't feel dead... that was the whole point. He could feel—his hands, the rough denim, the ground beneath his feet, the log he was sitting on. He. Could. Feel.

I can't be dead.

But if he was, it pretty much sucked. Where were the angels come to sing him home? And what about the light he was supposed to walk into?

Every adult he'd come in contact with as a child—parents, priests, nuns—had been very specific about what *Heaven* was like and the glories he could expected to find if he remained true to the faith of his fathers, which he had. *Gloria in Excelsis Deo.* And—*if he really was dead*—this didn't look anything like what had been described to him. No Pearly Gates, no Heavenly Choir, no luminous beings of joy and hope.

Conclusion: He couldn't be dead.

"FUCK!"

And, as if to confirm that little point, a deer took off through the mist-shrouded trees across from him like it was shot out of a cannon.

"How can I fucking be dead if a fucking deer fucking heard me?"

Good point.

Getting to his feet, Vince took a deep breath and ignored the fact that he couldn't actually feel the air moving into his lungs. There had to be logical explanations for that and everything else, especially if the guy was an actor. Yeah, he'd seen enough movies to know how what a good makeup man with the right prosthetics could do.

He smiled. *God damn.* They, Tess and the man, played him like a cheap guitar and, for a moment, only a moment, Vince felt something close to new respect for his wife. She must have been planning this whole thing for months...maybe from the very first moment her fucking brother showed her the millhouse.

Could be that's when she met him...the man in the costume.

She's not your wife. She's your widow.

"Bastard."

Vince took a step and felt the ground shift beneath him. *Felt it. Jesus, you would have thought they'd come up with a better plan. "I know Vince. He's so gullible he'll believe anything, he even believes me when I tell him I love him."*

"I did," he whispered, then laughed softly. She thought she knew him so well, his dear little wife, and, perhaps, she did... in certain respects. She knew, for instance, that he wouldn't stop until he got her back. "Because marriage is forever."

But she didn't know him that well...not if she thought this stupid plan would work.

"Convince him he's dead and he'll do something stupid to prove he's not...like run out in front of a moving car. Then we can be together forever."

"Wrong, baby...you're *mine* forever, and the sooner you accept that, the better."

Vince left the shelter of the trees and stopped when he felt the ground level out under his feet. He couldn't see the path beneath the mist, but the sound of water was louder which meant he had to be a little more careful about where he stepped. One inch too far and he'd find himself in the stream. *Going under. Suffocating.*

And if he were dead he wouldn't be worrying about that, now would he? Nope.

He started to reach for his throat, then tucked both hands into the pockets of his windbreaker. He wasn't going to play their games anymore, not for some two-bit actor who had a talent for makeup.

And was strong as a fucking bull.

"Got'cha." Vince rolled his shoulders and laughed. "Shit, you gonna try to convince someone he's dead, you better keep your hands to yourself. You can't touch a ghost, you moron."

Whistling silently through his teeth—the makeup must have closed off his throat or something—Vince slid his feet carefully across the ground until he came to a level patch. He couldn't see through the ground mist, but it wasn't very likely that the man—*actor*—could have dragged him too far from the millhouse. All he had to do was keep the sound of the water to his...right...left...no right.

And not step in any sinkholes.

**

He waited until the mist had closed between himself and the man before stepping out onto the path. The man was heading away from the millhouse, following one of the circuitous animal trails that crossed and recrossed the woods to the north of the old mill. A native woodsman would be hard pressed to find his way back...and he wished the same for this man.

For her sake, as well as his own.

There were already too many sins upon his soul to contemplate another. But if the man came back he'd have no choice but to protect her.

Again.

When her voice suddenly drifted through the trees at his back and he tensed and more than half expected the man—her husband—to come barreling out of the mist toward the sound. A moment's grace passed while he stood and waited, her voice rising and falling like lark's song, or a siren's call to the damned; but the wall of mist remained unbroken and he turned to follow the call himself.

When she left that morning, her face was ash-gray and her eyes hollow...but now, despite a sorrow he couldn't understand, she seemed more at peace. And it gave him hope.

He smiled when she hugged her brother and walked with sure steps into the millhouse. She was a strong woman, much stronger than his Victoria had ever been. As he passed through the stone and wood, he wished he could have thanked God for her strength, but that, he knew, would have been an affront too great even for his tattered soul to bear.

**

"Was it you?"

Tess hung her purse over the newel cap and looked up the stairs to the landing.

"Ghost, answer me, ghost. Were you standing in the doorway last night?"

The house held the quiet for a moment before a soft, hollow thump answered her and she smiled. To anyone else, including Robby, the sound wouldn't have meant anything; but Tess knew the sounds of the house now, every minute groan and whisper and scramble of squirrel claws across the roof... and she knew the sounds *he* made and this was one of them.

Tess stepped onto the first step and a creak echoed down from the landing above her. She couldn't see him, of course, but she knew he was there—standing on the stair looking down at her.

"I'm sorry I screamed like that, but I thought you were someone else. My husband, Vince."

Tess walked up two more stairs and sat down with her back against the wall and the toes of her sneakers pressed against the banister.

"But it couldn't have been my husband, because I killed him." She closed her eyes and tipped her head back against the plaster. "I forgot doing it, isn't that a strange? I killed him."

There, she said it, twice, and somehow the ground hadn't opened up and swallowed her. Maybe the third time would be the charm.

"I killed Vince. Do you think God will forgive me?"

**

Yes.
**

Great.

Vince stopped at what might or might not be the start of an *actual* trail and puffed out his cheeks. He wasn't tired, in fact he felt pretty good...except for the fact that he'd obviously walked in the wrong direction—*fuckfuckfuckfuckfuck*—and was in the middle of the woods.

Again.

The only bright spot—both literally and figuratively—was that the mist had finally burned off and he could see exactly where he was. In the middle of the woods.

Turning around, Vince took a couple of steps, stopped; wheeled a quarter-turn to the left and took another few steps... and stopped again. Nothing, including what he thought was the direction he'd just come from, looked familiar. He hadn't heard the stream in quite a while and he wasn't even sure he was still within the boundaries of the state park. For all he knew, he'd walked right out of one set of woods and into another; but he couldn't just stand there.

Well, yes he could. He could stay right there until someone —most likely cadaver dogs—found his body.

"Tess, you were right about your husband. He wandered off into the woods and died. Talk about stupid..."

"Oh *hell*, no!"

And from behind the wall of trees directly in front of him, a dog concurred.

"Snicker! Knock it off. Daddy's having enough trouble without your help."

"Real funny, Irene."

A man and woman...and dog.

Vince pushed his way through the dense boughs, following the sounds of their bickering—*"I told you to get a new map." "I don't need this right now, Irene." "Oh, excuse me, Daniel Boone." "Irene..."*—like a beckon. He found them in a small meadow maybe a hundred yards in from where he'd first heard them. Both were dressed at the height of urban-wilderness fashion— fanny-packs with clip-on water bottles, walking shorts and tank top for him, short-shorts and tube top for her; both with oversized hats, sunglasses and clunky-soled hiking boots from which erupted thick rolled socks. The man had a look of defeat about him, shoulders hunched forward as he studied a small square of paper in his hand.

They were only kids, mid-twenties the pair of them, obviously married.

And, just as obvious, she was a bitch.

"Can't you just admit this isn't the right trail so we can go back to the car? I'm getting all bug-bit."

"Like there'd be a bug brave enough to bite you."

"*What?*"

Vince's original plan was to stroll into the clearing as if he was just another nature lover out for a day hike, but he stopped a few feet short to listen. The only thing better than *having* a discussion that could erupt into violence, was watching one.

"Hit her," he whispered.

A low growl rolled through the air in front of him and Vince looked down into a pair of golden eyes. The chocolate lab was the size of a small, but well fed, pony. Hackles raised like porcupine quills and lips curled back to reveal ivory-colored fangs, the dog lowered its head and took a slow, stiff-legged step forward.

Vince froze, not wanting to give the dog any reason to attack. "Hey!"

The dog's growl deepened. Vince glanced toward the fighting couple. The man was still staring down at the paper in his hands, the woman still bitching at him.

"Hey, you two."

And not paying any attention to anyone but themselves.

"Look, let's just go home, okay? I'm tired."

"You wanted to go hiking."

"I did not!"

"Yes, you did. You wanted to take the day off and—"

"Yo!" Vince yelled. "Call off your dog, okay?"

He lifted his arms to attract their attention—since shouting apparently wasn't working—and the dog took it as a threat. It lunged forward a few inches and started barking like it'd cornered a bear. Vince had never heard sounds like that except in movies and it scared the crap out of him.

"HEY!"

The woman finally noticed. She turned and pointed. "*Your* dog's going crazy."

"*My* dog?" But the man was already folding up the map. "Snicker...hey, Snick, c'mer, boy."

Snicker ignored his master's voice and took another stiff-legged step forward. Vince skimmed one foot back as slowly as possible, but a twig must have rustled or something because the dog heard it and lunged again, the foam slathered jaws only a few inches from his crotch.

"CALL HIM OFF!"

"SNICKER! COME. HERE!"

"For God's sake, David, that's not doing any good. Go *get* him. He's probably cornered a skunk or something and I swear if he gets sprayed I'm taking the car and leaving both of you here!"

The man stuffed the map into the front pocket of his shorts and stomped toward them, muttering to the dog or himself. Vince couldn't tell which, but kept shifting his gaze from master to dog and back again. *Hurry up, asshole! I swear to God I'll sue your ass twelve ways from Sunday if it bites me.*

"Knock it off, Snicker."

The man walked up behind the dog and smacked it on the rump. It gave a quick little yelp and tucked its tail between lowered haunches, then turned, saw Vince and remembered why it was barking. It started again, gold eyes never leaving Vince's face.

"What is it, boy? What'cha got in there, huh? Let's go see."

Bending forward, the man took hold of the dog's collar and the dog, feeling its master's touch, charged forward. Vince stumbled back, hands out, protecting his vitals.

"Whoa, hey…knock it off. What the hell are you doing?"

From the clearing, the woman asked the same thing. "What the hell are you doing? I want to *go*. *Now!*"

Man and dog, both apparently well trained, stopped instantly. Vince curled his hands into fists to let the guy know he wasn't amused, but kept them between himself and the dog.

"You're real funny there, asshole."

The man looked at Vince and gave a little shrug. "Come on, Snick, there's nothing here. We'd better be going. *Mama* wants to go *home*."

"What the hell do you mean *nothing*? Hey! Asshole! I'm talking to you—"

Vince took a step forward just as the guy let go of the dog's collar. The lab shot forward, jaws gapping and teeth barred. Vince didn't have enough time to do more than tighten his leg muscles, close his eyes and wait.

There should have been pain and the rending of material and maybe even a little blood, followed by a wet crack as Vince broke the dog's neck. There should have been those things, but the only thing that happened was the dog's jaws snapping shut.

On nothing.

Vince opened his eyes and looked down.

The dog's muzzle was buried in Vince's leg up to its eyes… and those eyes were wide and white rimmed and staring back up at him. Vince moved back and the jaws reappeared. Both of them, Vince and the dog, knew something wasn't right, but it was the dog that reacted first. Shivering, it peed itself and then twisted back like a corkscrew and took off at a dead run—

Dead.

—that almost knocked its master on his ass.

"SNICKER!"

The man watched the dog go tearing past his wife, then turned around and stared right into Vince's eyes before his gaze shifted to look for whatever it was that frightened his dog.

"What happened?" The woman began walking toward the trees. "Did something bite him?"

"I don't know- might have been a snake or something. Where's Snicker?"

She reached the trees and stood on tiptoes, looking over her husband's shoulder. Right at Vince.

"Probably at the car by now. I don't see anything, but let's get out of here."

When the man turned, Vince made a grab for his arm. There was not even the movement of air against his finger as his hand passed through the man's flesh.

"Yeah, you're right." The man shrugged. "There's nothing here. Stupid dog."

Vince watched the couple slowly walk away.

"Jesus-humping-Christ," he said to himself. "I really am dead."

**

Robby and Chuck showed up just as Tess was making a salad for dinner. They came, like the Three Wise Men-minus One, bearing gifts: a picnic hamper filled with items Tess had only seen in the windows of gourmet shops, two bottles of Australian Shiraz and a half-dozen DVDs...all comedies.

"We planned to do this a week ago," Chuck told her as he spread a blanket across her living room rug. "But the patio's too hard and the ground is still too soggy, so we decided this would be the best solution."

"A picnic," Tess said, "in the house."

Chuck had looked at Robby and Robby had looked at Chuck, and both of them looked at her. "With movies."

She wasn't convinced. "So you didn't just come over here to keep me company tonight?"

"Why would we do that? Robby sprawled across one corner and began digging through the hamper. "What goes good with paté? Oh I know…how about 'Arsenic and Old Lace'?"

Tess glanced at the wine bottles as she sat down.

The movies were all comedies, light and cheerful, mostly 30's and 40's classics that got funnier in direct proportion to the amount of wine consumed. By the time they left, well after midnight, Tess couldn't stop giggling.

Convenient fabrication or not, it worked—she didn't think about Vince once. Until they left.

Then, waving until she could no longer see the beams of their flashlights through the trees, Tess took a deep breath of the still, thick air and remembered. Everything. Every lost moment time had taken from her came flooding back.

Vince on the kitchen floor, a bloody halo around his head.

Uniforms, dark blue trousers legs and black shoes moving so slowly toward her.

A light voice, a woman's voice, asking her to hand over the bloodied knife in her hand.

Another voice, just as soft, asking her what happened.

Robby…Robby to the rescue, telling the other voices to leave her alone.

Flashes of light. Photographs. White trousers, kind hands, a stretcher behind her back. A blanket tossed over her… another tossed over Vince. Someone saying no rush on this one, he's long gone.

Hospital room. Court room. Her lawyer smiling. Robby smiling. Vince was dead and he couldn't hurt her anymore.

And I killed him.

"Oh God."

Her stomach twisted up inside her as she lurched off the porch and into a light misting rain, barely heavier than the air. The rain didn't make a sound when it hit the ground, but by the time Tess reached the footbridge, she was soaked to the skin.

"He's dead. Vince is really dead."

A tiny shiver tickled the dripping hair at the back of her head. He was dead, Vince was dead and if she said it to herself long enough she might believe it...might have believed it if he suddenly hadn't moved through the shadows opposite the millrace.

It wasn't Robby and it wasn't a deer and, and even though Tess knew her slightly tipsy imagination—*guilty conscience*—could conjure up whatever it wanted to out of the shape in the shadow, there was something about it, the way it...he stood there looking back at her.

He's here.

"No, you're not."

The wet gravel crunched under her feet as she backed toward the millhouse, bur the shape in the trees never looked away, never moved...until she slipped and landed on her butt.

That's when he reached for her.

"NO!"

Tess scrapped both knees getting to her feet only to fall again after two steps. She crawled the rest of the way, leaving a mud-trail behind her as she scrambled up the porch steps.

"You're dead!" I killed you!" Her back hit the porch step and she scrambled onto it, leaving a mud-trail across the wood. "Go away! Leave me a—"

Lightning flared again and Tess collapsed onto the porch, laughing at the rain-tousled basswood sapling as it *reached* for her again. It felt like hours before she was able to catch her breath.

"Oh, God...I really am crazy." Closing her eyes, Tess listened to the misting rain turn into a shower that beat against the porch roof. "He's gone...Vince is gone and he's never coming back."

Flat on her back in front of the open door, Tess let the rain sing her to sleep.

She was safe.

**

He moved slowly through the rain, keeping to the shadows until he stood on the porch next to her.

She looked like as innocent as a child. The wet strands of her hair rested gently against her cheek and forehead and her lips curved into a smile as though she were dreaming.

His son had never lived long enough to learn how to smile.

Bending low, he traced the shape of her lips onto the air with his finger. Still asleep she frowned suddenly and curled onto her side toward him.

"Hush, now," he whispered. "It's all right. I'm here."

The smile returned to her lips with a soft sigh.

With the utmost care he brought her into the millhouse and made sure the door was closed—*and locked*—behind them.
**

He stood in the rain and watched as the door closed, and the lights in the millhouse windows go out, until only one, the glow from her bedroom, shown like a beacon in the night.

"Tess," Vince whispered. "My own little wifey."

CHAPTER 13
JUNE 25th

Tess woke up to a whirlpool.

Guilt, relief, horror, revulsion, acceptance...no, not acceptance, recognition of what she'd done—*I killed him...I killed Vince. I killed him...I killed Vince*—but she still couldn't completely believe what she'd done.

Or that he really was dead.

A man like Vince couldn't die *that* easily.

But he did, and I killed him.

Tess blamed the repeated bouts of nausea on the wine she'd had the night before. It was as good a reason as any and probably the right one, considering she couldn't actually remember taking off her wet clothes and crawling under the sheets...or closing all the windows so the rain wouldn't get in.

Time had slipped again, but not enough or in the right direction...Tess still remembered killing Vince.

God.

The millhouse was a sweat lodge, which seemed a fitting punishment for a murderess—*I killed him. I killed Vince*—but it wasn't enough. She kept the air conditioner off and, after Robby called to complain about his own hangover and asked if she needed anything, either 'some-of-the-dog' or Extra-Strength Tylenol, she'd lied and told him everything was fine. *Of course everything's fine...I killed her husband and got away with it. And didn't remember any of it.*

Her head was spinning slightly as she wandered into the bathroom and began going through the medicine cabinet.

The first pass was a disappointment. There was only three Advil left, which she took with a handful of tepid water. When the tablets had dulled the pain to a more-or-less constant throb, Tess went through the cabinet again...and noticed a small amber bottle partially hidden by a box of Band-Aids. *Dalmane*, a prescription 'sleeping aid'. Her name was on the label and the typed instructions warned her not to take more than two tablets within twelve hours, to keep out of reach of small children and not to operate any heavy equipment after taking one. Tess didn't recognize the doctor's name or when she got them.

The bottle had never been opened.

Tess broke the seal and poured the red and yellow capsules into her hand. Each capsule had the drug's name and 15mg printed on it. 15mg didn't seem like it would be enough to put someone to sleep, but there were—she counted—fourteen capsules in the bottle. Fourteen times 15mg equals....615mg.

That should be enough.

No note. She decided that as she carried the capsules back into the bedroom and lay down. She wouldn't know what to say anyway. *I'm sorry. Please forgive me. I can't live with what I did. It wasn't your fault. I love you.* It all sounded so forced.

Tess just hoped Robby would find her before the enclosed heat made her body too unbearable to look at.

They went down surprisingly easy without water...and almost immediately she felt as if she were floating on a calm sea. It wasn't unpleasant at all. Dying was comfortable, almost effortless...until her stomach objected.

Violently.

It felt like someone punched her in the gut with a sledgehammer—much harder than Vince ever hit her—and her body jackknifed, folding inward and onto its side as the first tidal wave of bile gushed out. The bedspread was spared, the rug, the front nightstand and her shoes weren't. Tess left a trail of jellied capsules and the partially digested remains of her picnic dinner all the way back to the bathroom.

She spent the rest of the day regretting her decision.

Tess had managed to drag herself to her feet a few times to rinse out her mouth and wash her face before returning to the cool tiles, but finally managed to leave the bathroom. Suffering be damned...she showered and turned on the AC before making herself a cup of weak tea and crawling back into bed.

Hell hath no fury like a woman's own stupidity.

Vince was right about that.

The rain continued, off and on, for the next two days while Tess cleaned and worked and remembered.

I killed Vince. He's not here.

When her cell phone rang, she didn't have to look at the name display to know who it was. She'd been expecting his call since opening an e-mail that morning entitled: *We're going to drown.*

"It's not that bad, Robby," she said before he could start. "The stream and millrace are high, but we already went through a flood...remember, and we survived."

Silence. "Yes, but...that was only a 'Flood Warning,' we're in a full scale 'Flood Watch' now."

Tess clamped the cell phone between her shoulder and ear and saved the file she'd been working on before he called. "A 'watch' is worse than a 'warning'?"

His sigh filled the phone. "Okay, let's forget semantics for the moment and concentrate on only one word...*flood*. As is drowning, hence the subject of my e-mail."

Tess read it again—*'We're on FLOOD WATCH. Pack up some things and get your bum over here ASAP. Chuck's buying supplies. Hurry!"*—and noticed the time stamp.

"You were up at five?"

"What do you mean up? I haven't slept in..." Tess heard shuffling through the phone. "Okay, only twenty-nine hours, but, hey, that's the price you have to pay when living in a flood plain. I knew this whole thing was too good to be true. How bad's the stream?"

Tess pushed her chair back from the desk, checking the millrace first—it was pounding against the side of the footbridge—before walking to the rain-splattered window on the far wall.

"Just like I said…muddy and fast and a little high, but not too high."

"What's 'not too high' mean in real terms?"

Tess watched a tree bob and weave its way downstream.

"It's still a few feet below the bank."

"Good. Pack a bag. Get over here."

"No. Robby, we've already had a flood and the millhouse was fine. I'll stay here."

"Listen to you, a regular Unsinkable Molly Brown. Look, baby, the ground's saturated if there's another flood it will be a hundred times worse than the little… overflow we just had. I'm serious honey; I'd feel better if you were over here with us. Jesus, will you look at the field."

Tess crossed the room saw and Robby on the back balcony, partially hidden by an oversized red golf umbrella. The field did resemble a rice paddy.

"Can you see it?" his voice whispered into her ear. "This is worse than last time, T… I'll—wait…update on the Weather Channel. Hang on."

Exhaling loud enough for him to hear, Tess sat down and keyed up another file.

He mumbled something.

"What?"

"Yeah, okay…the Weather Channel's radar shows the rain moving north. It *supposed* to end by midnight, but if you even *think* the water's getting high, you call and I'll be there even if I have to swim."

Yes, sir. Going to hang up, now. Bye-bye."

He was still muttering when she snapped the cell shut. Even if there wasn't another flood the water might be deep enough. Drowning couldn't be as bad as having your throat cut....

**

He stood behind her in the doorway, giving her distance but not leaving her alone. If the water rose to surround the millhouse, he'd be trapped inside with her, again, but that was the chance he had to take. He hadn't known what the tablets in her hand contained, but he had recognized the look in her eyes.

It'd been the same look he'd seen in Victoria's.

Forgive me.

It wasn't to God that he addressed the thought, but to the air. He couldn't find it in his heart to speak to the deity she has so loved above all else. More than her love for him and far more than her motherly devotion to their son.

"Samuel." Forgetting himself, he whispered the name of his son and she turned, looking over her shoulder.

"Did you say—" The flesh between her eyes furrowed as she stood, meeting his eyes for an instant before they continued on. "Was that you, ghost?" The wrong left her face as her shoulders sagged. "I need more coffee. Vince...my husband always said I..."

She shook the rest of the words away as if they were a bothersome horsefly and he stepped aside to let her pass, knowing she would not harm herself. It was strange how he seemed to know that about this woman and yet had not seen the danger threatening his own son. This would have been his room, had he lived to outgrow the cradle at the foot of their bed.

He should have known.

Even now it was hard to forget the look that had been on Victoria's face when he walked in to find her holding the body of their son against her breast. She was smiling, content, more at peace than the months she carried the babe within her.

"He's gone home."

He thought at first it was an accident or a chill that had carried him off. The autumn had been so cold and he was so small, come early because she'd slipped on a frost-coated rock by the stream and fallen.

A surprise, she'd told him when he asked why she was out by the water in her condition. She'd seen some berries near the stream and had wanted to gather them to make a pie. He should have known she wasn't strong enough. It was his fault for getting her with child too soon after their vows. She'd been but a child herself and he a man of forty. He should have waited, but the desire for an heir too strong within him.

He should have known what that would do to her.

When he found the marks of her fingers on the baby's throat, he lied and kept the truth like a cancer in his heart. He kept it, just as he kept the secret of her death a few days after he buried their son. It had not been an accident any more than the child's death, but he had attested to finding her cold and still in their bed, dead of a broken heart…and forfeited his soul to provide her a place in sanctified ground next to their son.

That had been his sin, not the way he died.

**

Tess spooned creamer into the oversized mug Vince had given her. *Instant Human…Just Add Coffee.* He'd known her so well.

**

Being dead wasn't all bad.

Vince turned his face toward the clouds and closed his eyes. If he hadn't known it was raining—and he knew that only because he could hear it and, before he shut his eyes, seen it hit the ground—it could have been a beautiful sunlit summer's day.

Or it could have been hellishly humid.

Didn't matter to him one bit.

He couldn't get wet and, although he could still feel—his hands, the ground under his feet, a stump if he sat down, the wound at his throat—heat and cold and everything else just didn't seem to bother him. It was as if everything in the world, besides him, had been turned into mist and cobwebs.

Although there were times if he remembered something she did, or didn't do—*his little wifey*—the world would turn solid again. Vince smiled and imagined he was taking a deep breath.

"Tess."

And a raindrop smacked him in the eye; tangible and real.

The test worked.

Vince opened his eyes and the world had once more become the density of dreams…or nightmares, depending on your outlook, and the rain fell through him without so much as a hesitation. He could hear it hit the puddles beneath his feet.

A heron flew overhead like some out of place pterodactyl and he watched it until a blast of thunder banked it toward the trees. Vince imagined the thin-necked bird spiraling down in flames like a WWII fighter and nodded.

He remembered as a kid watching old black-and-white war movies with his dad on Saturday mornings and cheering like crazy when a plane—friend or foe—went down.

He remembered a lot of things…like being alive, for one, and he remembered dying.

Vince fingered the wound at his throat.

And he remembered standing in the trees watching the young couple and their ghost-seeing dog *(Fuck, I'm a ghost)* hightailing it away when…

Vince dragged his teeth over his bottom lip, looking for dead skin to chew off—a bad habit he was going to have to break—and, couldn't remember what happened next. *Okay, so there's a still a few holes in the system.* Meadow…hikers…dog…

dog attacks…dog runs away…man and woman don't see him take off after dog…and then…

Fog.

Yeah.

A heat mist had started forming almost as soon as the hikers took off and, man did it get thick. Vince hadn't been able to see a foot…less in front of him so he sat down and waited and…

Then the rain came and the fog went away and he needed to get going.

And see the little wifey.

"Yeah!"

Vince punched the air as he started walking, wishing it were her face. The bitch had more than just a beating coming to her, she had eternity coming.

"Marriage is forever, baby," he said out loud because he'd always love the sound of that phrase. "We promised God, and I'm coming to make sure you keep your promise."

And with those words it finally made sense. *Jesus.*

Vince stopped so suddenly he felt the ground shift under his feet. *That* was the reason he was still around and not in Heaven receiving the just rewards of the righteous. He was there as The Lord's Own Holy Ghost…to see to it that she kept her promise.

To join him in the Life Eternal as his Immortal Wife.

Forever…and ever, amen.

"Goddamn, You do work in mysterious ways." Vince dropped his arms and felt his nails dig into his palms. *Felt* it… like he'd make her *feel* it.

Shoulders back, he took off as if the yellow brick road had suddenly been laid down before him. Now that he understood the reason behind his miraculous transubstantiation from flesh to spirit, he didn't have to worry about which direction he was headed…God would provide. God would prevail. God would see that nothing stopped him from—

Vince stumbled back, ice forming in his belly.

The gully might have started out as an animal trail, but years of erosion had widened it into a trench and the rain had turned it into a rivulet.

It was no more than a foot or two across; not even that in some spots...the spots where he could have easily stepped over without breaking his stride. Probably just like he had a hundred other times without noticing. Hell, he'd crossed water deeper than that walking across the parking lot. All he had to do was step over it and continue on his way.

Yeah.

He had a mission. He had to find Tess and meter out God's justice.

Right.

Squaring his shoulders, Vince shifted his weight forward and watched the ground spiral into a vortex...a dark gray mouth opening wide to swallow him whole...pulling him into a nothingness filled with sounds...voices...memories.

"NO!"

Vince staggered back, retching out something that looked like black smoke. *Shitgoddamnsonofabitch!* What the hell was happening to him? It couldn't *just* be the memory of almost drowning—*can a ghost drown?*—or whatever the hell it was that had happened to him in the water, it was almost like....

...like God was giving him a sign.

Vince took another step back and knew he was on the right track when the mist cleared and he was standing upright and whole, and looking down at the piddling little nothing of a stream without so much as a tummy flutter.

Okay, he wasn't supposed to cross here...God would let him know. *Got it.* All he had to do was, what? Follow it?

Taking another nibble along his bottom lip and keeping his eyes on the stream as if it were a coiled cobra, Vince eased his foot to the right, waited and let his body follow. No fog, no nausea, no blind terror.

"Let's do it."

Keeping the stream to his right, Vince took two more steps and the rain stopped. A few more steps and sunlight pierced the clouds.

It wasn't a burning bush, but for a cradle-Catholic it was a pretty good sign he was going the right way. Eventually God would show him a place to cross and show him the path to his own sweet little wifey.

Yeah, being dead wasn't bad at all.

CHAPTER 14
JUNE 26th

Tess put her mug of coffee down on the porch step to keep from dropping it when she saw Robby, covered in mud from mid-chest to the toes of his green hip-waders, coming up the path.

It wasn't what she expected to see, first thing in the morning and she didn't even know what was strangest...the time, her brother covered in mud or that he actually owned a pair of hip-waders; but it was all she could do to keep from laughing.

"Good morning."

His glare his reply.

"Can I ask what happened or would you rather just growl?"

He did a fair interpretation of Lon Chaney, Jr. as he stomped across the footbridge.

"Apparently there's another stream on the property that we didn't know about," he said. "While Chuck and I were busy keeping tabs on the millrace and stream, our newest little waterway flooded the basement."

"Oh, Robby."

"Yeah. It would have been okay except that the sump pumps got clogged. We're very lucky the rain stopped when it did."

"Is there much water?"

"About a foot, but it could have been a lot worse I guess."

"It's that muddy?"

Robby brushed at the front of his waders without looking down. "No...I fell a few times coming over here, the ground's like slush in some spots. I figured, as long as I was dressed for it, I might as well check out the pumps over here. Doesn't look like there should be a problem, though. You are pretty high and dry."

"I told you I'd be okay." Picking up her mug, Tess stood and fed him a sip. He made a face as soon as he swallowed.

"Eech...when are you going to stop using that artificial creamer and switch to real milk?"

"V... Very...possibly never. I like creamer." She couldn't remember if she liked it to begin with or not. Vince liked it and that's all they ever used. "Besides, preservatives are supposed to keep you young, right?"

Robby made a face as he backed up. "You're one sick little girl. Okay, I'll grab the hose from the back and wash off as much as I can...why don't you go inside and put down a couple of towels so I don't leave puddles."

"Why don't you just take off the waders?"

"Because I'm only wearing a smile...do you know hot these things get?"

Tess turned and started across the porch.

"Oh, and before I forget, don't plan anything for to night... you're having company."

"I am?"

"Yep. Say around nine. I know it's kind of late, but I have a business dinner meeting in Center City and Chuck will be showing houses until after eight, so plan on eating and we'll bring dessert if you make coffee."

"So it'll just be you and Chuck."

Robby gave her a wide, wicked smile. "Among others," he said and waved as he disappeared around the corner of the house.

"Rob— "

Leaving the door open behind her—*there was no longer a reason to lock it, Vince was dead*—Tess beat him to the back, coffee mug and two dish towels in hand. He finished the coffee for her, grimacing the whole time and pointed to the floor.

"Here," he said, giving her back the empty mug and taking the towels, "trade ya. Now you'll see why the Olympic Committee mourned my decision not to compete in Ice Dancing."

He laid the towels down and put one muddy wader-boot on each, then "skated" to the cellar door and opened it.

"Robby, who's—"

He put his finger to his lips and leaned into the stairwell, head cocked to one side. "Good, no dripping water...you may have lucked out, kid."

Holding onto the doorframe for support, Robby turned on the cellar lights and leaned forward. "And no standing water that I can see. Cool...but I'll take a look since I'm here anyway." He winked at her and started down the stairs.

"Robby!"

The clumping stopped and his head appeared at the lower right hand corner of the door. There was an all-too-knowing smile on his lips. "What?"

"Who's coming tonight?"

"Don't know," he said, "but I'm sure we'll find out."

Tess stopped herself from asking anything else. He was teasing her, just like he did when they were kids...making her play Twenty Questions instead of giving her a simple answer. It was just what big brother did to little sister, but it always made her feel stupid and worthless and maybe that's why she stayed with Vince...because he'd done the same thing and she was used to it.

"Okay."

"I don't... What?"

"I'm going for a walk. Be back later. Have fun."

"Walk? Wait, I—"

Tess walked down the hall and out the front door, closing it behind her with a smile. It was the first time she'd not played the game, not followed someone else's rules and it felt... *wonderful*.

Stepping carefully where the mud oozed up over her flip-flops, she followed Robby's tracks as far as the corner of the millhouse and turned right, away from the stream and toward the woods.

Birdsong and the whirring hum of insects echoed from hidden places among the thick, dripping branches as Tess picked her way through the underbrush. The storm had encased every trail leading into the State Park in a thick layer of shining mud.

The morning would have been perfect except for the heat. The sun seemed bent on making up for the time it lost during the storm, pulling moisture from her and the ground with equal voracity. Tess hadn't gotten more than a dozen steps into the tree before her tee shirt was glued to her body and the sodden terry-cloth shorts began bunching uncomfortably between her thighs.

Heat mist swirled in tendrils around her feet as she passed.

Stopping next to a wild raspberry bush, Tess used the hem of her shirt was wipe the sweat from her face and catch a much-needed breath. The bush had almost been plucked clean of fruit, but there were still a few berries deep within the labyrinth of barbed vines that looked invitingly ripe. She managed to avoid most of the thorns and found three berries that tasted like warm honey against her parched tongue. The fourth made her eyes water, but that didn't stop her from looking for more.

Vince had taken her berry picking every summer...it was one of the better memories she had of him.

Tess popped the sixth berry into her mouth, so ripe it'd left a stain—*like blood*—on her fingers, when she heard Robby cursing softly from the stand of trees to her left.

He'd come looking her. *How sweet.* Tess stayed hunched over the bush, pretending total concentration in the search for ripe berries and tried not to giggle as she listened to him stomp his way through the brush. He sounded upset. *Yes! I won. Nya, nya.*

"I'm over here, Robby." Tess popped another berry—sweet and ripe—into her mouth. "I found some berries. Come on... better hurry or I'll eat them all."

She heard him say her name as he started to run.

**

He had kept the faith and been rewarded.

Vince stopped running *around* the trees and started going through them. It was going to take some time before he remembered to take full advantage of his new *life*, but with God's help and his little wifey beside him...*again*...there was no telling what he could accomplish.

He was truly blessed.

**

Run!

Tess' hand closed around the berries she'd gathered, crushing them until they bled down her arm.

Her mouth began to form a word—a question? A call?—but she never got a chance to find out what it would have been. Her body took control and began backing away.

He called her name again—"Tess! Tess!"—and the heat did something to his voice...changed it, made it deeper, angrier...

It's not Robby. Run!

When they were little and played 'Keep Away,' Tess always pretended Robby was a fierce monster and never looked back because, even then, she knew it would spoil the fantasy.

But she didn't turn around this time because she was afraid the monster was real.

**

Vince stood in the middle of the path and watched her race across the footbridge. Three vaulting strides farther and she was on the porch, hanging onto one of the supports as she turned and looked right at him.

But didn't see him, of course.

He wasn't worried, there'd be time for that.

Soon, baby…you won't see anything else.

**

"Hey, you're back."

Tess pulled herself onto the porch and looked through the open front door *(Didn't I close it?)* to see Robby, boots firmly planted on what would never again be her dishtowels, slip-sliding down the hallway toward her.

"Have a good walk? Jesus, what did you do to yourself?"

Tess looked at the mulberry-colored stains running down her arm. It did look like blood. "I…I found some wild raspberries."

"So you decided to wear them?" Stepping onto the porch, Robby picked up the ruined towels and found a relatively clear corner to dab at the streaks. "You are *so* lucky you didn't run into a bear."

"No, I was going to bring some back but… We have bears?"

"Not personally, but this is a State Park and it covers a lot of ground. If New Jersey has bears, I'm sure there has to be a couple here."

Maybe that's what it was—Run!—maybe it was a bear.

"But I wouldn't worry too much about it. We've been here a while and the scariest thing we saw was a 'possum-skunk grudge match. Not a pleasant sight, let me tell you." Robby gave up trying to clean her arm and tossed both towels over his shoulder. "I'll wash them and bring them back tonight. Nine o'clock. Oh, and the next time you want to go berry picking let me know…we have buckets for that."

He jumped the porch steps instead of walking down. "A perfect Ten…and the crowd goes wild."

He looked back over his shoulder and winked. "Guests. Nine o'clock."

"Okay," Tess surrendered. "Who's coming?"

Robby shrugged. "We'll have to see. Later, 'tater."

"I hate you."

"Likewise." He waved without turning around and Tess walked into the house, locking the door behind her.

Because maybe there were bears.

**

They arrived at 10:25: Robby, Chuck and a string-tied pink bakery box.

"Kolache," Chuck said, shaking the box. "Just like mama used to buy. And before you decide anything about tonight, I just want to say that if you're not one hundred percent comfortable with this we can drop it. Okay?"

Up until that moment Tess, after noticing that the porch behind them was empty, had only been wondering where the guests were. Now she was confused. "Um…okay, but…"

"Robby and I have been talking about this for a while now. I wanted to do it the first night you got here, but it might have been too much, too soon. Now that you have a…have your memory back I think it might help." Chuck took a deep breath and smiled. "This isn't the end, Tess, we go on."

She shook her head. "I have no idea what you're talking about."

For a few seconds after Robby pulled the narrow rectangular box out from behind his back, the only thing Tess marveled at was how little the cover design had changed since they'd last played it. The colors were different, the one her cousins had was black and white; this was done in shades of blue, but the white letters were stilled outlined in red so they seemed to float a few inches above the lid.

It was just a game…then.

Tess backed away from the Ouija board as if it'd been a loaded gun. "Vince…"

Robby quickly lowered the box to his side. "No, baby, don't even think that. This has nothing to do with…what happened. It's just for fun—"

Just a game.

"—and to be honest, I really don't believe in it, but I thought, if you wanted to find out about your ghost...the miller's ghost, I mean, we could—"

My other *ghost...the one that's already here.*

"We did it at our place," Chuck said. "After your brother yelled at them, I thought it was the only polite thing to do and it was really amazing. It not only confirmed the information I was able to get from police records and the Historical Society, but...it seemed to establish a rapport with them, and I thought...we thought..." Chuck took a deep breath. "We don't have to do this."

Tess looked at the box in Robby's hand. *I don't have to do this. All I have to say is no and they'll take it away. Why not? It's just a game, just a silly game. The dead can't talk to the living...it's only the living who try to talk to them. What am I afraid of? Vince is dead and I know I killed him. Even if he is a ghost what can he do to me now?*

"Will the kitchen table be okay?"

Robby kept the box low when he hugged her. "You sure?"

"Sure she's sure." Chuck was beaming as he took the game out of Robby's hand and carried both it and the cookies into the Keeping Room. "Give me a second to set up."

Tess felt her brother's arm close around her shoulders. "Thank you. He's been like a kid in a candy store ever since we got it as a House Warming present...the gift that keeps on giving, right? It really is silly, but, you know...it seems to work. I guess. Sort of. We stayed up *playing* after the last guest went home and...well, we got a couple answers that were really a little creepy. I Googled some of the references and the information was spot on in most cases. For instance, you know that little girl in the backyard...the one from the train accident...I read a copy of her obituary. Her name really was Abigail."

Tess felt the night breeze whisper past her ear. Beyond the porch, the night looked very dark. She ducked out from under her brother's arm and closed the night out.

"You don't really believe that, do you?" she asked as she turned.

He rolled his eyes. "Yes, and I believe in the Easter Bunny, too. Honey, give your big brother a little credit, will you." Robby glanced toward the kitchen, then stepped toward her, his voice low. "There are a hundred explanations for the answers we got and most of them can probably be traced to one source." He crooked his index finger toward the Keeping Room. "Chuck started researching the history of the property before our bid was even accepted. There's probably not a footnote he hasn't memorized and, even if he thinks he's forgotten it, that information is stuck to the inside of his subconscious like bugs on fly-paper.

"So, take whatever it is we 'find out' tonight about your ghost with a grain of tequila salt. It'll be historically accurate, and I'm not saying we don't have ghosts, but...."

"Ready!"

Robby winked and offered Tess his arm. "Our master's voice, shall we?"

Tess stopped at the threshold and caught her breath. Chuck had turned off the overheads and lit the half-dozen candles she'd placed around the room for decoration. It was lovely...and terrifying. The flames danced in the cool artificial breeze from the vents and the wavering light made Tess feel as if she was underwater.

And turned the Ouija board on the table the color of bone.

"Cookies?" Robby ask as he led her to the table.

Chuck gave him a *look*. "On the counter with the coffee. For later."

"You're mean, you know that?"

Chuck ignored the comment and walked around the table, sitting with his back to the café-curtained window. The empty box sat of the far end of the table.

"Okay kids...get comfortable. Robby, head of the table, please, Tess across from me."

Tess sat down and folded her hands in her lap, looking over the top of Chuck's head to the darkness between the valances and closed lower half. *Why didn't I get full-length curtains?*

"And this," Chuck lifted the box lid and pulled out a manila file folder, "is our proof against whatever may happen tonight. I did a little more research on your ghost, Tess, and it's all right in here. Names, dates...the Historical Society even gave me copies of their daguerreotypes—pictures. His wife was very pretty."

Tess felt the cool air ruffle the back of her hair as she reached for the file.

"No, no. This, like the cookies, comes *after*." Chuck closed the box and laid the file on top. "I already know what's in it, but you don't. And..." He looked at Robby. "...I have very good hearing."

Robby's blush was dark enough to see even in the candlelight. "I didn't mean you cheated or anything, but you know how these things work. The players move the plastic... thingie—"

"Planchette," Chuck corrected.

"Planchette...and I'm not saying you'd move it on purpose, but...."

"But you're right; I do know the answers to probably most of the questions we'll ask tonight. Just like I knew the answers at our place...so it's suspect because, really, that's how this thing works.

"So..."

Chuck pulled a large white handkerchief from his back pocket and held it up, showing them both sides as if he were a magician about to perform a trick.

"I'll keep my eyes closed beneath it," he said, gathering the handkerchief into a serviceable blindfold and tying it around his head. "Now, one of you spin the board so I won't know which end is up."

Robby turned the board so that it faced Tess and winked. Game or not, she suddenly didn't want to play.

"It's getting late; shouldn't we have to cookies first? Or how about some wine?"

"Mm, wine would be nice."

"I'll just go get a bottle." Her chair's legs scraped against the floor at almost the same moment Chuck clapped his hands together and pointed. The gesture, along with the blindfold, made Tess think of Tiresias, the blind seer of Greece.

"Sit." He commanded and she sat. "Afterward. You can't be drunk and commune with the spirit world."

"Says who?" Robby wanted to know. "I've had many a fine commune with spirits…the bottled and bond kind."

Stony silence.

Robby sighed. "Okay, we're going to play this straight… pardon the obvious pun in that. Okay, fingertips resting lightly on the planchette. Here, give me your paws, Chuckles. Come on, T, you've done this before. Lightly, you're not trying to squash a bug."

Tess lifted her hands and hoped Robby would think the trembling was only an optical illusion caused by the shifting candlelight.

"Okay, who wants to go first? Tess."

Question and answer in the same breath. Tess closed her eyes for a moment and tried to remember if *the game* had felt any different when they played it as children. It didn't…it was still scary.

"Okay." Opening her eyes, she looked down at the planchette beneath their fingers, and asked the same first question everyone asks: "Is there anyone here?"

There was a moment of near disappointment when it seemed the weight of her stare was sufficient enough to keep it still, then—slowly—as it always did, the planchette moved under her fingertips, pulling her along. She wasn't doing anything so Robby had to be moving it, since Chuck couldn't see and she was definitely *not* pushing.

The planchette stopped above YES.

Big surprise.

"What'd it say? What'd it say?" Chuck whispered.

"It said Yes," she answered. "But we already knew that would be the answer, right?"

Robby winked at her across the table. "Would have been boring if it hadn't been, but now we have confirmation...so ask something else."

What's your name? always followed the first question, but it almost seemed too personal so she asked and all of them knew he was the ghost of the miller. Frowning, she tried to remember some of the questions her cousins asked.

"Oh, I got one... how many spirits are there?"

Robby was impressed— "Good."—and Tess watched the planchette slide across the glowing board and stop above the wrong number.

"Two?" She shook her head. "That's wrong. The miller's ghost is the only one here."

"No, the miller's ghost is the only one we know of," Chuck said softly. "This could be his wife or child, although if you haven't heard what sounds like a baby crying, I think it's more likely to be his wife...or maybe it's the spirit of a Lenape warrior..."

The thought that there was another ghost in the millhouse had never occurred to her...why should it? Robby had only mentioned the miller's ghost and he was the only one she ever spoke to, but if there was another...a second pair of eyes that followed her every move...

Tess hunched forward as the skin across her belly tightened.

"Can I ask a question?"

Tess nodded before she remembered Chuck couldn't see her. "Sure."

"Okay..." There was the slightest hint of a smile on his lips. *He's enjoying this.* Tess looked at her brother. *They both are.* "Are you the miller?"

The planchette moved quickly across the board. NO

"No," Robby echoed.

"The plot thickens." Chuck licked his lips. "Are you of this house? The miller's wife?"

The planchette shifted slightly to the left, then returned to its original spot.

"No."

"I got one," Robby said. "Were you a man or woman?"

"Just like you to ask that," Chuck mumbled under his breath.

There was no hesitation in the answer. The planchette moved so quickly Tess felt her fingers almost slip off. It moved twice—pausing briefly on the I before stopping over the M.

"I. M?" Chuck asked after Robby called out the letters. His forehead wrinkled above his closed eyes. "Imo?"

"No, it's not a name." Robby's voice dropped softer than a whisper. "He's using present tense. *I am...male?*"

The planchette shot across the board. YES

"Whoa...that was interesting."

"What happened?"

While Robby explained to Chuck, Tess felt a chill settle across her shoulders as if someone sitting next to her had put their—*his*—arm around her. *He's here.*

"Okay, then I'll ask," Robby said. "Who are you?"

The chill around Tess' shoulders deepened as Robby leaned closer to the board, his shadow from the candlelight rippling against the curtains.

Vince hated candlelight.

"What are you hiding, huh? Did my little wife do something she doesn't want me to see? Turn on some fucking lights and show me, bitch!"

She was on her feet and moving toward the light switch before she realized what she was doing.

"Tess?"

Tess turned in anticipation for a blow that never came. Chuck had pulled off his blindfold and both he and Robby were staring at her.

"Honey...are you okay?"

"I—I just thought...." She looked at the switch beneath her fingers and let her hand drop. "I don't know what... Sorry."

"No problem." Robby leaned over and patted the chair she'd just left. "Come back and join the fun. Chuck, blindfold back on please—" When Tess sat down he turned the board 90°. "Okay, fingertips down Now, were was I? Oh, yeah—ghost...if you're not the miller *or* his wife...who are you?"

The planchette didn't move. And, a minute later, when it still hadn't moved, Chuck cleared his throat.

"Ask something else and we'll come back to that. Sometimes, they're a little shy. Why don't you ask something Tess."

"Maybe later."

"Okay, I'll go. If you aren't the miller, or a member of his family, did you die in the millhouse?"

Tess' stomach did backflips. "God, Robby!"

"Shh. Is that why you haunt this place."

The planchette moved forward an inch and backed up. NO.

"You don't have to tell me," Chuck whispered. "I felt that. So, why do you haunt this place?"

T

"T...trauma? Terror? Toothache?"

"SHH!"

The planchette gathered speed, pausing only a second or two above each letter before moving to the next.

"E. S. Tes...Tess? You're here for Tess?"

YES

"Looks like you have a secret admirer, baby."

Tess stared at her brother. "Robby, did you do that? I won't be angry."

"No, I didn't but..." The planchette suddenly shifted beneath their fingers and began to move.

P. R. O. T. E. C. T.

"Protect?" Chuck asked. "You're here to protect Tess?"

YES

"From what?"

T.H. E. O. T. H. E. R.

Chuck pulled off the blindfold after Robby read off the letters and winked at Tess. "See, what did I tell you.? All right, ghost, who are you protecting Tess from? The miller's ghost?"

The planchette shot across the board—NO—at the same moment Tess answered. "No. He...the miller's ghost has never tried to hurt me."

"Then who are we talking about?"

T. H. E. O. T. H. E. R.

Robby kept his fingers on the planchette, but sat back in his chair. "I don't know about the two of you, but I'm confused. Okay...who are we talking to right now—the miller or the new entity?"

Tess could feel a tiny vibration beneath her fingers as the planchette shifted under them; first to the left, then right, and left again like a miniature tug-of-war before it broke free.

M.I.L.

"The miller?"

YES

"Okay." Robby motioned for Chuck put the blindfold back on. "So we're talking to the miller's ghost now, great. And you're protecting Tess."

YES

See, Tess wanted to say, *I told you he wouldn't hurt me.*

"From the other one?"

YES

"Do you know this other entity? Does it belong here?"

YES   NO

"What'd he say?" Chuck asked.

"Yes, he knows it," Robby translated, "no, it doesn't belong here?"

YES

Robby looked up at Tess. "I'm impressed. I like your ghost."

So do I.

"All right. If the other doesn't belong here, how did it get here?"

C. A. L. L. E. D.

"Who called it?"

. . .

"Guess he doesn't know."

Tess leaned forward. "Ask who the other one is."

"You just did, baby."

But the planchette didn't move.

"Do you know this other entity?" Chuck asked.

YES

"Then who is it?"

. . .

Robby looked at Tess. "Is he always this stubborn?"

He'd asked the question the way someone would ask a wife about her husband. And it sounded very natural.

"He can be," Tess said. "A little sometimes."

The planchette did another little jump and return. YES

"Well, at least he has a sense of humor. Let's go back to the second question. If you are the miller tell us your name. "

M. A. T. H. E. R. S.

"Mathers?"

"Yes!" Chuck's grin stretched from ear to ear. "And your first name?"

The planchette slid across the board and off the edge.

"Now he's just being cute. Tess, you ask him."

"Me?"

Robby moved the planchette back to the center of the board. "He's probably more comfortable with you."

"Do you know his name?" Tess asked and while Robby shook his head, Chuck gleefully bobbed his up and down.

"Oh, yeah. It's in the file…along with a facsimile of the statement of death. So, it's all right, Mathers…you don't have to hide anything."

…

Robby pushed the planchette back to the center of the board. "Go on, Tess, let's get acquainted."

The chill ran down her arms into her fingers. *He doesn't want me to do this.* "Tell us your name."

NO

"Why not?"

…

"Look, Mathers," Chuck said softly, "it's not a secret. I know your name and if you won't tell, I will."

"Hard ball," Robby whispered as the planchette slowly began to move, then began calling out the letters, one by one. "T. H. O. M. A. S. We got a Thomas."

Tess pulled her hands away. *Thomas?*

"Bingo." Chuck pulled the blindfold into a headband and nodded at the board. "Now *that* was pretty amazing. Unless Robby went on line and did he own research—"

Robby crossed his heart and held up his right hand. "Never."

"—then I was the only one here who knew the miller's name was Thomas Mathers. I'll show you the papers in a minute, but if you want more proof we can ask the name of his wife and—"

Tess stopped listening.

It was a coincidence. Thomas was a common name—she'd known a number of Toms, Tommys, Thomases growing up. She knew a Thomas now who worked for the Parks Department as a costumed docent. Oh God. *He knows so much about the millhouse...he's a good actor. His name might not even be Thomas...that might only be a part of the character...to keep the tourists happy...*

"Thomas," she whispered and the planchette moved under their hands. YES

Chuck smiled at her. "See, he does like you better than your crotchety older brother."

Robby blew him a juicy raspberry.

Tess looked at the file folder on the top of the box. "Show me his pictures."

"What?" Robby asked. "Now? Don't you want to wait until we have more—"

Chuck picked up the file and opened it across the top of the Ouija Board. The planchette still resting above the YES.

"The quality of the photos is pretty good," Chuck said as he pushed it toward her, "But if you'd like to see the originals they're over at the Historical Society headquarters. I'll give you the name of the curator, any time you want to come by—"

He was still talking, Tess could hear him but the words floated on the air as insubstantial and meaningless as candle smoke. The top pictures was an exterior shot of the back of the mill with the name and date inscribed in a flowing hand, white lettering against the dark, in the lower right-hand corner.

Mathers Mill (originally More Hope Mill) from Wissahickon Stream—circa 1800

She went through the rest of the photos quickly, the faces looking out from the glossy finish unfamiliar—

Victoria Whitney, age ten, copy of oil on canvas—1874

Victoria (Whitney) Mathers, wedding photo—May 18, 1870

Chuck was right, she was pretty.

Samuel Whitney Mathers, Memento Mori—8ᵗʰ November, 1883
—except one, the last:
Thomas Mathers—circa 1870

The picture showed a young man, barely out of his twenties, dressed in a stiff-collared white shirt and dark waistcoat staring grimly at the camera. A young man forced to have his picture taken against his will. A young man who would age and eventually lose his wife and child and life a hundred plus years before she was born.

A young man who would become a ghost.

Thomas.

Tess shook her head. "It's not possible."

A hand touched her shoulder, but she didn't jump.

"What's not possible?"

"I just…" Tess shook her head and picked up the baby's photo. If she hadn't known what she was looking at, the image could have been a doll, a sad little doll. There were shadows gathered in the sunken eyes and hollow cheeks…and one tiny fist was curled tight against the stiff linen ruff of its christening gown. *No wonder he killed himself…* "Nothing."

Tess closed the folder and handed it back.

"I should have taken that one out, I'm sorry." Chuck put the folder into the box where she couldn't see it. "It's getting late, maybe we should stop and have the cookies before they dry out. Nothing worse than a dried out prune kolache."

"You bought prune? You know I like the apricot and sesame seed better."

"I have those, too."

"Robby…"

They were looking at each other, not her and not at the board.

"I'm only joking, T, the prune isn't bad…as long as you think of them as plum. But how 'bout we ask a few more questions."

"It's getting late."

"Yeah, I know...and I know you have a walk-through at 8:30, but come on—"

"Robby...look..."

"Hang on a minute, sweetie." He gave her a quick look, and then turned back to his partner. "There's a whole lot more going on here than just a simple haunting."

"Oh, *now* you believe."

Robby. Chuck?"

"Minute... Whether I do or not doesn't matter right now, we have proof...something I've very big on having...that the miller's ghost is not only haunting this place but feels it needs to protect my sister. I want to find out who this other one is, don't—"

"Look at the board!"

Tess had thought it was just a trick of the candlelight, or her eyes, but when she heard the sharp intake of breath; she knew she hadn't imagined it...that it wasn't an illusion. While the three of them watched, the planchette slowly moved across the board by itself.

"Jesus."

The candles drew in their light as the room grew colder.

"Chuck, do you see it, too?"

"Uh-huh."

"What's it spelling?"

Tess already knew, she'd been watching the planchette move while they'd been arguing...repeating the same pattern over and over and over again. Up—across left and down—up to the right—over two to the left—down right— Up and across to the left, then down again and up to the right; over two, down...up...across...up—

"I," Robby whispered.

Across to the left and down.

"N."

Up to the right.

"C."

Two over to the left. E, then left and down.

"Oh God." Robby looked at her, then down at the board where pattern had started again. "This can't be happening."

"Vince," Chuck said, "it's spelling out Vince's name."

Something moved past the window behind Chuck, a shape without form, like a shadow crossing the moon. Neither her brother nor his partner saw it, their attention was still held by the board, but it didn't matter...she was the only one who was supposed to see it. And she did. And knew exactly what it was.

"Jesus Christ, I—"

A sound—indistinct, directionless—buffeted against their ears and every candle went out as if a wind had suddenly swept into the room. Robby and Chuck were both on their feet, shouting, telling her and themselves everything was okay, don't panic.

But she wasn't afraid, Vince always liked scaring people.

Robby came around the table, kneeling next to her chair, as Chuck turned on the overhead light. The room was so bright it hurt her eyes and made them water.

"Tess."

The light had turned the window into a mirror, reflecting the ceiling, but she knew the shadow was still there—watching—she knew he was there.

Vince.

"Tess? Please, baby, look at me." Robby exhaled loudly and sat back on his heels when she finally turned toward him. "There's got to be a logical explanation for what just happened. Okay?"

Tess shook her head.

"I tried to tell you, Robby," she whispered. "He's here."
**

Vince felt the vibrations of the millrace through the soles of his feet as he watched their shadows dance across the curtains. He was probably too close to the water, but he couldn't make himself back away. Something had happened that he didn't understand.

He'd seen Robby and Co. walking up the path and shadowed them from the opposite side of the race; stopping when they crossed the footbridge and watching from the trees as Tess opened the door.

Maybe it was just the fact that she was alive—for the moment—but he didn't remember her ever looking that good before. *My little wifey.*

After the door closed, Vince stayed in the shadows, hunkering down so he wouldn't be seen...until he remembered that no longer was a problem. If Tess had gotten a dog, then he might have been worried, but since that wasn't the case, he stood up and strode down the middle of the path like he was the King of Bohemia.

The millrace was still a bit high, but the footbridge looked a mile wide—sturdy and whole—and Vince stepped on it with confidence and...

He was standing in a candlelit room *(what are you trying to hide, bitch?),* at the kitchen table he'd bought her... answering questions?

What the fuck?

The three of them, Robby, his partner *(what's with the blindfold?)* and Tess were huddled around some stupid board game.

"Oh God. This can't be happening."

"Vince, it's spelling out Vince's name."

And then he was back outside, staggering back from the footbridge and staring at the man who slowly walked down the porch steps toward him.

Tess' boyfriend.

Vince wasn't exactly sure what happened, but he had a pretty good idea the guy was responsible for whatever had gone down. Ghost or not, the guy could apparently see him, so Vince decided not to waste the opportunity and shot him the bird.

The man reached the opposite end of the footbridge and stopped.

"You're not wanted here."

"I'm not?" Vince folded his arms across his chest, a gesture that had never failed to impress...or intimidate. "Funny, I could have sworn I heard my name mentioned. She wants me."

The man shook his head. "She doesn't know what she wants."

"Oh, yeah?" Vince didn't like the way the man talked about Tess, *his wife*...his stupid, murderous bitch of a wife. "You're full of shit, pal. I belong here. With her."

"No," the man said. "You belong in Hell. With me."

Vince never saw him move.

One second he was on the opposite side of the bridge, the next...the very next the man's hands were around Vince's throat and he was staring into his own face twisted with rage, his own voice screaming in his ears.

"Bitch!" "Goddamned cunt!" "What are you trying to hide?" "Think I'm stupid?" "Think I'm weak?" "Brainless...stupid... bitch...mine, you're mine...Goddamned bitchcuntwifey...

Images of his face and echoes of his voice filled his head, overlapping one another as the hands...*his* hands tightened around his throat.

"*This* is what she remembers—" Another voice cut into his brain like a knife. "This is what you did to her."

"Vince, please." "Vince, don't." "Vince!"

Then a different knife flashed and it was her face he saw, sprayed with blood as he fell to his knees.

When Vince finally looked up the man was gone.

CHAPTER 15
JUNE 27th – Morning

I go to join them…
Last journal entry of Thomas Mathers
November 19, 1886

The pictures sat in a neat row on the table in front of her, the morning light infusing the sepia-toned images with a soft rosy tint.

They ate the cookies and drank the coffee and put the game away and never said a word about it—about the planchette moving by itself or the name it had spelled out. It was almost as if, somehow, they'd silently agreed that it couldn't have happened, so there was no point in mentioning it.

If it hadn't been for the folder she'd taken out of the box, Tess might have believed that.

But here they were…proof that at least *something* had happened.

Tess continued stirring creamer into her coffee even though it had gone cold. She wasn't really interested in drinking it—it was only a quarter after six and her stomach was complaining about the three cups she'd already had. It was just something to do, a sound to cover the sound of Robby's snores from upstairs.

He'd stayed the night when she refused to leave. For no reason…since nothing had happened.

Just to keep her company, he said. So she wouldn't be alone.

With the ghost.

With Thomas.

Tess stopped stirring and pushed the mug to one side. Elbows on table, she leaned forward and stared down at his picture.

"Why didn't you tell me?"

A soft chill brushed through her hair.

He's here.

"It is you, isn't it?"

**

He moved his hand away from her hair, but kept looking over her shoulder at the photographic images before her. It'd been so long a time he'd almost forgotten how beautiful Victoria was and it shamed him to acknowledge that he *had* forgotten what their son looked like...and how much of his mother there was in the delicate features.

Forgive me, Samuel.

"It is you, isn't it?"

He stepped back when she lifted her head.

"I know you're there, Thomas."

His first thought was to scatter himself to the air or melt into the grains of wood, and become nothing, but he didn't move.

"Why don't you answer me?" She kept her back to him, but picked up the image of himself that his father had pressured him to sit for—*'It's what gentlemen of quality do, boy, and you're as good as any o'em.'*. "It's a little late to pretend you're not there, Thomas.

"Please...say something."

It was a plea, edged with madness...an echo of Victoria's voice that last day—

"Say something."

"What? What am I to say? Oh God. Why, just tell me why."

"Why are you crying, Thomas? He's happy now, our little one. He wasn't happy here you know that…you heard him cry. He cried all the time."

"Babies cry, Victoria."

"Only unhappy babies, don't you know that? You understand… please, tell me you understand."

"I— Yes, I understand. Now please, come to bed. You need your rest."

Smiling, she handed him their son, the marks of her hand still on his throat.

"See how peaceful he is now?"

"Yes."

Her eyes were so bright when she looked at him. "He wasn't happy here. He wanted to go back to God."

And she started to laugh as a child laughs at Christmas-tide and he wanted to strike her down, to wring the life out of her as she had their child…but it was all he could do to stand and hold his son's cold, limp body against his beating heart.

When the women came to comfort and sit watch that night, he had already washed and dressed the tiny body in what would have been his christening robes. He wouldn't let the women touch Samuel, lease they see the marks, and they accepted that as part of his grief, the same way they accepted the laughter as part of hers.

He kept her secret, and still she laughed until the sound became as constant as the autumn's wind in the rafters of the mill. The mourners who'd come back to the millhouse with offerings of food and comfort had fled before it, crossing themselves in their hurry to escape what they thought was only grief madness.

She slept through the day he buried their son and woke singing, and he thought she'd forgotten her crime and cursed God for letting him be the only one to remember. For two days she sang and he hated them both—her and God—then the millhouse went silent.

He found her slumped over the empty cradle, a smile on her black-tinted lips and the bottle of poison still clutched in her hand…

He kept that secret, too, so she could be buried next to their son in hollowed ground. How the Fates must have laughed at the irony when they came and found him.

"Please, Thomas."

"I'm here."

"Oh God." Her back went rigid. "Why didn't you tell me the truth?"

"Would you have believed me?"

She turned so slowly the dust motes riding the morning light barely stirred in her wake. Had she screamed or run or damned his soul as others had, it might have been easier for both of them. But she just sat there, staring at him.

"No," she said, "I wouldn't have."

"Tess..."

He foolishly reached for her and she started, got up from the table as clumsily as a newborn foal and stumbled back, away from him; a half-strangled moan rushing past her lips. There was resignation in the sound, like that of a trapped animal as the hunter approaches.

Thomas let his arm fall to his side.

"Am I so much changed, Tess?"

"Yes." Then she shook her head. "No. I don't know. You can't be a... Prove it. Dematerialize or something."

He laughed because no one, not once in all the years he'd been bound to the earth, had ever asked that of him: to prove himself a ghost.

Her eyes were glistening when he stopped.

"I'm sorry. Forgive me."

She pulled the loose-fitting robe tighter across her breasts and he looked away. Had he been able, Thomas would have blushed for all the times he had not...but that was yet another sin he could not bring himself to ask forgiveness for.

"This is hard." She took a deep breath, shaking her head. "I can't... You're not just some crazy man in a costume who broke into my house, are you?"

Thomas smiled. "No. If I take off my head and carry it under my arm, will that be enough proof?"

She went pale and he was immediately sorry for the jest. "You can do that?"

"No, but I can give you the answer to a question you once asked."

"A question?"

"You asked me if I thought God would forgive you for killing your husband." He moved slowly, closing the distance between them. "The answer is yes, I'm sure He will."

Her eyes went big for a moment, but only a moment, then her eyes cleared and she nodded.

"You really are a ghost."

"Yes."

"T?"

The call echoed down the stairs and she looked past him, toward. "That's my brother. He stayed here last night after— But you probably know that."

"Yes."

"He'll freak when he sees...."

"Don't worry." Thomas walked toward the shadows clinging to the side of the hearth. "He won't see me."

The hollow thud of his feet on the stairs stopped. "Tess?

"I'm in the kitchen, Robby."

She looked at him once more—and smiled, the fear gone from her face—before hurrying to pour out another mug of coffee. Thomas melted into the stone as her brother clumped into the room.

Her brother had the look of a man who'd slept little and badly, as Thomas could attest. He'd watched the man throughout the night wrench himself from sleep to tiptoe across the narrow hallway and listen at her door. He looked older, haggard, his eyes red-rimmed and half closed. His body, limp beneath the wrinkled clothes he never bothered to remove, seemed to move only with the greatest effort and collapsed into itself when he sat down at the table.

Thomas watched as she placed the steaming mug down in front of him and began to gather up the images of his long dead family. Her brother frowned. "Please don't tell me you've been up for hours looking at those things."

"No," she lied. "Not hours."

Her brother turned, squinting at the room's timepiece for a moment before giving up.

"So, who were you talking to when I came in?" He pulled the mug closer but didn't raise it to his lips. "The ghost?"

"Yes, Thomas."

Her brother took another sip and shook like a dog stripping its coat of water. "God...how strong did you make this stuff? Okay, it did its job. One sip and I'm wide awake. Tess, about last night...."

But she shook her head and both of them seemed relieved when he nodded.

"Well, as much as I'd love to stick around all day, I've got a couple major projects in Lancaster that need my personal touch. Want to come with me? We can find one of those 'All You Can Eat" Amish places and gorge ourselves silly on Shoofly pie."

She carried both their mugs to the sink, shaking her head. "Can't. I work, too, you know."

"I'm serious. Take the day off and come with me."

"No, but bring me back some apple butter."

"Tess—"

From his place within the stones, Thomas watched as if what was happening before him were a simple mummery. Her brother standing at the doorway; Tess with her back to the room, continuing to wash long after the mugs were clean. It was a sad little play at best, but one that worked.

Her brother shook his head and walked to the front door, shouting back for her to hear. "Okay, have fun, working girl. I'll give you a call when I get back. Shouldn't be later than seven or eight. Come up to the house and we'll have drinks."

If she answered at all it was even too soft for Thomas to hear.

**

When the front door slammed shut, Tess felt the vibrations through her feet. They'd done a wonderful job renovating, but the millhouse still had its quirks. It felt every disturbance no matter how small. A shift in the wind's direction and the eaves in the attic hummed softly. A door closing anywhere and the floorboards trembled. And when the ghost walked at night... *Thomas*...the density of the air changed.

Like now.

Tess turned off the faucets and wiped her hands. "Are you still here?"

"Yes."

When she turned around Thomas was standing in front of the fireplace looking back at her.

"Can't you leave?"

His body began to fade as she watched. "Of course, I'm sorry. You'd rather be alone."

"No, that's not what I meant."

Vince had trained her too well...that was the only reason she ran to him, her hand extended. It was always the same thing—he'd apologize, for something small, and pretend to leave and *know* that she'd run after him, begging him not to go. She hadn't even stopped to think who or what or where—she ran and reached for his arm....

And watched her hand move through the patch of cold air that was his arm. Her fingers felt numb but she didn't scream and she didn't back away.

He looked more embarrassed than anything else. "I didn't know you were going to touch me or I would have... I'm sorry. I'll leave you now."

"No, please. I don't want you to go." Tess slipped her hands into the robe's pockets as if it was the most natural thing in the world, to be standing in the kitchen of her home, taking to its previous and long dead occupant. "What I said before, I just meant…I was wondering if you could stop haunting?"

"I don't know."

He turned and walked to the back window overlooking the Wissahickon.

"My wife believed there to be a Heaven and a God who could be merciful in the forgiveness of all sins, but I could not believe or accept such a…fancy after—after they died." He reached out and drew a line through the condensation on the glass. When he lifted his finger, the bead of water continued down the glass. "I still can't. After their deaths I imagined I heard her and the child, here, in the mill, and I cursed God for tormenting me. If you believe is such things, I damned my soul long before I placed the rope around my neck."

"Oh, Thomas."

He shook his head. "No, no pity. My faith at the moment was only the belief that my death, by my own hand, would be the only way we could be together. Not in Heaven, certainly, but at least Hell."

He laughed softly and Tess bit her lip to keep from crying.

"I was wrong. Perhaps she was right…perhaps eternal belief is more powerful than mortal sin, and if the Almighty can hear me, I pray that it's so." Thomas turned around and his eyes fell on everything but her. "She's not here. Victoria and the child don't haunt. They went home to God as she believed she would."

His eyes flickered toward her and moved on. "And I am where I belong. By your leave."

Tess held onto the mantle as he walked across the room, fading for an instant as he crossed a patch of morning sunlight that streamed in through the front window. When he reached the entrance hall he stopped; his back still to her.

"Would you do something for me?" he asked.

"If I can."

"Don't leave the house today."

"Why?"

"There's another storm building to the north and the creek's already high. You don't want to get caught out if there's a surge. It won't take much this time for the water to rise. It was the same when the mill was taken." Nodding, he walked into the hall. "You'll be safe. Stay here."

There were no creaks from the floorboards or the sound of the door opening and closing, but Tess knew he was gone.

She hadn't planned on leaving the millhouse, hadn't even thought about it. If the 10:00 News weatherman was even partially right, it was supposed to be hot and humid and horrible...the only sane thing to do was stay inside and crank the AC down to 65.

But a sane woman doesn't talk to ghosts...or get angry with one.

Or kill her husband.

Tess walked to the front door and locked it. *Don't leave the house today.*

Stay here. It hadn't been a request, not even a question—it was an order. He *told* her what she was going to do and left with the full and certain knowledge that she'd do exactly that.

Just like Vince.

**

Being dead was really starting to piss him off.

It wasn't all *that* different from being alive but the rules had changed and no one had given him a playbook to study.

He must have spent the entire night standing there at the footbridge...because that's where he was when the sun came up. And he didn't remember falling asleep.

"What do you plan on doing with that? Kill me? Is that it? Is that what my little wifey wants to do? Kill me? Well come on then, take your shot. Come on.... COME ON!"

Okay, so maybe he did fall asleep.

A flicker of movement caught his eye and he bent down for a closer look. A small golden moth, the kind he used to catch and feed to his cat when he was a kid, was playing a solitary game of hopscotch across a stand of dandelions without a care in the world. She was like that—small and fragile and mindlessly going about her business as if nothing else existed.

He reached out and the moth fluttered through his hand as if it wasn't there.

"It was my fault." If he was going to be honest with himself—and being dead didn't give him the right to go back on his principles—then he had to admit it, even if the only thing that heard him was an insect. "I taught her too well. When I said jump, she jumped." *Well come on, then, take your shot. Come on…. COME ON!* "She just wasn't smart enough to think for herself, that's all. I bet she's really sorry for what she did."

He reached for the moth again and this time his solid flesh closed over it. He could feel its wings beat against his palm—so soft, so frantic—an instant before he crushed it.

"Yeah, real sorry."

Vince wiped the remains of the moth off on his pants as he stood up. The curtains in the upper left-hand window parted and she looked out.

Not at him, just out into the morning.

His little wifey was wrapped in a towel, her hair tangled in wet strands around her face. He loved it when she just stepped out of the shower—all warm and pink and smelling of Ivory soap, her back dotted with water for him to dry. That'd been a lover's game between them—to finish drying her off before he got her wet again.

He could still remember the feel of her body opening to him, the smell of her skin.

Vince raised his hand—*I'm here, I'm back*—but she turned and walked back into the dark room before he could get her attention. *Bitch, didn't even look.* And then he saw why.

A moment before the rising sun mirrored the glass into a mirror, the man took her place at the window and smiled down at Vince, touching two fingers to his forehead in a condescending salute.

So sorry, pal, the gesture said. *You can go away now.*

Yeah, they were both sorry…but not sorry enough.

Smiling, Vince took a step forward—

CHAPTER 16
JUNE 27th — Afternoon

Time had gotten away from her again, but she was too tired to chase it. If time wanted her, it could come back and find her. Right here, right now…no waiting.

Her original plan, to storm out of the millhouse as soon as she showered, had gotten waylaid. First, she managed to shave off a quarter inch of skin from her left anklebone, which required wrapping toilet paper around her foot while she hunted for the box of bandages which had *somehow* fallen out of the medicine cabinet into the hamper. Then, the computer developed a problem. A real one. Then the office called and… Robby called and…time went away for a while.

When she finally noticed the change in the light coming in through the windows, she was standing at the kitchen window with a glass of iced coffee in her hand and it was 1:45 in the afternoon.

The next time she looked up, it was half-past three and she made sure the back door slammed shut behind her as she left.

Seated on a gnarled coil of exposed root, Tess leaned back against the Sycamore and watched the sunbeams try to pierce the mist that hung in the air, suspended like a curtain between earth and sky. Occasionally the sun would break through the haze and leaves and the pile of stones would be illuminated. Then the muggy, sluggish wind would shift and the light would blink out.

Wiping the back of her hand across her forehead, she closed her eyes and just listened. Everything, from the slow rustle of leaves and droning buzz of insects to the soft, measured drops of moisture falling from the trees in a warm, mock rain, had a muffled quality to it. It could have been peaceful if it hadn't been so hot.

God it was hot.

Leaving the comforts of the millhouse and its steadily regulated 72-wonderfully dehumidified-degrees had been a mistake. Leaving because a ghost made her angry was a *bigger* mistake. And, leaving even after she saw that the stream was flooded, went so far beyond a mere mistake that it probably required an entirely new term for "error in judgment."

That—watching trees, pieces of cut firewood, water bottles, numerous toys and even a car tire go bobbing by—had almost made her change her mind. Knowing there was no easy way across—the broken dam was probably a good few feet underwater and the hollow tree was just a bit too far to walk in the heat—*should* have changed her mind.

If her car hadn't had air-conditioning, she would have changed her mind. Would have, could have, should have.

But here she was, at Thomas' grave.

Something small and multi-legged crawled across Tess' knee and she kicked it away without opening her eyes. Anything dangerous, like a spider or hornet, would have already bitten her and anything that wasn't dangerous would forgive her. Either way, she didn't care...because it finally all made sense.

It wasn't time she'd lost, it was her mind.

Maybe she wasn't pathologically insane—and she might even get better...one day—but if she crazy enough to kill her husband but forget that fact, then she was certainly crazy enough to conjure up a ghost.

Or two.

There was no Thomas except for what lay under the pile of stones in front of her: bones and dust and stories to tell gullible tourists and amateur historians. Not that she hadn't made up quite a nice little story herself...one perfect for light summer reading: murderess suffering from convenient bouts of amnesia moves into a haunted millhouse—

No. She moves into a millhouse her brother tells her is haunted.

—where the tormented ghost of the miller still walks and where, as in every good Supernatural-Romance, they—ghost and pathetic, lonely heroine—fall hopelessly and helpless in unrequitable love.

By page 209.

A perfect guilty pleasure, as long as you don't let your friends see you reading it.

But not so good in real life.

Tess opened her eyes and watched a large carpenter ant march across the top of the tombstone.

LOST

How appropriate—for *all* of them...her two ghosts, Thomas and Vince, and herself.

A drop of moisture hit her right shoulder and tickled down her arm, feeling like the caress of a fingertip against her skin. If she hadn't watched it slide that's probably what she would have imagined it to be...that Thomas—or Vince—had touched her to let her know he was there.

Poor Vince, he'd always known she was crazy. That's why he'd been so hard on her—*Oh God, I'm sorry*—he'd been trying to make her better—*so sorry*—to make her behave like normal people. *He loved me.*

He'd loved me from the start...

**

"I can't believe you, you know that. I really can't. I thought you wanted me as much as I wanted you, but... Shit, what are you, some kind of a Goddamn cock-tease?"

Tess had never seen anyone get that angry and it frightened her. He moved through the small, cluttered dorm room like a tornado—scattering books, clothes and papers into the air. Naked, his body still glistening with sweat, he alternately swung at the air or slapped his chest leaving red marks shaped like his hands…that matched the ones he'd left on her upper thighs when he pried her legs apart.

"You…you…"

"What?" He swiped at a squat beige dresser identical to the one in her dorm room and knocked off a bottle of *Old Spice* after-shave. It shattered against the edge of the built-in closet and the familiar scent Tess had always associated with her father filled the air. This time the smell almost made her sick. "Look what you made me do?"

She pressed her back against the wall when he charged across the room.

"I said *look* what you made me do!" He grabbed her chin and wrenched her head to the side. "That was a gift from my grandmother. She's not rich, you know…she wasn't lucky enough to have rich parents who left her an inheritance."

Tess wanted to tell him she didn't have an inheritance, that her parents—what she remembered of them besides the scent of her father's cologne—were regular people with regular jobs who died too soon…but the rage on his face made her shrink back.

"I—I'll buy you another."

He slammed her back against the wall.

"Jesus, you rich bitches are all the same. You think you can buy your way out of anything."

He raised his hand and its shadow fell across her face. "No…please."

The shadow fell away, trailing over her body as he backed up. He sat down on his roommate's bed opposite her. For a moment he glared at her; then he leaned forward over his splayed knees and shook his head.

"Why don't you just get dressed and go, okay? I mean, I thought we had something special."

He sighed and Tess felt a different kind of pain. Moving slowly so the other pain, the one that radiated outward from between her legs, didn't get any worse, she crawled to the edge of the mattress and carefully lowered her feet to the floor. He must have been watching because he suddenly leaned back away from her.

"Why are you doing that? I didn't hurt you."

Tess couldn't say anything for a moment. "You did, Vince, you hurt me."

He waved her comment away and looked toward the blinds covering the window. It was only four in the afternoon and they were in his ground-floor room...if he'd left them open like he wanted to, anyone walking past would have been able to look in and see him raping her.

"Vince?"

He kept his face turned away from her. "I *love* you and I thought you loved me. How the hell can you say I hurt you?"

Tess bent forward, readying herself to stand, when she felt a warm oozing sensation between her legs and looked down to see bright red blood staining the inside of her thighs and sheet. Her first thought was that her period had come two weeks early and she clamped her legs together.

"Don't worry about it. Here."

Tess looked up—mortified, embarrassed, wanting to die— as Vince threw her a threadbare *Eagles* towel and watched while she wiped the blood off her legs.

"You know, I would have been easier on you if you'd said you were a virgin. But, hell, a lot of girls say they are, nowadays, you know. Just stick it under you and I'll wash it with the sheet. There won't be much; there never is the first time."

Tess wanted to ask *how* he knew that but didn't want to know the answer. After putting the towel between her and the mattress, she pulled her clothes toward her with her feet. Her T-shirt and bra were okay, but the zipper was broken in her jeans and her panties were a total loss. He'd torn them off her as if they'd been made of paper.

She slid the shirt on over her head and used it to cover herself while she snapped her bra in place. Wadding the panties into the back pocket of her jeans, Tess stood up and waited for him to turn away so she could finish dressing with some privacy.

He didn't move and she felt her legs start to tremble.

"I—I have to go."

"Tess." He got to his feet and stood between her and the door. "I don't want this to end. I don't want us to end. I love you."

"Vince, you raped me."

"I did not!" He moved so quickly Tess didn't have a chance to back away or scream; all she could do was stand there and let his fingers dig into her arms. "I did *not* rape you. *We* made love, that's all."

That's all?

"And if you can't tell the difference you're crazy."

"I'm not...Vince you—"

He shook her until her head snapped backwards and forward like a rag doll's, then held her out at arm's length.

"If you say that again I swear to God I'll kill you. Do you understand me?"

"Y-yes."

"And it wasn't rape, was it?"

"No."

Vince smiled and Tess remembered why she went out with him. When he smiled he looked like a little boy—all dimples and curls. Harmless, like he wouldn't hurt a fly.

"Okay, then. Okay." He pulled her to him. "See, I'm only worrying about you, baby... You go around telling people I raped you and they'll put you in a loony bin. I don't have to rape anyone to get what I want...I wanted you, Tess, and that's why we made love. We made love because you wanted it as much as I did. Right? That's right, isn't it?"

Tess nodded against his chest as he pushed her back toward the bed.

"That's my baby. See, you just got scared, that's all, and I understand that. It's hard for a girl, the first time...especially with a guy as big as I am down there, but it'll get better, you'll see."

IIe pulled the sheet out of her hands and pushed her down on top of the bloodstained towel, then climb on top of her.

"Just relax. Come on, open your legs...that's right, wider. Relax, I said, you're just making it worse. Shit!' He punched the pillow next to Tess' head and she went limp. "Yeah, like that...that's right. Oh, yeah...that's good, isn't it? You like that, don't you, baby?"

They both screamed when he came.

"Don't worry, baby," he panted, "I'll teach you everything you need to know. Now kiss me and say you're sorry."
**

Tess crossed her arms over the top of her knees and buried her face against them and wished time would leave for good.

"I'm sorry, Vince."

**

—and jerked back from a large and hairy-legged gold-and-black spider hanging less than an inch in front of his nose.

"Jesus!"

It wasn't that he was afraid, hell, he liked spiders, but it was just so sudden. Anyone would have reacted the same way....especially if it shouldn't have been there.

Vince stopped backtracking and the spider, along with most of the surrounding landscape, became vague and unrecognizable shapes that seemed to drift in and out of the mist that surrounded him.

Where the fuck am I?

The mist made it impossible to tell where he was, but Vince knew for sure he was nowhere near the millhouse...which he should have been...just about to step across the footbridge and pay his little wifey *(widow)* an unexpected 'howdy-do.'

But now here he was—

He heard the sound of water, just a trickle somewhere out in the mist, just enough to pucker up the old sphincter, and knew *exactly* where he was.

—out in the middle of the fucking woods.

Again.

Vince kicked at the closest recognizable thing—a moss-covered rock—and watched his foot sail through without the slightest hesitation.

Shit.

The question, now, was why.

And God gave him the answer.

"—sorry, Vince."

If he smiled any wider Vince thought his face would tear in half.

She's here.

Something like a chill moved through his body and he had to grab a nearby branch to keep from falling. *She's here.* Vince tightened his grip on the branch, moving his hand slowly back and forth against the rough bark. *She's here. Goddamn, I can't believe it. What's the chance…?*

A piece of the bark fell to the ground.

I'm back.

But when he tightened his hand again, Vince watched his fingers pass through the branch without resistance.

No! What the fuck?

He tried again and again his hand moved through the branch as if it were air. Whatever had made him solid and whole had gone just as quickly as it had—

"I'm so sorry, Vince."

Tess. His hand struck the branch with enough force to send a half-dozen leaves swirling to the ground.

It was her, her love—*guilt*—made him whole.

"My own sweet little wifey."

Who would have thought it.

"Vince."

Her voice became the beacon and he the lost ship steering his way through the fog to safety. Unfortunately, the image wasn't as fanciful as he would have liked. Underscoring her voice was the constant low thrum of water that came at him from every direction and, more than once, caused him to stumble or sidestep or backtrack to avoid the numerous small creeks that seemed to spring up before him.

"Forgive me."

She couldn't be more than a few yards away, just over the rise—*I'm coming, baby*—and he had to bit the inside of his cheek—*ow!*—to keep from cursing when a branch he'd pushed aside snapped back and caught him in the eye. It hurt, but damn it felt good to be...*solid* again. Even if it didn't last, Vince was sure he'd have enough time to do what was needed.

With her.

He broke through the last of the brambles and felt the ground give way under him. Pinwheeling, he twisted to one side and managed to wrap one arm around a sapling just before he went over the edge. *Shit.*

The pool of water lay in front of her, filling the narrow hollow and lapping at the base of the tree where she sat all huddled up like a kid playing hide-and-seek instead of the heartless siren that just tried to lure him to his destruction.

Again.

Jesus, she really is a bitch.

Vince got his footing and snapped the sapling in two. The sound sent a shock wave through her and she jumped. *Good, she hasn't forgotten.*

"Tess? Wake up, baby."

She lifted her head. "Vince?"

"Up here."

She turned, looked up and he saw her bones go rigid under the skin. "Oh God."

"Did you really think you'd get away from me?"

"I—I'm..."

"Sorry?" *No, but you will be.* "It's okay, baby, I forgive you."

Hope, or something like it, misted her eyes.

"There's nothing to forgive." Smiling for all he was worth, Vince held out his hand. "Come on, give me your hand."

She leaned forward over her knees and reached for him even though the distance was too far. And that's what he counted on. She'd go into the water head first and, if she was very, very lucky, she'd hit a submerged rock and die instantly.

"That's right," he whispered, "come to daddy."

"Tess, *no!*"

Vince turned, snarling at the man who'd suddenly appeared on a narrow outcropping of rock to his right. But Tess' costumed lover wasn't even looking in his direction—his attention was focused downward...and then Vince heard the splash.

By the time he looked down, the water had already filled the hole she left in it and the rings, rippling outward across the surface, were smoothing out.

Vince blew her a kiss, posthumously, then looked across the quiet pool and smiled.

"I win, asshole, she's mine. So why don't you take a flying —"

The water exploded in a geyser of mud-brown rain.
**

Tess broke the surface gasping for air and trying to get her feet under her. The water wasn't deep, maybe not even waist high, but it was thick with mud and the ground had become the consistency of pudding, sliding out from under her every time she tried to stand up. For a moment there was air and light and sound, then the ground slithered away and water closed over her head.

Blind, without direction, hearing only the pounding of blood in her ears, Tess fought the claustrophobic panic to draw breath and kicked hard for what she hoped was the surface.

Her hand glanced off something hard and she twisted toward it, her fingers scrabbling across the words carved into the stone as if she was reading them in Braille. When her hands reached the top she pulled herself, straight-armed, into the air and felt the pile of rocks shift under her weight.

L O S T

Bracing her forearms across the top of Thomas' headstone, Tess wiped the wet hair out of her eyes and shuddered at what she saw. *God.* The hollow was filled with water, the smaller shrubs and bushes drowned and only the trees jutting up through the dark surface. He'd been right about the flood... she should have listened to him and stayed in the millhouse.

Rain pockmarked the surface and reversed gravity, splashing water *up* into her face.

"Tess!"

She turned and felt the rough granite scrape against her skin. Thomas stood on a rocky ledge to her right, leaning forward, his hand extended toward her. A figment of her insanity or straight run-of-the-mill delusion he looked real... and he looked scared.

"Get out of the water, Tess. Now."

"Aw, leave her alone, lover-boy. She's fine right where she is."

The water churned a frothy chocolate brown as Tess spun to the left. Vince was standing on the rise where she'd first seen Thomas.

He's here. And he's real.

"Oh God...please let me be crazy."

Vince winked at her.

"Tess!"

Thomas was pointing to something behind her.

"Snake! Get out of the water!"

She saw it out of the corner of her eyes—the small triangular shape gliding across the water toward her, twin wakes rippling outward from its undulating body. Tess didn't have to see the dark chestnut bands on the tan skin or the copper color of the head. The Copperhead was swimming by instinct toward high ground …and she was it.

"Tess! Move!"

Tess put the headstone between her and the copperhead and pushed off. She'd miscalculated the depth of the water by a few inches, it came up to her chest and felt like molasses, but the snake was the perfect incentive to move and move quickly. She tripped only twice before reaching the outcropping.

Thomas took her hand and pulled her onto the rocks and for a moment, neither of them moved. His skin was cool, but his fingers were firm and the bones solid.

"You're real."

Thomas gently squeezed her fingers before he stepped back.

"As real as thought, but there are times when will is strong enough to make flesh whole. He knows that now," Thomas looked across the flooded hollow then at her, "and it's a weapon he'll use against you. You have to get back to the millhouse, you'll be safer there."

Safer, not safe. A small difference, but Tess noticed it.

"But you have to hurry, the water is still rising." Thomas moved backward across the rocks and motioned for her to follow. Tess could feel Vince's eyes burning lines across her back. "The heartless tree is still above water, you can cross there if you hurry."

"But I drove here. My car's in the parking lot."

"You'll not be able to get there. We're on the highest ground this side of the creek, the flood's taken everything else."

"But my car…" Tess shook her head as if that, her car being underwater, was somehow less possible than the fact that she was standing there talking to one ghost while her husband's ghost watched.

"Tess!"

Tess began turn and felt a small tug against the side of her cheek.

"No," Thomas said, "don't look at him and for God's sake and your own, don't *think* about him. You're the one who's called him, Tess. You're his tie to this world, but you can break that."

"How?"

Thomas' gray eyes locked onto hers. "You must want it broken, Tess. *You* have to make that decision."

But how—"

"Tess! You listen to me, you bitch, and you listen good. I'm finished playing games. You're mine and you always will be. Now get your ass over here before I really get mad. Tess! TESS!"

She flinched at the command, but Thomas' hand—solid and real and strong—closed on her arm and pulled her away. Vince's voice followed them through the rain—"TESS!"— gnawing at the back of her mind like a starving dog. It would be so easy to pull away, to let go of everything and just turn around and go back. *End it. Now...here...*

And then she saw it through the trees...the undulating surge of jaundiced foam and waves the color of dead leaves. The swollen creek had swallowed the path and crawled onto the land. When Tess looked down she saw the new shoreline, just a few yards away, creeping ever so slowly toward her and backed away.

"Oh my God."

Thomas stepped in front of her, blocking her view for the moment.

"*That* is the only thing you need to think about, Tess. I haven't seen it this bad in nearly a hundred years...but it's not over yet. If the surge comes it will wash over the land like God's own judgment. Get to the millhouse and stay there."

Tess nodded, looking over his shoulder. "But..."

"Don't speak his name." His voice snapped her attention back. "Don't think of him, Tess. There is nothing back there but a grave and memories...none of which matter anymore."

"Thomas, he's—"

He took a quick step toward her and she ducked her head, ready for his fist. It would have been an easier pain than the words that came instead.

"Dead and you killed him. It's you, Tess, you've called him."

Tess folded her arms over her belly and shivered even though the rain falling through the branches was warm.   "I never called him."

"Every time you think of him or say his name, even to yourself, you call him to you. Just as you called me."

Is that you, ghost? The water's roar covered the sound that escaped her throat.

Thomas stepped to one side and walked into the woods. "The heartless tree...the hollow tree is only a few hundred feet ahead. She's survived worse that this, but get to her and get across as quickly as you can. Remember what I said...don't think of anything but the water."

"Thomas?"

He stopped, but didn't turn around. His body was fading, growing dimmer.

"My wife...believed in the power of prayer. If I could, I would offer mine. Go, now."

"Come with me."

"I can't. If anything happens, Tess, and he gets past me, keep water between the two of you. It's...difficult for us to cross running water."

We're nothing, Tess, he and I...nothing but shapes and shadows. If you have to remember anything, remember that and he won't be able to hurt you.

He dissolved into the rain and Tess turned and ran and hoped...*prayed* that her screams were only in her head.

CHAPTER 17
JUNE 20th – Into Evening

"Tess!"

"Tess! God*dammit*."

"This is your last warning, *bitch*. You get your ass over here *right now* or I'm going to—"

"To do what?"

The man stepped out from behind the trees and smiled the kind of cold, satisfied smile that a man gets when he watches his dog lay a fresh pile of steaming reality on some lawn-Nazi's beloved Kentucky Bluegrass. It was a smile Vince was used to giving, not getting, and he wasn't sure how to take it...even if he was dead.

He was putting on his own kind of smile when a ripple caught his eye and he looked down to see the big Copperhead pull itself from the water between his feet. Vince backed up so quickly he left a stream of vapor.

"Fuck!"

"It can't hurt you."

The man's smile was gone when Vince looked up.

"Nothing can hurt you now," the man said. "Except me."

**

It wasn't in blind panic...Tess ran in a very *purposeful* panic with Thomas' words setting the cadence. *Don't speak his name. Don't think of him. Don't speak his name. Don't think of him.*

Vince.

And time, which had been very considerate up until that moment, hiccuped...and brought back every moment, every abuse, every word he'd ever threatened her with. And she finally saw what he was...and what he'd made her.

Time recovered and moved on, but Tess stood there, ankle deep in a newly formed estuary, and lifted her face into the rain. She'd been such a fool. He never loved her...he just wanted something to control.

Tess!

Her head snapped forward, eyes wide, and the water that had encased her ankles was suddenly lapping against her knees. A twig or branch—*snake*—bumped against her leg and Tess churned the rising waters white as she crawled onto a narrow spine of rock. The ground on either side had been turned into tracks of thick mud, quivering beneath the constant, pounding rain. Breathing hard, Tess pushed the sodden coils of hair away from her face and shivered despite the murky heat. Despite the steady downpour she could still hear the roar of water.

The flood was catching up to her. There was no way of telling how far inland the water had come. There was no telling if hollow tree was still there...or if she even going in the right direction.

Doesn't matter. Keep moving.

Tess brushed against the branches of a dripping cedar and instantly the wet air was filled with the scent of freshly sharpened pencils.

'The woods are lovely, dark and deep.
But I have promises to keep.
And miles to go before I sleep,
And miles to go before I sleep.'

But at that moment she wished to God she'd never heard of Robert Frost.

**

"What the *hell* are you talking about?" Vince had never had to ask more than once for anything in his life, especially when he put on the kind of emphasis he was giving the words right now. But the man just stood there looking at him. "You think *you* can take *me*?"

"Why would you even ask?"

It was all Vince could do to keep his jaw from dropping open. Either *Thomas* had balls as big as Gibraltar or was a few cans short of a six-pack or didn't know *what* he was dealing with.

In which case it was time he found out.

The guy didn't have a ghost of a chance.

Vince pulled every inch of his full, imposing stature into play. "Do you have *any* idea who you're talking to?"

"Yes, but you don't."

"Oh?" Vince let the laugh come...and the man vanished into thin air.

A cold chill raced down Vince's backbone as he stared at the spot and might have gone on staring for a while longer if he hadn't suddenly been grabbed and spun around.

The man was smiling again.

"*Now* do you understand, friend?"

Oh fuck.

**

"Damn!"

The land looked solid enough, until she stepped on it... then it oozed out from under her and disappeared beneath the flooded field. The water was only a few inches deep, but the mud was the consistency of ready-mix concrete and took her left sandal when she pulled herself back into the relative protection of the trees.

Her first thought was to retrieve the sandal. The second, to sit down and put it on. The third was that she was absolutely insane to be standing there thinking about doing either of those things. The water was still rising.

Keep moving.

Tess took off the other sandal and fed it to the flood...a sacrifice for her safe passage. And she had to admit that slogging through the muck barefoot was easier, even if she did suffer the occasional stubbed toe. The willows provided just enough handholds to keep her semi-upright and that's all Tess concentrated on: staying semi-upright as the floodwaters slowly climbed her legs.

Eighteen, nineteen, twenty steps and the mud around her feet decreased enough that she was stubbing her toes with every step. Twenty-two, twenty-three and the willows were thick enough that Tess had to muscle her way through. Twenty-eight, twenty-nine and Tess felt a subtle strain in her calves. She was walking uphill.

Thirty-four steps and she climbed onto a rain-slick boulder.

"Oh, God."

**

Now that he had the man's attention, Thomas let him go and stepped back. There wasn't any need for a show of strength now—fear, shock and, finally, understanding shown equally in the man's eyes. "You're...you're a—"

Tess' late husband shook his head as if the word was a blasphemy beyond all right to say it aloud. If their first meetings had been different, or he had any doubt that the man, even now, might change, Thomas might have felt pity for him.

As it was, he felt nothing but the absolute knowledge that what he was about to do was right and just.

"It's over," he said as gently as he could. "She knows what you are—"*What we both are.* "—and she's not afraid. There is *nothing* you can do to her now but leave her in peace."

The man's eyes widened. "Leave?"

Thomas walked to the edge of the overlook and looked down, watching the concentric rings made by the rain ripple across the surface. The water was so muddy he couldn't see his grave.

"I know your fear—" He waited, even though he knew there'd be no denial, before continuing. "—and there's a reason for that. We come from the earth, and to the earth we are bound. The light of the sun and moon affect us as little as the wind can lift a shadow from the ground. Water is different."

"Bullshit."

"No, it's not...I know."

It was as if it had been only the day before...the first time he tried to cross at the wooden bridge he and his father built to span the creek; the same place where, years later, other men would build a dam. But on that day, the day that had lost all reason, crossing the bridge had seemed but a simple thing. He woke to murky sunlight, standing beneath the frayed end of a rope that had been looped—*six times*—around a crossbeam and heard men speaking his name.

The men were neighbors and stood before a small covered dray. They were dressed solemn as if going to the Meeting House and spoke softly as befit the Sabbath; but there were no women with them, nor children, nor prayer books. And never once did they look up when he called to them in answer to the repetition of his name.

He thought them jesting, playing a prank as they had as children, then, as the noon bell began to toll, the men fell silent and he with them. On the twelfth chime one of the men, a friend he'd known half his life, climbed onto the dray and clicked the pony into motion. The others followed alone or in pairs, hats in hand, and Thomas followed them, his questions still unanswered. At the bridge only the sounds of the pony's unshod hooves and boot heels against wood played against the sound of water falling over stone.

He called to them once more, and when they still wouldn't answer, Thomas ran onto the bridge and felt himself torn apart.

Clarity beyond anything he had ever imagined possible stripped away the questions and doubts and lies he had clothed himself in and he saw—*dearest God in Heaven*—what he was and what he'd done in his life. Every sin, large or small, every slight, every failing he had ever committed was brought forth in a blinding light. The water took away the blinders he'd placed upon his life and left behind a soul naked and trembling in despair.

It seemed an eternity to crawl back to land, but in that time he knew with no uncertainty what the dray carried and why there were no women or children present. The men were there to bury the cursed remains of a suicide...not next to his wife and child or those who gave him life or anyone who had ever known him. The dead man they conveyed had committed the most heinous sin and they, his reluctant pallbearers, would find a place apart and alone where his soul could molder forever in torment.

They had cursed him for committing a sin against himself, but Thomas wondered if anyone had cursed the dead man standing behind him for the sins he had committed upon another.

"I know the fear..."

"I'm not afraid of anything."

Thomas didn't turn around. "Yes, you are, but you don't have to be. Water is life, that's why it affects us, but if you're brave enough it can wash you clean." What was one more lie to a condemned soul. "The fear is but a passing thing...a memory of what had been and lasts but a moment. When it passes you're free."

"To go to Heaven?"

Or Hell. "You believe in Heaven and a just God?"

"Of course I do."

Just as Victoria did. "Then if God truly is just, you'll be where you belong. You don't belong here. Tess— She kept your spirit bound to this world, but not with malice. She didn't understand."

"She didn't understand," the man said and his voice grew bitter, "just like *I* didn't understand. But *you* fixed that little problem, didn't you?"

Thomas nodded. "Yes.

"Fuck, you must think I'm a real idiot. I'm not afraid of water and I'm not buying what you're selling. There's got to be a lot more that you're not telling me. I know what you're trying to do. You want me out of the picture so *you* can have her all to yourself, isn't that right?"

"I have as much right to her as you, friend."

"Then you admit it?"

Thomas stayed quiet and let the fire grow.

"God damn you, you son of a bitch. You want her but it's not going to go down like that. She's *my* wife and when I go I'm taking her with me."

The man charged and Thomas calmly stepped to one side.

**

When she'd first seen the waterfall, it had frightened her by its sheer power...now that power from tripled even though the fall itself had diminished in size by half. The flooded stream was only a few feet beneath the ridge, but now the water shot almost perpendicularly out from the rocks with the force of a fire-hose...directly against the upstream side of the hollow tree.

The leaves and smaller branches were gone, stripped away by the water, and even from where she stood, Tess could see the giant tree vibrate against the constant battering. As if to dramatize it just a bit further, an anchoring root snapped and the tree lurched.

There was no *way* she could cross that. It could go any moment, with her in it. She could already see her body—drowned and bloated, flesh torn—somewhere downstream wedged into a culvert with all the other flood debris.

Robby would have to come identify her body, if he could.

I can't do this.

But time didn't pay any attention to her. One minute she was on the rock, immobile, the next Tess had both hands around thick, rain-slick roots and was pulling herself up into the tree's fire-blackened interior.

Time wasn't going to let her die...just yet.

Turning, Tess turned back toward the woods. It could have been so different. "I'm so sorry, Vince..."

**

Thomas watched the man go over the edge toward the water and blink out like a candle in a storm.

"Tess...NO!"

**

"...forgive me."

This time Vince didn't stop to think about the how or why or wherefore, and apparently *not thinking* was the key. As long as he *acted* he was solid and whole and real...and they both knew it.

But it didn't last.

And it was all her fault.

But when wasn't it?

It had been fine, perfect, in fact...up to the point when he found himself standing at the base of the big hollow tree. All he did was reach up and grab a handful of her rain-snarled hair. Okay, so maybe he snapped her head back a little too hard, but, hell, he'd kissed her, didn't he? Kissed her a good one, too...a nice big *smack*, right on the lips and then...

Then she opened her fucking mouth and screamed.

And the sound passed through him like he was nothing.

Which, of course, he wasn't.

The bitch.

**

Thomas was right.

Tess stepped down into a foot of rainwater that had collected inside the tree and watched him flex his fingers. He was only a shape moving between the raindrops, vague and indistinct—now. A moment before he'd been solid and real and her scalp still burned from where he'd grabbed it.

"Go away."

He looked up... *Vince* looked up and smiled and the rain splattered against his shoulders.

"Don't think so, baby. At least not without you."

He pulled himself higher on the roots and Tess moved deeper into the tree.

It's my fault he's here.

**

Vince didn't have to look to know he was solid again. He could feel the rain on his face and the rough wood in his hands and if it hadn't been for the look on her face—shock and terror equally combined—he might have shown her, right then and there, what those solid hands could do.

But that would have been too easy. He wanted her around, for a while yet, so she could keep him real.

So he could lay one fucking ghost to rest before he took her with him.

"Forever and ever, baby," he said, keeping the smile on his face even though she was moving away from him. "And this time death does not part."

She said something, his little wifey, but even inside the shelter of the hollow tree, the sound of water was too loud for him to hear. It looked like she said 'no,' but that wasn't likely. Not from her, not even now.

Vince tipped his head to one side. The rain was doing a real job on her, making her squint and plastering down her hair that had, in his opinion, gotten a little too long and shaggy…but, on the plus side, it'd reduced her tee-shirt to something resembling a nearly transparent second skin.

He was still having trouble with temperature, but it must have been chilly, because her nipples were giving him a double thumbs up.

Then he looked a little closer and noticed the bra beneath the shirt. It was thin and lacy and not one he recognized. She'd always worn plain white bras with enough padding to make up for her lack of size, but this one…this was the kind of bra a woman bought with the sole intention of showing to a man.

Goddamned round-heeled bitch didn't even wait until my body was cold.

Vince stepped off the root he was standing on and into the tree…and felt a shiver pass through him when his foot hit the water.

He backed up but kept smiling like nothing was wrong.

"So," he said. "How've you been, baby?"

But before she could answer, Vince glanced out of the corner of his eye at his nice firm, solid hand…and lunged forward. She hadn't backed up far enough, or else she'd forgotten how long a reach he had, and the sound she made when his hand closed over her arm rose like a startled bird above the water's roar.

But it ended all too quickly when he pulled her to him. He could feel her body, *feel* it squirm against his own…and his body responded.

Vince knew she'd felt it, too, because he watched her eyes go big and round.

"My own sweet little wifey." Vince reached up under the thin layer of wet cotton and pulled the lacy little bra away from her right breast; then squeezed until tears replaced the rain on her cheeks. "Did you miss me, baby?"

Her lips trembled, formed a word.

"Didn't quite catch that, baby." He found her nipple and crushed it between his thumb and forefinger. Her body arched into his. *God, what a slut.* "You'll have to speak a little louder…being dead is murder. Oh, but you already know that. Go on, you were saying."

She took a deep breath and Vince's chest rode the swell of her lungs up and back down as she released it in a piercing scream.

"THOMAS!"

Vince let go of her breast and grabbed her throat, the shirt bunching between them as he squeezed.

"You fucking bitch!" He tightened his grip and felt her windpipe jerk as she tried to breathe. "You think *he* can help you? Shit, he's *nothing*…less than nothing." Vince leaned down until he was looking into her eyes. He wanted to see the exact moment, the instant she became his again. "No one can help you, baby…you're mine and you're coming with me."

She made a little gasping sound and her eyes, instead of dulling, shifted away from him. Vince only caught a quick glance of the man's face as he turned—

**

Thomas pulled her to her feet and held her while she gasped for breath and choked on the rain that came with it. The first thing she saw, when she was able to see clearly enough, were his eyes…and they were the color of the flood.

"Why didn't you listen?" He wasn't shouting, but Tess could hear him even over the pounding of blood in her ears. "He only has the power you give him…don't give him any more than you already have. Now, turn around and brace yourself."

Tess pulled away, remembering all the times Vince had told her to do the same thing—*come on, baby…we both know how much you like it this way*—and saw something materialize out of the rain behind Thomas. At first it was nothing more than a swirling gray-black mist that writhed and twisted among the roots like a fish caught in a net, then a familiar shape began to emerge....

Thomas slapped her across the cheek hard enough to set her back on her heels.

Vince's face melted back into a harmless mist.

"Stop it! See *me*, Tess, listen to *me*... I can't help you if you won't help yourself. Now..." He took her shoulders and turned her around. "Brace your arms against the tree, woman."

Tess reached up and grabbed the rough edges of the lightning blasted fissure.

"She should hold," Thomas said, "her roots are sunk deep, but I want you move as quickly through her as you can. Keep to the center and look straight ahead. Keep moving, don't look back and don't stop until you get to the millhouse. Do you understand?"

Tess nodded and felt a small touch against the small of her back.

"Go!"

He pushed her and Tess' feet almost went out from under her. Going as quickly as Thomas probably wanted her to was not an option. Even if the tree were perfectly still—which it wasn't—the water had turned the interior bark to mush and skating her feet as if she were on ice proved very little help. Each step was a scramble to keep her balance.

Something hit the side of the hollow tree with enough force to knock it, and Tess, to one side. Twisting as she fell, Tess dove flat into the water and let her momentum skim her forward a few feet, then began slithering toward the broken crown like a newt. And this time she did what he told her to do—she looked straight ahead toward the brighter dull gray patch of daylight and didn't stop moving until she was across.

Don't stop until you get to the millhouse.

Panting as she scrambled onto the rocks, Tess got to the top of the ridge before she allowed herself to turn around.

**

Thomas ignored the blasphemy and said a small prayer of thanksgiving when he saw her reach the rise on the opposite bank. The dead man standing behind him seemed less pleased, if the number of curses he fed to the sky were any indication.

"She's safe," Thomas said as he turned. "You can't get to her."

The man stepped deeper into the heartless tree and Thomas felt a moment of doubt. If the man realized he could cross without fear, it would be harder to stop him. They were equals now...but fortunately, Thomas alone knew that.

For the moment.

"There's nothing you can do to—"

The man struck the edge of the bark with his fist. A piece no bigger than a child's fingernail broke off, but it was enough. *I've misjudged him.*

"Shut the fuck up, okay? I'm tired of listening to you." He took another step and Thomas braced himself. "Especially when you're talking crap. I know she wants me...and you know it, too. Hell brother, all I have to do is wait and I'll get her." He smiled. "I got all the time in the world, isn't that right?"

It would have been too simple a thing to lie. "Yes."

"Then I'll get her." The man started to laugh. "Shit, she doesn't even care. Take a look for yourself if you don't believe me."

Thomas glanced over his shoulder and saw her through the curtain of rain. She was still on the ridge looking at them...looking at him. *God, Tess.* The man was right, she didn't care any more than Victoria had.

He couldn't let that happen again.

"Believe me now, asshole?"

Thomas turned back to the man and nodded. "Yes."

God forgive me.

Moving quickly so the man had no time to ready himself, Thomas closed the distance between them.

"You're right, *brother*," he said, "she doesn't care, but not for the reasons you think. She feels blame for what she did and probably always will in some way. It's her guilt that calls you..."

His hands closed on the front of the man's over-shirt.

"But I can make damned sure you'll not answer again."
**

Vince looked down at the man's bony knuckles and snorted a laugh through his nose. A lot of guys, usually those who thought themselves stronger or braver than they actually were and generally too drunk to know the difference between showing off and blind stupidity, had done the same thing—got up close and way too personal.

And he'd let them.

For a minute, minute and a-half before giving them a valuable lesson in both reality and humility by driving his fist, knee, or forehead into them. Of course, he'd never beaten up on a ghost before, but, then again, he'd never been one either...so it should be pretty interesting now that he understood the rules.

Vince leaned back, adding a little tension to the man's arm and sighted down the hollow log to where Tess stood watching, his little wifey. And for her sake, she'd better have been watching *him*.

When the man—*Thomas*—pulled him forward, Vince played along even to the point of dragging his feet through the water. Neither of them looked down to see if he was making waves, but Vince could *feel* the pressure against his ankles and fought hard to keep his face blank. There was always a danger of losing the pot if you showed your hand too soon, so he twisted and muttered and waited until they were in the middle of the tree.

Then...let go...and watched the man's hand slide through the front of his chest.

This time it was the man who studied his clenched fist. When he finally looked up, Vince smiled.

"I'm a fast learner...brother."

Vince had only seen one other man that angry in his entire life...or after...and that had been his father after little Vincey, age fifteen, had taken the family sedan on an unscheduled...or insured joy ride. His father had almost killed him that day, and the look on the man's face was pretty damned near identical. He hadn't been able to get away then...or now. Using Vince as a counterbalance, Thomas grabbed the front of the windbreaker and spun, slamming them both into the side.

There was an only a moment of resistance—

"Go in peace, brother."

—then Vince saw the boiling spray come up to meet him and made a blind grab.

It wasn't only Tess or anger that made him whole, fear—absolute and mind numbing—did a hell of a good job, too.

They went into the water together.

**

Tess screamed into her open hands, but wasn't even sure which one she was screaming for...

**

His arms felt like they were being ripped out of the socket a sinew at a time and rocks tore his flesh, but those weren't even the worst pain....

Pain. God, he'd almost forgotten what pain was. It'd been so long since he felt anything, but even the physical pain was infinitesimal compared to the sensation of life and memory that the water returned to him one moment only to take away the next.

Tumbled, backwashed into the roots of a drowned tree… trapped, the water began to wear away everything that he was or ever had been, to wash it downstream with the rest of the debris. He was dissolving into nothing…finally… dwindling into oblivion.

Let go…just to let go.

NO!

Kicking free he reached toward the surface.

**

Clinging to the broken branch that had saved him, he watched the water race by below him. Pulling himself up, he relaxed his grip and slipped back through the wet wood to the drier core.

There was only one reason he'd been saved…God had finally noticed His mistake and was trying to make amends.

He began running and the hollow tree echoed his steps.

**

…until she saw who was coming toward her through the rain.

He's here.

CHAPTER 18
JUNE 27ʰ – The Flood

He's gone. Thomas is gone. Oh God, he's gone.

Her stomach tightened at the memory of seeing him fall into the water, his body winking out as the flood took. It had been worse than watching Vince die, because this time she cared.

This time she would have mourned and prayed for his soul…but she couldn't even follow his last instructions.

Keep moving. Don't look back. Don't stop until you get to the millhouse.

One out of three wasn't bad—she kept moving.

Don't look at him—she couldn't help herself. That was an instinct in all prey animals. Every time she found a path above the rising water, she'd turn and he'd be there—sometimes whole, sometimes nothing more than a shape or gesture, a leering grin caught somewhere between the light and shadows of the trees. This wasn't, as she once hoped, an illusion or madness or a game.

It was real.

He was real.

Don't think of him was impossible.

Time ran at her side and played catch up, filling in all the missing pieces—the pain, the beatings, the terror, the fear, the relief when he collapsed in a pool of blood on the kitchen floor of the condo…the raw hate she felt for him.

He was dead…*it was self-defense*…and buried…*he was going to kill me*…and she'd stood at his grave…*why didn't you stay there*…and wished she had killed him sooner.

"Tess."

A shadowy arm reached for her and she twisted away, holding back the scream even as she slid down into the flood. The water closed over her head and carried her away. Roots along the bank snagged the hem of her shirt and pulled it up around her neck, twisting into a noose.

Bright spirals and pinwheels of color flared and died in the muddy darkness before Tess' eyes. The surface was only a few inches above her, she could feel, grab at it with her hands…only a few inches above her upraised face…but it might as well have been miles.

"Give it up, baby, you're only prolonging the inevitable. Come on, come back to papa."

It would be so easy.

And just want he wanted. Maybe he'd even forgive her.

"We'll be together…forever."

A fear worse than dying swept over her. Not this way… not after everything she'd been through. Planting her feet against a submerged log, Tess clawed at the material twisted around her neck and pushed off.

She didn't know if the shirt tore or the roots broke, but suddenly she was gulping air as fast as her lungs would work. Tess didn't stop to take inventory or give her trembling body a moment's grace. Pulling off her shirt, she left it hanging on the barbed roots of a half-downed scrub.

Her breath gave out when she reached high ground; and even thought her mind was screaming at her—*keep moving, keep moving*—her body collapsed against the trunk of a tree and stayed there.

Okay, but just for a minute.

Her body thanked her and got comfortable, closing her eyes and lifting her face to the rain that found its way through the leaves. Tess didn't mind, it felt good…soft and warm and gentle.

Even the sound of the water seemed peaceful at the moment.

He's here.

Her head snapped forward and she saw him—*it can't be, I didn't think about him*—Vince walking slowly toward her, his arms open.

"Come here, baby…give daddy a kiss."

Tess backed up two steps just to put a little more distance between them.

"It's over. Come on…make it easy on yourself."

"Go to Hell."

The last thing she saw, before she turned and started running, was the sardonic grin turn to a grimace.

**

The rain stopped a few minutes before she reached the clearing, but the damage was already done and the floodwaters were still rising. The path was little more than a foot wide—a tiny marshy strip of land dotted with puddles that separated the two halves of the flood. Where the creek had become a churning, debris-strewn river, the flooded millrace had inundated the lowlands and turned the field into a lake. The footbridge and flower garden were drowned, the bottom porch step half-submerged. Only the millhouse remained, an island in the middle of a mud-gray sea connected to the world only by the thin ribbon of land Tess was standing on, sat on the crest of the hill like a fortress in an ancient fairy tale.

And all she had to do, like any good princess, was escape the dragon, get to the castle and be reunited with her knight in shining armor.

So they could live happily ever after.

She always hated fairy tales.

Tess pulled a ragged breath into lungs that felt suddenly too small. Her knight was gone, never to return…only the dragon remained, and *he* wasn't getting tired.

Vince had always been the runner in the family. When they were dating, he'd been content to let her sit in the stands and watch him do laps around the track at the high school. After they were married he decided she needed to get some exercise.

"I didn't marry some fat-assed lazy house-frau and I'll be damned if you're going to turn into one."

They both found out she couldn't jog to save her life. Halfway around the track she'd start to loose her rhythm and gasp for breath. When she finished, if she finished, it was all she could do to stagger onto the grassy center field and not throw up.

But Vince still signed them both up for a "little" Five-K marathon a month after the honeymoon.

In a field of 3304, Vince had come in 39th.

She never made it across the line.

Vince told the officials she'd dropped out a mile into the race because she'd taken a tumble and sprained an ankle. The judges awarded her Number 3304 as a consolation and tsk-ed when then saw the livid bruises that covered her arms and legs.

Vince framed the Number 3304 and hung it in the master bathroom over the toilet…so she'd never forget how she embarrassed him.

That was the one thing he was really good at, not letting her forget anything.

Including himself.

A hand brushed against the back of her head and Tess hunched forward, turning as she ran a hand across the tangles. There was nothing behind her, this time, but that didn't matter…she knew exactly what was going on—

"Tess."

—he was playing his favorite game: Cat and Mouse.

"LEAVE ME ALONE!"

A few feet from the rise, the path shrank down to the width of a pencil, the flood nibbling away in bits and pieces at the final barrier almost as she watched. In a few minutes the millhouse would be surrounded.

"TESS!"

She turned and felt her overworked lungs catch.

They ran toward her, the two of them...Vince in the lead, the runner, Thomas his pale, transparent shadow. It was Thomas who'd called her name and Thomas who waved his arms over his head as if he knew she couldn't believe what she was seeing.

His voice was hollow and drifted on the air between them like cattail fluff.

"Get to...millhouse. Hur— Tess, I... good—"

What had he tried to say—*I love you? Good-bye? Good riddance?* As Tess watched, his body flickered and went out, then reappeared directly behind Vince. Their eyes met, once— *get into the millhouse. Now*—then Thomas grabbed Vince around the neck and jerked him to a stop.

When she reached the back door, Tess turned—*she was safe now, she was at the millhouse, wasn't she?*—and watched a nightmare. At times it seemed Vince fought empty air, throwing punches at nothing and reeling when the nothing struck back; other times she almost saw him clearly...Thomas.

No more...no more...

But she couldn't look away.

Vince threw another punch, and suddenly was jerked up off his feet and held over the surface of the water. He hung there for a moment, clawing at nothing, when Thomas flickered back into existence. His face grim, he looked over Vince's shoulder at her, but faded again before Tess could read the expression in his eyes. Vince screamed—she'd never heard him scream before—as his feet hit the water and disappeared.

Tess turned away, pressing her face against the doorframe. She couldn't watch him die again...not like this.

Tess kept her back to the water as she opened the door. The rain and heat had swelled the frame and a harsh metal-on-metal snap of the lock echoed into the empty house ahead of her.

A gentle hand cupped her elbow.

"Thomas?"

"Wrong, baby."

The last thing Tess saw before Vince took her by the throat and propelled her backwards into the millhouse, was Thomas kneeling on a tiny patch of dry ground surrounded by water.

His lips moved.

"I can't help you. Tess... He's nothing, he's—"

Here.

**

He almost felt sorry for her.

She fell, landed smack on her ass on the floor...but it was her fault. All he did was give her a little push so he could step in and close the door; but she'd gotten all dramatic—eyes wide, skittering backwards down the hall like some kind of fucking crab. Hell, you would have thought he'd backhanded or something.

Which, if she didn't stop giving him those big *'what did I do'* cow eyes, he might just have to resort to.

Soon...but right now he enjoyed just following the butt-wide mud trail she'd left on the floor and listening to the soft, but discernible sound of his cross-trainers against the wood. Vince slid his hands into the pocket of his windbreaker and felt the smooth lining against his knuckles. Man, he could follow her like this all day.

It wasn't like she could go anywhere.

If she ran outside and tried to swim, she'd drown and he'd win.

If she stayed in the millhouse....

Hell, it wasn't going to even be a challenge and that's why he *almost* felt sorry for her.

His death, now that he remembered it, had been *relatively* easy. There hadn't been much pain and, up until those last few seconds when he realized he couldn't breathe, it'd been a pretty easy passing.

She wasn't going to be that lucky.

He wanted her to feel every exquisite moment as her life slipped away and not just because she deserved it for what she'd done—even though she did—but because he wanted her to carry the memory of those moments with her.

Forever.

"Forever and ever." Vince took one hand out of his pocket and held it out to her. "'*Finish vitae sed non amorius…in spiritus.'* Amen."

She hit the front door. "Go away."

He touched his chest in mock surprise. "It speaks. Not very nicely, but it does speak. The question is, why is it speaking when I didn't say it could?"

Vince closed the gap between them and squatted down, tracing a spot of drying mud on her left ankle with his finger. She pulled her leg away so quickly she almost kneed herself in the chin.

"You felt that, did you? Pretty amazing, isn't it?" He held up his hand and turned it forward and back. "It took a while, but I'm getting the hang of it. And it's not so much different than being alive. It just takes a little patience and practice… you'll find that out soon enough."

She tried to get away…she actually tried to get to her feet and run. While he was talking to her.

Vince grabbed her chin and squeezed until tears formed in her eyes. Man, it felt good, it felt right. He added just a bit more pressure and she whimpered.

Strike Three. He sighed, shaking his head.

"I can't tell you how disappointed I am right now, Tess. I tried to be a good husband and teach you what it meant to be a good wife, but look how much you've forgotten. First—"

Vince pulled her head toward him. "—you talk without permission."

He slammed it back against the door and felt a tear hit his hand.

"Second—" He pulled her forward again. "—you moved while I was speaking."

Slam.

"Third, you're crying and you *know* how much I hate that."

Slam.

Her eyes were going half-mast so he shook her until she fluttered back into full, and painful, consciousness.

"Jesus, just look at you...you're pitiful. I don't even know why I bother. Can you tell me? Can you give me one reason why I should care?" He was hoping she'd try and was disappointed when she didn't. "I asked you a question."

Slam.

She blinked, confusion dulling her eyes.

"Jesus, you're making it hard on yourself. I asked you a question and you don't even respect me enough to answer. Don't you remember how this goes?"

Before he could add another knot to the back of her head, she whispered "Y-yes."

"Ah, good. So you *do* remember."

"Yes."

"Tell me."

She looked up into his eyes. "I remember I killed you."

It must have been shock...he couldn't believe she'd say something like that...but suddenly the delicious pressure he was exerting on her chin was gone.

**

Tess watched his face as he stood up and backed away—glaring, angry, hands balled into fists. There was something wrong, something different about the way he looked... moved...

"What did you say to me?"

Tess held on to the doorknob as she got to her feet. He was fading, his body growing dimmer until she could see the stairs and newel post through him. It was like watching a photograph being *un*-developed, the colors and shapes disappearing…leaving the picture going blank and clean and empty.

And she finally understood what Thomas meant.

Tess took a step toward him and met his eyes for the first time in her life.

"What the fuck are you looking at, bitch?"

She almost laughed.

"Nothing. I'm looking at nothing, don't *you* understand." He lifted his hand but she shook her head. "You can't hurt me…not anymore. You're dead…you're nothing more than a few bad memories that I couldn't let go of. But I can now."

Tess took another step and he backed away.

"It's over, I'm not afraid of you anymore. Thomas was right, you're nothing, Vince…nothing at all. Go to hell."

Tess took a deep breath. She was alone in the entranceway.

"Tess?"

"Thomas?"

She ran down the empty hall and opened the back door into a blazing red-orange sun, so low in the sky that, for a moment, Tess couldn't see the shape trudging toward her from the water's edge. And for a moment she thought…

Even when he wrapped his arms around her and pulled her close, she let herself pretend it was him. *Thomas.*

"Oh, God, baby…I was so worried." Robby's voice vibrated through her chest. "I left Lancaster when I heard the first reports and that was almost four hours ago. The off-ramp and most of Fort Washington is under water. I had to get off at Willow Grove and backtrack from Jenkintown. I now know every side street and dead end between here and—"

Tess stepped back but didn't get very far away. "You are okay, aren't you?"

Shielding her eyes, she turned and looked out over the water's unbroken surface. The path was gone. The flood covered everything.

"Yeah," she said, nodding. "I'm okay." She hoped her brother would think her eyes were tearing from the glare of the setting sun. "How *did* you get here?"

Robby jerked his thumb over his shoulder to the flat-bottom duck boat bobbing gently at the water's edge. A man in a mud-splattered Park Ranger uniform stood at the bow, holding a mooring line. He nodded to Tess and smiled.

Tess moved her arms up to cover as much of the fact that she was wearing only shorts and a bra.

"Oh, don't worry about it, baby. Wayne's a professional."

Tess hoped her nod looked convincing, but didn't drop her arms. "It's bad enough that you need a boat?"

"In places, apparently, and *this* is one of the places. Most of the house is...okay, but the dining room and butler's pantry are pretty much soaked ...thank God it's a stone floor. The pool and basement are flooded—not a real surprise. Power's out, which, with all that water, is a good thing. It could have been worse."

Robby touched her chin. "What... God, you're bruised. What happened?'

"Nothing. Slipped, I'm fine now."

"Sure? Well, Chuck will be glad to hear that. He was coming home to get some papers and called me when he couldn't get through...then he tried to call you. When he couldn't get you he called me and I started trying."

"Sorry, I must have turned off the cell phone."

"I'm going to take you down and have one surgically implanted." He ruffled the top of her head and made a face. "You're wet... Oh God, you were out in this, weren't you?"

"Just for a little while. I wanted to see it." She smiled up at him. "I know, I'm nuts...but I'll get better."

"You don't have to do anything of the sort. I love you just the way you are. Anyway, when I couldn't get you, I got as close as I could...that would be the Bent Elbow's parking lot and that's where I met Jim and his boat. He told me this is the worst flood the area's had in over a hundred years. A couple people have died—" Robby's sigh ruffled the still air. "So...go pack a few things and the three of us—you, me, and Chuck... not Wayne—are going to as grand a hotel as can be found in these parts. I think we deserve it."

Tess looked over her brother's shoulder and watched the alchemist in the setting sun change the water from lead to gold.   The opposite bank looked farther away, the half-submerged trees casting ebony shadows.

He might have been able to get to them. He might still be there.
"Tess?"

"I'd rather stay here. Look, the millhouse is still on high ground. I'll be okay."

Robby held her face gently between his hands.

"You're right, you *are* nuts. Yeah, the millhouse if on high ground, for the moment, but if it rains again...here or north of us, that'll be all she wrote. So, clothes—packed...now. No argument or I'll throw you over my shoulder and I'll dump you in the boat as you are. I love you, okay?"

Tess smiled at her less-than-shining knight. "Okay. And I love you, too."

"Good. Glad to hear it. Go. And if you're not out in five minutes I'm comin' in after you."

Tess left the back door open, letting the golden light fill the hallway as she raced up the stairs. The light helped to scatter the darkness that had gathered in the corners and along the walls. She couldn't remember the millhouse ever being that dark before, or that quiet.

There'd always been some small sound to let her know he was here...*Thomas*, even when she'd only thought of him as the ghost. But the rooms were silent now, the air still. Empty.

He's not here.

Tess tossed shorts, tops, underwear, nightshirt, and her toothbrush into a small overnight bag, and grabbed a pair of tennis shoes from the closet on her way out. Tying the laces together, she hung them over one shoulder so they wouldn't get wet.

She left her cell phone in the recharger. There was no one she needed to call.

Robby was in the boat and the water had turned back to lead when she closed the door behind her.

The Park Ranger smiled as he took her case and helped her on board. "We'll be doing patrols until everything's back to normal, so don't worry about anyone getting in."

Tess looked back at the empty millhouse. "No, I won't."

EPILOG
NOVEMBER 16TH

History repeated itself.

The British may have won the Battle of Fort Washington, but everyone watching knew how the war would end and acted accordingly.

Tess stood on the sidelines, cheering Robby and the other members of General Washington's brave troops, and jeered at Chuck and the lines of straight-backed, red-coated "British" soldiers who'd marched up from Mathers Lane to do battle on the lawn of the Lodge House.

Afterwards, when the dead rose and congratulated each other and their executioners on a job well done, with the exception of Robby who'd fallen early and demanded a recount, Tess rewarded her two "heroes" with cups of steaming apple cider.

It'd been five months since the summer flood and there were still parts of the park, those less visited by tourists and school groups that still hadn't been completely restored. The hiking trails through the woods were the most obvious, although Chuck told them that a number of local Boy Scouts troops had already volunteered to come and clear the paths.

But that wouldn't be until after the spring rains…minus another flood, of course.

The small cemetery, one of the favorite tourist and tour group stops, had been the Historical Society's first project.

But Thomas' grave in the hollow was gone.

The force of the water had scattered the pile of stone and leveled out the ground, covering the grave itself with a thick layer of mud and debris. A Park Ranger found his tombstone, muddied and chipped in places, in the middle of a field a quarter mile away.

Because of its significance, however, once they saw the name, the Historical Society had the tombstone cleaned and hauled to the cemetery where it was placed above an empty grave.

Thomas was gone.

**

He stood in the doorway and watched her still form on the bed. Autumn had come and brought with it a peace he'd never known. With each day, the light changed a little more from the sharp clarity of crystal to the mellow gold of candlelight.

Winter would come and the light would change again. Then it would be spring and summer and autumn and the cycle would continue, as constant as the millrace and the stream…while he waited for her.

**

Tess heard the bedroom door close and closed her eyes with a smile.

He's here.

The End

AUHOR'S NOTES

While there is not a cemetery, at least as described, in Fort Washington State Park, Mather Mill and Hope Lodge are quite real and were the sites of a major Revolutionary War battle. The battle was lost by the Colonials and from there General Washington took his army to Valley Forge...and we all know what happened there.

The millhouse, unfortunately, is a fabrication, but its model, Thistledown, is very real and I'd like to thank Geno and Tracy Ciavarelli for letting me wander around their home and take notes. Special thanks, too, to Rob Dunbar and Chas Henrickson for allowing me to do the same with their home, the Bark House.

P.D. Cacek
Fort Washington, PA
2007

www.ingramcontent.com/pod-product-compliance
Lightning Source LLC
Chambersburg PA
CBHW020410260626
47156CB00007B/2314